Praise for Deborah Hale

"Deborah Hale has outdone herself to the complete advantage of the reader."
—*RT Book Reviews* on
A Gentleman of Substance

"This is a pure pleasure to read."
—*RT Book Reviews* on *Border Bride*

"*The Wedding Wager* is a delightfully written story."
—*RT Book Reviews*

Praise for Louise M. Gouge

"Gouge's story has romance, mystery and laughter."
—*RT Book Reviews* on *Love Thine Enemy*

"Gouge's interesting read has romance, intrigue, spies and secrets."
—*RT Book Reviews* on *The Captain's Lady*

D0959214

DEBORAH HALE

After a decade of tracing her ancestors to their roots in Georgian-era Britain, RWA Golden Heart Award winner Deborah Hale turned to historical romance writing as a way to blend her love of the past with her desire to spin a good love story. Deborah lives in Nova Scotia, Canada, between the historic British garrison town of Halifax and the romantic Annapolis Valley of Longfellow's *Evangeline.* With four children (including twins), Deborah calls writing her "sanity retention mechanism." On good days, she likes to think it's working.

Deborah invites you to visit her personal website at www.deborahhale.com, or find out more about her at www.Harlequin.com.

LOUISE M. GOUGE

has been married to her husband, David, for forty-six years. They have four children and six grandchildren. Louise always had an active imagination, thinking up stories for her friends, classmates and family, but seldom writing them down. At a friend's insistence, in 1984 she finally began to type up her latest idea. Before trying to find a publisher, Louise returned to college, earning a BA in English/creative writing and a master's degree in liberal studies. She reworked the novel based on what she had learned and sold it to a major Christian publisher. Louise then worked in television marketing for a short time before becoming a college English/humanities instructor. She has had eleven novels published, five of which have earned multiple awards, including the 2006 Inspirational Reader's Choice Award. Please visit her website at www.louisemgouge.com.

The Wedding Season

DEBORAH HALE
LOUISE M. GOUGE

Love Inspired

Recycling programs
for this product may
not exist in your area.

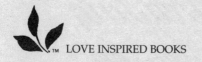

™ LOVE INSPIRED BOOKS

ISBN-13: 978-0-373-82873-9

THE WEDDING SEASON

Copyright © 2011 by Harlequin Books S.A.

The publisher acknowledges the copyright holders of the individual works as follows:

MUCH ADO ABOUT NUPTIALS
Copyright © 2011 by Deborah M. Hale

THE GENTLEMAN TAKES A BRIDE
Copyright © 2011 by Louise M. Gouge

www.LoveInspiredBooks.com

Printed in U.S.A.

CONTENTS

MUCH ADO
ABOUT NUPTIALS

Deborah Hale

In memory of my beloved grandmothers,
Edna MacDonald and Agnes Graham,
who were such a loving, inspiring presence
in the lives of their many grandchildren.

Bear with each other and forgive whatever grievances you may have against one another. Forgive as the Lord forgave you.
—*Colossians* 3:13

Chapter One

⟋⟍

The Cotswolds, England
1814

"Miss Leonard, I presume?"

The question, posed in a rich, firm baritone voice, startled Rebecca Beaton as she stooped to pluck a fragrant purple hyacinth in the garden at Rose Grange. Had Hermione decided to abandon her sketchbook and venture outside to help gather flowers?

Rising, Rebecca scanned the garden. But she saw no sign of her former pupil, to whom she now served as companion.

The only other person in sight was a well-dressed gentleman, presumably the one who had spoken. He was tall and broad-shouldered with dark brown hair, a high brow and a proud, jutting nose. His piercing slate-blue eyes regarded her with a mixture of surprise and disapproval.

But that was ridiculous. How could he possibly disapprove of her when he did not even know who she was?

Realizing he must have mistaken her for Hermione, she was about to correct him when he rushed on. "I beg your pardon for presuming to address you without a proper introduction, Miss Leonard. But since we might soon be quite intimately connected, I hope you will permit me the liberty of introducing myself."

How was Hermione going to be *intimately connected* with this gentleman?

Again he refused to give Rebecca an opportunity to inquire, but continued speaking as if he did not care whether she objected. "I am Sebastian Stanhope, Viscount Benedict. I have just come from London after learning, to my considerable dismay, that my brother has gotten himself engaged to you."

So that's what this bewildering visitation was all about. Rebecca felt on firmer ground at last, though it grieved her to hear the viscount was displeased with his brother's betrothal. She must explain his mistake at once and fetch the real Hermione to speak with him, though she feared such an interview would upset the dear girl.

But Lord Benedict still refused to let her get a word in. "I am certain you have many fine qualities, Miss Leonard. Indeed, I can understand how your beauty must have secured my brother's admiration."

Her *beauty?* Even if his lordship had paused just then to let her speak, Rebecca doubted she could have produced a sound. Her teachers at school had always impressed upon her and the other girls their deficiencies of appearance. Whenever she peeped in the looking glass long enough to check that she was neat and tidy, all she saw was an unattractive square jaw, unmanageable hair of a commonplace brown shade and brows far too full and dark for beauty.

Was the viscount trying to flatter her or mock her?

He sounded sincere enough in his brusque, imperious

manner. "I am pleasantly surprised to discover you are not some green girl barely out of the schoolroom."

That must be a polite way of implying she was so firmly "on the shelf" it amazed him that she'd managed to secure any marriage proposal. Even if his lordship had put the case in so blunt a manner, Rebecca could not have disputed it. With her lack of fortune and beauty, she'd never had much hope of securing a husband. Each passing year had only whittled away at whatever unlikely dreams she might have had. Dreams of a poor but kindly curate, perhaps, or a widower who needed someone to care for his motherless children and could not afford to be particular.

Firmly turning her thoughts from such modest romantic fancies, Rebecca forced herself to concentrate on what Lord Benedict was saying. "Your manner of dress suggests a character not afflicted with frivolity and I approve your reticence. It is refreshing to meet a woman who does not chatter on like a magpie."

Rebecca barely stifled a hoot of laughter. Though no magpie, she would have had plenty to say for herself, if only his lordship would give her an opportunity. The viscount was certainly talkative enough, though she could hardly compare the mellow resonance of his voice to that of a squawky bird.

"My brother's taste in women has clearly improved." He swept a glance from the toes of her shoes up to the crest of her bonnet. "Still, I fear it would be a terrible mistake for him to marry you."

"Why is that?" Rebecca managed to squeeze in the question when Lord Benedict paused for breath, though she wondered why she hadn't used the opportunity to reveal her true identity.

His lordship started at the sound of her voice. Had he

begun to think she might be mute? Or was he not accustomed to having his pronouncements questioned?

Whatever the cause of his surprise, he quickly recovered from it. "For a number of excellent reasons, I assure you. Though my brother is a fine young fellow in many respects, he is impulsive and changeable in his affections. You are not the first woman with whom he has fallen in love. Fortunately I was able to end his other dalliances before they reached the troublesome stage yours has."

Lord Benedict was a fine-looking gentleman of great consequence who had paid her more compliments in five minutes than she had received in her whole life. Yet Rebecca found herself forming a decidedly poor opinion of him.

For one thing, it sounded as if he was trying to run his brother's life. For another, she did not care for the way he dismissed Mr. Stanhope's feelings for Hermione as a meaningless dalliance without ever having seen them together. She *had* seen the way the young gentleman looked at Hermione and spoke to her. Though admittedly no expert in matters of the heart, Rebecca believed she could recognize the difference between a transient fancy and true love.

His lordship must have sensed she was not swayed by his reasoning.

"There is also the matter of your birth and fortune." He dismissed the fine old manor house with a flick of his gaze. "The woman my brother weds will one day be Lady Benedict. It is not a position that should be assumed by someone who is unprepared for the demands it will entail."

Once again Rebecca had a chance to get a word in, and once again she let her curiosity get the better of her. "Why will your *brother's* wife become Lady Benedict? Surely, if you have a son one day…"

She lowered her gaze, chiding herself for raising such a

delicate subject with a man she'd just met. A man who didn't even know who she truly was.

"I will have no sons, Miss Leonard, nor daughters either. Carrying on the family line is a task I will leave to my brother and his wife, which is why it is of the utmost importance for Claude to choose his bride wisely."

The viscount's answer piqued her curiosity further still, but this time Rebecca refused to indulge it with more questions. It was clear Lord Benedict wanted his brother to select a wife using his head rather than his heart, and the only qualifications should be fortune and rank. Hermione Leonard might not be the daughter of an earl with a large dowry, but she was well bred and accomplished. What was even more important, in Rebecca's opinion, she would make a loving wife and devoted mother.

Lord Benedict reminded Rebecca of the haughty relatives who had tried to prevent her parents' marriage. "Is that everything you wish to say, sir?"

"Not quite. I have an important request to make of you. After hearing me out with such civility, I hope you will be inclined to grant it."

"Request?" Rebecca arched one eyebrow.

The viscount thrust his arms behind his back and drew himself up to his full, impressive height. "Having heard some of my reasons for opposing the match, I must ask you to promise you will not wed my brother."

Though her conscience prodded her to explain his mistake, Rebecca could not bear to expose poor Hermione to this dreadful man without proper warning. Besides, Lord Benedict would discover the truth soon enough. "I give you my word, sir. I will not marry your brother under any circumstances."

"Truly?" Her reply seemed to take some of the starch

out of the viscount. "Just like that? You're certain you won't change your mind?"

"Entirely certain." Rebecca reminded herself she was telling the truth. "After everything you've said, nothing could induce me to make such a match."

Once he believed he'd gotten his way, Lord Benedict became far more affable. "That is very sensible of you and most obliging. I came here fearing I might have a fight on my hands. Many women, once they'd accepted a marriage offer from a man with my brother's prospects, would have clung to it against all appeals. Your willingness to act in everyone's best interests speaks well of your sense and character."

His cordiality made Rebecca begin to regret misleading him. Lord Benedict had misled *himself,* she reminded her nagging conscience. She'd never once claimed to *be* Hermione. If he'd given her an opportunity to speak in the beginning, rather than rattling on in that arrogant manner, he would soon have learned of his error.

"If you will excuse me, sir, I must retire." If she stayed in the garden any longer, Rebecca feared Hermione might come looking for her and expose the whole mistaken identity.

"Of course." His lordship paid her the compliment of bowing very low. "I will not detain you any longer."

With that, he marched away looking greatly pleased with himself, while Rebecca hurried into Rose Grange to tell Hermione everything that had transpired.

"You did *what?*" The Honourable Claude Stanhope hurled down his silver fork with such force it might have chipped his china dinner plate.

Leaping to his feet, he glared down the length of the

dining table at his half brother. "How dare you speak to Miss Leonard without my knowledge, let alone demand she break our engagement?"

"I did not *demand* anything of the lady." Sebastian continued to consume his helping of roast pork with a better appetite than he'd had since he learned of his brother's latest romantic entanglement. "I simply explained the situation and requested her cooperation. To my surprise, she was most agreeable."

"Agreeable?" Claude huffed. "She's a perfect delight! And I refuse to believe she consented to break our engagement at a mere word from you. Tell me the truth. Did you threaten her? Try to bribe her? Did you tell her despicable lies about me?"

"Nothing so nefarious, I assure you." Sebastian tried to dismiss his brother's description of Hermione Leonard as a *perfect delight* but found he could not.

Though her looks were not perfect by any objective measure of feminine beauty, there was a strength about her jaw and brow that appealed to him more than the porcelain delicacy currently in fashion. Her eyes were very fine, too. The warm golden brown suggested prudence and constancy, while flickers of emerald betrayed lively intelligence, perhaps even an impish sense of humor. Ever since their meeting, he'd found himself recalling those eyes and the mystery he'd sensed in their beguiling depths.

Now he strove to put them out of his mind so he could concentrate on this discussion with his brother. Having rescued Claude from his latest scrape with such ease, the last thing he needed was for his brother to run back to Miss Leonard and urge her to change her mind. Not that he suspected the lady could be easily persuaded, in spite of his experience to the contrary. Sebastian flattered himself that he had made a good case for breaking the engagement. It was also possible Miss Leonard had been having second thoughts even before he spoke to her.

"I simply explained my reasons for objecting to a union between you," he continued. "Then I requested her promise not to proceed further. I must admit, I was surprised by her willingness to oblige me so readily. I was prepared to pay well to secure your freedom."

It would have cost him a pretty penny to extricate his brother from an engagement to any of the grasping beauties with whom Claude had been besotted in the past. What a relief that Hermione Leonard had proven to possess far more sense and strength of character than those others. Sebastian had considered offering her generous compensation for her cooperation, but Miss Leonard's admirable behavior had made him fear she might take offense at such a suggestion.

"I don't want to be free of Hermione!" Claude pounded his fist on the table, making the silverware jump and the crystal shudder. "Why can't you understand that, Sebastian? I want to spend the rest of my life with her."

To his considerable dismay, Sebastian found he *could* understand his brother's desire for something more than a passing flirtation with Hermione Leonard. For that very reason, he was relieved he'd been able to break the engagement. He would not relish the prospect of feeling more than brotherly concern for his attractive sister-in-law.

"You didn't want to be free of the others either, remember?" he snapped, unsettled by the interest Miss Leonard had stirred in him after such a brief meeting. He'd believed himself immune from those sorts of feelings and wanted it to remain that way. "Yet later you were always grateful for my intervention. I have no doubt it will be the same this time."

In truth, Sebastian was not quite as confident as he strove to sound. Though he had many reasons for hoping this latest dalliance would end like all the others, he would lose considerable respect for his brother if Claude recovered too easily from his feelings for the intriguing Miss Leonard.

"It will *not,* I tell you!" Claude's boyish features clenched in a resolute scowl that made him look older. "Hermione is nothing like those other girls."

Sebastian could not gainsay that. Miss Leonard was as different from those simpering coquettes as a modest, fragrant spray of lily-of-the-valley was from a patch of showy Oriental lilies with their cloying scent.

"Consequently," Claude continued, "my feelings for her are quite beyond anything I felt for them."

His blazing hostility seemed to moderate, as Sebastian had known it would. His brother had always been prone to strong, sudden passions that quickly burned out. His infatuation with Miss Leonard, however intense at the moment, would be no different. Sebastian assured himself that what he'd done was as much for the lady's benefit as for Claude's. He would not want her hurt when his brother's ardor waned.

"I am grateful to you," Claude admitted in a grudging tone, "for saving me from myself with those other ladies. If you hadn't, I would not be free now to commit myself, heart and soul, to Hermione."

Sebastian pushed his plate away. His brother's sentimentality was taking a toll on his appetite.

"I believe the vicar would advise you to commit your soul elsewhere," he informed Claude in a tone of driest irony.

The young man responded with a withering look. "Make light of my feelings if you must, Sebastian. At least *I* am not afraid to risk my heart again after one bad experience."

Sebastian rose to confront his brother. "I will thank you to refrain from raising that matter."

Claude moved from his end of the table, taking a few steps toward Sebastian. "Why am I not permitted to comment on your private life when you are free to meddle in mine? I hardly call that fair."

"Fair or not, I am your elder and the head of this family." Sebastian moved toward his brother. "If I *meddle,* it is for your own good, so you will not make the same mistake I did."

"Being head of the family does not make you my master!" Claude stabbed his forefinger into Sebastian's chest. "And being older does not make you right about everything!"

"So," Sebastian sneered, "you rebel against the advice of an older man, yet you are hopelessly besotted with an older woman?"

He knew his allusion to the lady's age was ungallant. Miss Leonard could not be more than three years his brother's senior. But Claude's jibe about being afraid to risk his heart had struck a nerve.

"Older woman?" His brother stared at Sebastian as if he'd taken leave of his senses. "Hermione is four full years younger than I."

"That cannot be." Sebastian shook his head. "The woman I spoke with was very handsome, but she had to be at least five-and-twenty."

"It could not have been Hermione, then." Claude crossed his arms in front of his chest, daring Sebastian to contradict him. "If anything, she looks *younger* than her years."

"Of course it was her." Sebastian had never heard anything so ridiculous. "She told me…that is…she was picking flowers in Squire Leonard's garden and…"

A look of amused comprehension and overwhelming relief

made Claude's face light up. "The lady you spoke to, was she about this height with brown hair and hazel eyes?"

"That's right." Why was his brother grinning like a fool?

"Well done, Sebastian!" Claude began to sputter with laughter. "You managed to persuade Hermione's *governess* not to marry me!"

Governess? Sebastian's jaw clenched. To think he had been fooled and foiled by that sly creature with the traitorous collaboration of his own unaccountable interest in her. Clearly his brother was not the only one who needed to be kept from repeating past mistakes!

Chapter Two

"I still cannot imagine how Lord Benedict came to make such a mistake." Hermione shook her head in puzzlement as she and Rebecca walked toward the village church for Sunday morning service. "How could he possibly suppose you were me?"

"It is a mystery beyond my power to fathom." Rebecca refused to take offense at Hermione's remark, though it did sting a little. Since she'd come to Rose Grange as a grown woman of twenty to teach Squire Leonard's twelve-year-old daughter, perhaps it was only natural the girl should think of her as hopelessly ancient. When Hermione reached the advanced age of seven-and-twenty, she might consider it more flattering than ridiculous to be mistaken for nineteen.

"His lordship struck me as the type of man who takes little notice of a woman's age or the fashion of her garments," Rebecca continued. "To him, I suspect one female, of lesser rank than a peeress, looks much like another."

She wished she could dismiss the top-lofty viscount from her thoughts with such ease. But he intruded upon them as insistently as he had upon her solitude in the garden yesterday. Whenever anything blue caught her eye, she found herself recalling his eyes. Snatches of his conversation drifted through her mind in the bothersome way pieces of music sometimes did. In his case, it was a resonant baritone melody in a minor key.

Hermione let out a soft trill of laughter that banished the viscount's voice from Rebecca's mind…for the moment. "What amazes me even more is your audacity in leading his lordship on so he never suspected his error."

"I did *not* lead him on," Rebecca protested, relieved to spy the old stone church quite near ahead. She was not certain how much more of Hermione's teasing on the subject she could abide. "I told you, he scarcely let me get a word in. Mine was a sin of omission, which I only did to spare you. I hope that will count in my favor when I make my confession and beg Divine forgiveness."

"Of course it will." Hermione seemed to repent her levity at Rebecca's expense. "I am very grateful to you for keeping him away from me until Claude can introduce us properly. I hope once he becomes acquainted with me, Lord Benedict will withdraw his objections to our betrothal."

"I hope so too, for both your sakes." Having spoken with the forceful viscount, Rebecca doubted he would be so easily dissuaded.

Behind them, the beat of horses' hooves and the soft rumble of carriage wheels approached. Then a familiar, cheerful voice called out, "Miss Leonard, Miss Beaton, good morning to you!"

Hermione spun about. "Mr. Stanhope, this is a pleasant surprise. What brings you to church in Avoncross this morning?"

The Stanhope estate belonged to the neighboring parish, and the family provided a living for its vicar. Rebecca had never seen the gentlemen attending this church.

As Rebecca slowly turned around, Claude Stanhope uttered a sentence that sent a guilty shudder through her. "It was my brother's suggestion we come here this morning. Miss Leonard, may I introduce Viscount Benedict? Sebastian, it is an honor to present my fiancée, Miss Hermione Leonard."

By this time Rebecca had turned toward the fashionable gig which had halted behind them. As the Stanhope brothers alighted, Lord Benedict tossed the horses' reins to a young footman.

"Miss Leonard, we meet at last." The viscount acknowledged Hermione with a stiff bow while she swept him a deep, graceful curtsey.

"Lord Benedict, it is a pleasure to meet the beloved brother of my betrothed."

Often, in the company of ladies and gentlemen, Rebecca felt as if she were invisible. Now, she wished she was so she would not have to confront the viscount in her true, humble identity—a penniless governess he would scarcely condescend to notice.

But she was not invisible, and Lord Benedict most certainly *did* notice her. Turning away from Hermione without responding to her greeting, he fixed Rebecca with the icy intensity of his slate-blue stare. "Miss Beaton, I presume? Or am I mistaken about your identity once again?"

"Lord Benedict." She strove to keep her back straight as she curtsied, determined not to let the viscount intimidate her. "Since you have kindly given me an opportunity to answer this time, I am pleased to inform you that you are *not* mistaken."

The excessively polite impertinence of her reply made Claude Stanhope sputter with laughter while Hermione let out a girlish giggle.

Lord Benedict tried to scowl, but one corner of his mouth appeared to resist. "In the course of our previous conversation, I gave you a number of opportunities to correct my error. Yet you allowed me to persist in making a fool of myself."

Put like that, her well-intentioned actions sounded quite mean-spirited. Did Lord Benedict assume she'd kept him ignorant of her true identity simply to amuse herself at his expense? Once again Rebecca found herself unable to answer the viscount, but not because he gave her no chance to speak.

To her relief, the church bell came to her rescue, summoning them to worship.

"Come, Miss Beaton." Hermione tugged on her arm. "Or we'll be late."

"Sebastian," Claude Stanhope beckoned his brother. "Perhaps we can speak to the ladies after church."

With a mixture of eagerness and reluctance, Rebecca followed Hermione into the fine old sanctuary of golden-brown Cotswold stone. She knew very well why she was anxious to escape Lord Benedict and his disturbing suggestion that she had behaved deceitfully. What baffled her was a contrary desire to remain near him. Perhaps it was that discerning gaze of his, which seemed to see her in a way few others did. Or perhaps it was the compelling music of his voice that made her want to listen even when the words were not agreeable to her.

As the service progressed, she was acutely conscious of the viscount's fine voice as he joined in the prayers and responses of the liturgy, from two pews behind her.

"Reading from the Gospel According to St. Matthew," announced the vicar, "'Judge not, that ye be not judged. For with what judgment ye judge, ye shall be judged; and what measure ye mete, it shall be measured to you again."'

Was that what she and Lord Benedict were doing? Rebecca wondered as she listened to the familiar passage with uncomfortable new insight. She had judged him to be just like her haughty relatives while he had judged her to be a mocking liar. It troubled her to consider which of them might be closer to the truth.

"'Therefore,'" the vicar concluded, "'all things whatsoever ye would that men should do to you, do ye even so to them.'"

How would she feel, Rebecca's conscience demanded, if Lord Benedict had allowed her to persist in a mistaken belief when a few words from him might have set her straight? While she might not have strictly deceived him yesterday, she had strayed far from the Golden Rule. Though her pride rebelled at the prospect, Rebecca could not escape the feeling that she owed the haughty viscount an apology. Whether he would accept was quite another matter.

Hard as he tried, Sebastian found it difficult to concentrate on the service that morning. Against his will, his gaze kept straying from his prayer book to the women seated two pews ahead.

No wonder his brother considered it such a fine joke that he'd mistaken Miss Beaton for Hermione Leonard. Claude's fiancée had proven to be precisely the sort of silly chit Sebastian expected. Her fluttering lashes, whispery voice and grating giggles told him all he needed to know about her within a minute of their introduction.

Claude had been right in saying she looked younger than her years. Sebastian did not count that in her favor. He had no doubt she acted younger too. In his experience, young ladies as pretty as Miss Leonard had little enough sense to begin with. They tended to be selfish, sometimes cruelly so, and they scarcely knew their own minds from one minute to the next.

If only he'd been able to speak to her yesterday before she'd been put on her guard, he might have persuaded her to release his brother from their ill-considered engagement. No doubt Miss Beaton and her pupil had enjoyed a good laugh at his expense. Perhaps she'd congratulated herself on matching wits with a man like him and coming out the winner. Even as that notion vexed him, he could not quell a stubborn flicker of admiration for such a capable adversary.

Thinking back on their conversation, he was forced to admit Miss Beaton had not spoken a single untrue word, yet she had given him no reason to doubt his mistaken assumption about her identity either. It could not have been an easy balance to maintain. Neither could he deny the misunderstanding was partly his fault. If he had not been so determined to have his say, without interruption or argument, Miss Beaton might have been compelled to reveal the truth.

The moment the service concluded, Sebastian was accosted by a talkative acquaintance and detained for several minutes. Once he managed to break free, he looked around for the women but saw no sign of them. Given the accusing way he had addressed Miss Beaton earlier, he could hardly blame her if she'd fled from the church with all haste. He could not shake an unaccountable sense of disappointment.

Emerging from the dimly lit sanctuary, he squinted against the brilliant spring sunshine as he scanned the churchyard.

Over beside the gig, he spied his brother absorbed in deep conversation with Hermione Leonard. In Sebastian's opinion, it was grossly unfair that once a man had made an offer of marriage, he was honor-bound to go through with the wedding, no matter what the circumstances. Only the lady had the right to change her mind.

"Lord Benedict?" At the unexpected sound of Miss Beaton's voice behind him, Sebastian turned swiftly.

Seeing her standing to one side of the vestibule door, he found himself uncharacteristically at a loss for words.

She seized the initiative. "If I may, sir, I wish to continue our conversation from before the service. Upon reflection, I realize I behaved badly yesterday, when you came looking for Miss Leonard. I ought to have informed you at once of your mistake rather than encouraging your continued belief that I was she."

Her whole being radiated sincerity. During his career in Parliament and his past dealings with women, Sebastian had seldom encountered that quality to such a degree.

"I have given you good reason to doubt my veracity," she continued. "But I swear, when I acted as I did, it was never my intention to make a fool of you."

Her assurance soothed Sebastian's indignation more than he expected.

"I'm certain you must have had your reasons." He was not accustomed to backing down, but Miss Beaton's candid admission of fault left him with few options.

Her indomitable chin lowered a little. "At the time, I believed I had good reasons for what I did. I gave myself a whole variety of excuses, most to do with protecting Miss Leonard. I see now that I would not have needed to work so hard to justify my actions if they had been right and proper."

Sebastian found the lady's whole air quite disarming. How could he continue to blame her when it was clear she reproached herself even more?

He shrugged. "It seems we both made mistakes yesterday, Miss Beaton."

"Perhaps so." Her high, clear brow furrowed slightly. "But I fear my error in conduct was much worse than your error of fact."

One corner of Sebastian's lips curled upward, as it had been itching to do since he'd laid eyes on her again. "Is it to be a contest, then, which of us was more to blame?"

Her full lips pursed then spread in a smile that refused to be kept in check. It illuminated her face like a stray shaft of sunlight hitting a stained-glass window. "That would be rather foolish, wouldn't it? You are most gracious, Lord Benedict."

If there was one thing Sebastian could not resist, it was a sincere compliment. "I've been called many things in my time, but *gracious* has never been one of them."

"Indeed?" She glanced toward his brother and Miss Leonard, then headed slowly toward them while Sebastian strolled along beside her. "What do they call you, then?"

He thought for a moment. "Arrogant…stubborn…ruthless…"

Miss Beaton did not rush to contradict him. But as Sebastian searched for more insults, in which he took perverse pride, she asked, "Do they say anything good?"

"Those *are* the good things," he quipped, feeling ridiculously pleased when she laughed. "I am not being entirely facetious. All those so-called faults can have their place when put to good use."

"What sort of use?" She sounded doubtful.

"Fighting in Parliament to get our Army and Navy the support they needed to defeat Napoleon."

"That *is* a very good cause." The warmth of admiration in Miss Beaton's voice gratified him. "You must be overjoyed the war has been won at last."

Sebastian held open the churchyard gate for her. "I must confess my feelings are more of relief than exultation, especially when I think of all the lives lost on both sides. Even that relief is tinged with a sense of futility, that I was not able to do as much as was needed. Those brave souls accomplished far more than should ever have been asked of them. They did it in spite of the Government's neglect and interference rather than with our support."

What was he saying? Sebastian snapped his mouth shut. He could not recall the last time he had confided his feelings so fully to anyone, much less a woman he'd been so thoroughly vexed with an hour ago. "Pardon my nattering on, Miss Beaton. I am more accustomed to Parliamentary debates than polite conversation with a lady."

As the pair drew nearer to the gig, their footsteps slowed until they were barely moving. "Do not apologize, sir. Your conversation may not be *polite,* if by that you mean trivial and insipid, but it is most stimulating. There are a great many questions I wish I had time to ask on the subject, but you and your brother must want to get home."

He should fetch Claude home at once, rather than let the young fool linger there fawning over his unsuitable fiancée. But Sebastian found he did not wish to forsake the agreeable company of Rebecca Beaton.

Then an idea struck him—one that might kill two birds with one stone. "If you have questions for me, that sets us even. Claude tells me you were Miss Leonard's governess before you became her companion and chaperone."

"That is not a question, sir." The lady's lips blossomed into a playful grin. "Unless you mean to inquire whether your brother's information is correct, which it is. Squire Leonard hired me to be his daughter's governess not long after her mother died. In addition to educating her to the best of my ability, I hope I have been able to supply her with some of the companionship and advice of a mother."

Though Sebastian knew he ought to follow up on the perfect opening Miss Beaton had provided, the only words he could produce were, "Not a mother, surely! You are far too near her age. I refuse to believe you could be more than a slightly elder sister."

His words clearly pleased the lady. "You are most chivalrous, Lord Benedict. I assure you, Hermione considers me more than equal to her late mother in years."

To Sebastian, that further demonstrated Miss Leonard's immaturity. "Chivalrous? I cannot allow that. I have been called it even less often than *gracious*. You must mean to atone for the little trick you played on me by turning my head with flattery."

"No indeed!" she cried. "If I have a fault in that regard, it is being far too blunt-spoken for my position."

"Others may consider it a fault, Miss Beaton, but I do not." He found it refreshing to converse with a woman who did not simper or act coy, one who owned to her mistakes and possessed a sense of humor that was pleasantly infectious. If only more of the marriageable ladies in London were like this insignificant country governess, Sebastian would have had fewer reservations about letting his brother come to town.

Claude finally took his eyes off Hermione Leonard long enough to notice his brother and her governess.

"Bravo, Miss Beaton!" He swept her an exaggerated bow.

"I don't know how, but you seem to have a knack for managing my irascible brother."

Sebastian bristled at the notion of being *managed* by any woman.

But before he could summon a cutting retort, Miss Beaton spoke up. "You give me too much credit, sir, and your brother not enough. Considering the regrettable beginning of our acquaintance, he has been most forbearing, gracious and chivalrous."

Claude's eyebrows shot up. "Then there can be only one explanation. This man must be an imposter! Confess, villain, what have you done with my brother?"

The ladies burst into laughter. Though Miss Leonard's shrill giggles still grated on Sebastian's nerves, they sounded far more pleasant in harmony with Rebecca Beaton's warm chuckle.

"Enough of your impudence, boy." Sebastian assumed a mock scowl to prove his identity. "Why don't you invite the ladies to Stanhope Court for tea so Aunt Eloisa and I can become better acquainted with your fiancée?" He mentioned his widowed aunt so there could be no suggestion of impropriety.

"I should like nothing better! What do you say, ladies? Will you grace the dull old place with your presence?" Claude's handsome young face beamed with such pleasure, it gave Sebastian a twinge of guilt, which he promptly suppressed.

His brother must assume this invitation signaled Sebastian's acceptance of the betrothal. In fact, nothing could be further from the truth.

"We'd be delighted to accept!" Hermione Leonard exclaimed. "Wouldn't we, Miss Beaton?"

Her companion's response was less hasty, which Sebastian

approved, even though it made him anxious that she might refuse.

After thinking for a moment, she nodded. "We are not otherwise engaged. And I doubt your father will be sufficiently recovered from his cold to want our company."

"Excellent! We will look forward to your visit." Sebastian felt more confident of accomplishing his goal than he had since learning how Miss Beaton had duped him. If he could enlist her able assistance, he was certain his brother's imprudent engagement would be as good as broken.

Chapter Three

"You certainly managed to charm Lord Benedict." Hermione glanced around the elegant interior of the viscount's carriage a few days later. "Fancy him sending this to fetch us to tea."

"I'm certain it has nothing to do with me," Rebecca protested, smoothing the skirt of her neat but unfashionable dress. They had not even reached the viscount's mansion and already she felt hopelessly dowdy. "No doubt it is his lordship's compliment to you as his brother's fiancée."

"Hardly." Hermione grimaced. "Did you not see the way he looked at me the other day or hear his tone when he deigned to address me? It positively dripped with scorn. I'm certain Lord Benedict is still violently opposed to my wedding his brother."

"Dripped with scorn? Violently opposed?" Rebecca shook her head. "You are exaggerating. His lordship may have been a trifle cool, but surely that was my fault for misleading him as I did. I expect he did not feel kindly disposed toward anyone connected with me."

Hermione's delicate features tightened into a doubtful frown. "At first, perhaps, but you soon won him over. By the time the two of you finished talking, Lord Benedict seemed quite taken with you. Yet he still appeared to regard me as the most odious creature he had ever beheld."

Reaching across the carriage, Rebecca caught Hermione's ice-cold fingers and gave them a reassuring squeeze. "Lord Benedict is barely acquainted with you. He objects to your match with Mr. Stanhope on general principles—and not very sound ones, in my opinion. Once he gets to know you better, I'm certain he will be delighted to welcome you into the family."

"I hope you're right." Hermione caught her full lower lip between her teeth. "I fear I am not at my best around his lordship. He is so haughty and severe, I am quite afraid of him. When he gives me that cold blue stare, I feel every bit as foolish as he seems to regard me."

"Perhaps he is a little proud, but given his wealth and position, that can hardly be surprising." What did surprise Rebecca was hearing herself rise to Lord Benedict's defense. "Yet he is not too proud to make a jest at his own expense. And when he laughs, he doesn't seem the least bit severe."

Why did she feel compelled to stand up for anyone who was being criticized—even a powerful man more than capable of taking his own part? It must be a habit from her school days. The one thing that had made that miserable place bearable was the close friendships she'd forged with a group of fellow pupils. They had banded together to comfort, cheer and defend one another.

Hermione regarded her former governess with a rather superior smile. "It seems his lordship has succeeded in charming you in return, though I would not have believed him capable of it."

That pointed observation threw Rebecca into confusion. Hermione made it sound as if there were romantic feelings between her and the viscount. "Now you are talking foolishness. I simply tried to keep an open mind and not let my opinion of the gentleman be prejudiced by a bad first impression. You should do the same."

"Of course!" cried Hermione. "You've given me the most brilliant idea."

"To keep an open mind about your future brother-in-law? It is a good idea, but hardly brilliant."

"Not that." Hermione leaned toward Rebecca as if imparting a secret. "Since Lord Benedict is so partial to you, could you use your influence to persuade him to give our engagement his blessing? Please, Miss Beaton!"

"What influence could I possibly have over a man like his lordship?" Rebecca firmly dismissed the notion—from her own mind as much as Hermione's. "He is not *partial* to me, only polite."

Seeing the younger woman's crestfallen look, she relented…a little. "Still, you may rely on me to acquaint Lord Benedict with your many good qualities."

Eager to turn the conversation from that awkward topic, Rebecca pointed out the window. "Look, there is Stanhope Court. What a fine house it is. And what superb views it must command from the hilltop!"

A few moments later, the carriage came to a stop before the viscount's magnificent mansion. Rebecca had often glimpsed it from a distance, but had never before seen it up so close. The front façade, of honey-brown Cotswold stone, looked very grand and imposing with a high portico supported by six lofty pillars. A pair of great wings swept behind the house on either side, no doubt enclosing a rear courtyard that gave the place its name.

As she climbed out of the carriage behind Hermione, Rebecca was torn between wonder and an acute sense of her own insignificance. Though she recalled living in houses almost as impressive as this one, she had never been welcome in any of them. Only in more modest surroundings had she found a measure of acceptance and affection.

To her surprise, Lord Benedict and his brother came out to meet them.

"Thank you for accepting our invitation, ladies." Claude Stanhope swept them a deep bow. "This house has been empty for so long, it is a pleasure to have company at last."

Offering Hermione his arm, he escorted her toward one of the sets of stairs that led up to the portico.

That left Rebecca alone in the presence of the viscount and feeling self-conscious after her conversation with Hermione. It had been one thing for Lord Benedict to treat her as something approaching his equal when he'd mistaken her for Squire Leonard's daughter. His manner on Sunday she attributed to the time and place, for were they not all meant to be brothers and sisters in the sight of God?

Now, with his large, splendid house towering in the background, she could not fail to realize what an enormous gulf separated a powerful peer of the realm from someone little higher than a servant.

But Lord Benedict bowed and offered her his arm, as if she were an honored guest. "I fear I am to blame for Stanhope Court being neglected."

The blue gaze he fixed upon her did not seem cold at all. In spite of Rebecca's determination to resist any such foolish fancy, she could not ignore a warm glow of sincere regard.

"Why are you to blame?" She slipped her hand into the crook of his elbow, steeling herself to betray no sign that this first contact between them gave her any particular enjoyment.

But it did, hard as she tried to persuade herself otherwise.

There was a solid dependable strength about his arm that appealed to her far more than it ought to.

"This poor house was a casualty of my mission to secure more support for our men at arms," he replied with a mixture of pride and chagrin. "When Parliament wasn't sitting, I twice made the voyage to Portugal. I wanted to see firsthand what our troops needed to win the war. The rest of the time, I cadged invitations to house parties where I could meet with other Members of Parliament and promote my views."

Rebecca's respect for the viscount grew with every word he uttered. Though he made it sound as if he were apologizing for his actions rather than bragging about them, it was clear he had worked tirelessly for something he believed in.

"Perhaps *you* should have hosted a party," she suggested, as they passed through the elegant entry hall with its fine marble floor, "and invited those people here."

"I'm not certain who would have accepted an invitation from me in the end." His firm mouth briefly arched into a wry grin. If Rebecca had not been watching his face so carefully, she might have missed it. "I had become such a notorious bore on the subject. Besides, everyone knows married gentlemen make far better hosts."

"Were you too busy promoting your cause to seek a wife?" Rebecca recalled something he had said during their first meeting about never having children.

Surely now that the war was over, such an eligible and attractive man would have no difficulty securing a bride. Somehow the thought of him having a wife provoked a rush of contradictory feelings in her. On one hand, it seemed wrong that so good a man should always be alone. Yet at the same time, she resented the thought of him belonging to another woman.

Rebecca chided herself for such ungenerous feelings, especially when Lord Benedict flinched at her words. She hoped her offhand remark about such a private matter had not offended him.

But before she could stammer an apology, the viscount recovered his spirits and continued their conversation. "I fear I neglected a number of things in my zeal to do my duty, Miss Beaton. This house…my brother's welfare…"

He gave a rueful nod down the wide, portrait-hung gallery toward young Mr. Stanhope, who was ushering Hermione into a sitting room.

Was that why Lord Benedict had taken such a forceful interest in his brother's engagement, Rebecca wondered, because he felt guilty for failing in his brotherly duty? She could understand such feelings all too well. With a pang of shame, she recalled promising to advocate on Hermione's behalf with his lordship. Yet she had not said a single word about the poor girl.

"As for that," she hastened to rectify her lapse, "Mr. Stanhope does not appear to have suffered any neglect. He possesses most engaging manners and has become a general favorite in this area ever since he took up residence. Though you may not approve of his attachment to Miss Leonard, I can assure you she is an excellent match for him in every way that truly matters."

A doubtful frown darkened Lord Benedict's striking countenance, but it was too late for him to say anything disparaging about Hermione for they had reached the sitting room.

They had not been ten minutes at tea before Sebastian wondered why his brother could not see what was altogether obvious to him. A country squire's daughter such as

Hermione Leonard was simply not cut out to be the wife of a future viscount. Apart from a brief greeting to their aunt, he'd scarcely spoken a word since she arrived, and not for a lack of effort on his part to draw her out.

"Another plum puff, Miss Leonard?" He held out the overflowing tray of cakes and pastries. "You've eaten so little, I fear our hospitality does not meet with your approval."

"Not at all." She reached toward the plate with wary hesitation as if she feared the walnut tea cake might be poisoned.

"For pity's sake, Sebastian," his brother snapped, "don't hound Miss Leonard to eat if she's not hungry! I told you this was twice too much food for the five of us."

With a shrug, Sebastian offered the plate of sweets to her companion. "Can you find anything to tempt you, Miss Beaton?"

"Indeed, sir." She picked up a rout cake and set it on her plate, then reached for a jam tartlet. "The only difficulty lies in choosing between so many temptations."

"Then by all means have as much as you wish of everything," Sebastian urged her. "I like to see a lady with a healthy appetite."

It accorded well with the rest of her character. She did not pretend excessive delicacy as so many ladies of fashion did. Sebastian was certain she could not be prone to swooning or any other such affectations. It surprised him how much at ease she seemed in his house. Though clearly impressed and appreciative, she was not overawed by the grand old place. Her demeanor presented such a contrast to Claude's gauche, uncommunicative fiancée, he could not help but be impressed.

"That is most generous of you, Lord Benedict." She cast

a cheerful smile around at all the others. "But I fear my digestion will suffer if I overindulge in such rich fare."

How would he have borne this visit, Sebastian wondered, if not for Miss Beaton's presence? Somehow she managed to keep up an engaging flow of conversation to cover for Miss Leonard's sulky silence.

"What a marvelous art collection you have, Lord Benedict," she remarked, effortlessly filling yet another awkward pause. "That portrait of the young lady with the long curls is very fine indeed."

"You have a good eye for painting, Miss Beaton. That lady is our great-great-grandmother. She sat for the Restoration Court painter, Lely. It is one of the most valuable in our collection."

"I'm certain Miss Leonard recognized the artist's style," Miss Beaton continued. "She is an accomplished artist herself. She has done some very clever sketches of our acquaintances and a charming series of watercolors of the garden at Rose Grange."

Her praise of Miss Leonard put Claude back in good humor. "Hermione tells me you are quite skilled at drawing and painting, Miss Beaton. Might I persuade you to undertake a commission for me?"

Sebastian marked the lady's hesitation and approved it. As she took a slow sip of tea, he sensed she was searching for the right words to frame a polite refusal.

"I should be reluctant to disoblige you, Mr. Stanhope, but I fear Hermione has been too kind in her praise of my skill. You would be much better served bestowing your commission upon her."

"I would, of course." Claude helped himself to another pastry from the tray. "But I fear the task might be beyond even her considerable powers. I desire a sketch of *her,* perhaps tinted with watercolors. I am certain you possess both the talent and appreciation for your subject to render a flattering but accurate likeness."

Miss Beaton's reluctance vanished in an indulgent smile. "Very well then, sir. If you have faith in my powers, I shall be happy to make the attempt."

Would the lady be as willing to undertake a different sort of commission which he intended to offer her? Sebastian bolted a mouthful of tea. Though she had not known him long and the acquaintance had gotten off to a bad start, Miss Beaton did not appear to hold it against him. Indeed, he sensed a deep bond of mutual respect and sympathy between them that he fervently hoped might win her over.

Their tea was not a success, Rebecca was forced to admit, in spite of the quantity and variety of baked delicacies on offer. Though Lord Benedict made an effort to be civil to Hermione, the poor girl seemed to sense his veiled hostility, which dampened her spirits. Afraid of saying the wrong thing, she spoke hardly a word even when the others tried to draw her out. Her wary silence only made his lordship impatient and Claude Stanhope irritable.

Desperate to fill the tense pauses in conversation, Rebecca found herself talking far more than she was accustomed to. She seized every opportunity to pay tribute to her former pupil's cleverness, good nature and many accomplishments. Yet she feared her praise rang hollow in the face of Hermione's wooden silence.

The only thing that made the experience bearable was Lord Benedict's attentiveness. He seemed to hang on her every word. He laughed at her feeble efforts to lighten the atmosphere with a jest. He continually offered her dainty cakes and pastries. Surely Hermione could not be correct in supposing the viscount had taken a fancy to her? Hard as Rebecca strove to dismiss such an unlikely but appealing notion, Lord Benedict's gallantry made it difficult to deny the possibility.

At last his lordship rose and bowed to his aunt. "Thank you for the fine tea, but if I swallow another crumb, I fear I may explode. Would you ladies care to take a stroll around our gardens? They are quite fine, though I can take no credit for them. That is one area in which my neglect has served a useful purpose. I reckon good gardeners are like good generals. They achieve their best results when given plenty of supplies and a minimum of interference."

The quip and his invitation broke the brittle tension among their small party.

"A splendid idea!" Claude Stanhope leaped to his feet and held out his hand to his fiancée. "Come, Hermione, you must see the view from the Fountain Garden."

"I should like that very much." Hermione seemed to shake off the bemusement that had held her mute. "The fresh air will do me good."

As the young couple hurried away, Rebecca rose to follow at a discreet distance, as she had so often during their brief courtship. Only this time, rather than tagging along on her own as a grudgingly tolerated chaperone, she was escorted by Lord Benedict. The viscount diverted her with stories about Stanhope Court and his ancestors whose portraits thronged its walls.

Once outside, Rebecca was immediately enchanted with the gardens, beginning with the one behind the house. It nestled between the east and west wings of Stanhope Court like a beloved child cradled in the arms of a caring parent. The colors of the flowers stood out in vivid contrast against the background of greenery.

Next Lord Benedict led her down a brickwork path that wound through a succession of vine-covered trellises to a smaller terrace garden cut into the side of the hill. Surrounded by box hedge walls, it had the air of a secret room decorated in shades of pink and gold. Rebecca wished she could linger in it, but since Hermione and Mr. Stanhope had already moved on, they followed.

When she entered the final garden, Rebecca let out a gasp of wonder mingled with a sigh of delight. This tiny hillside bower was not planted with bright-colored flowers to draw the eye. Instead it was edged with greenery and contained only a few pale but fragrant blossoms. At its heart, a small stone fountain splashed and tinkled a soothing liquid melody. The focus of this garden was not upon itself, but outward at the breathtaking view of the Vale of Avoncross.

"How lovely!" cried Hermione. "I could stand here all day and never grow tired of such a view."

As Hermione extolled the panorama before them, Rebecca could not help wishing her young friend would now hold her tongue for a few minutes. This glorious prospect deserved to be savored, with only the gentle babble of the fountain and the subtle fragrance of flowers to enhance the experience.

Despite Hermione's vow that she could stand and stare all day, it was not long before her interest waned and she and Mr. Stanhope wandered back up the path. Or perhaps she wanted to escape the brooding presence of Lord Benedict.

Rebecca's reaction was quite the opposite. She welcomed the opportunity to enjoy such a rich feast for the senses in his company.

Eventually, however, duty won out over inclination. "I suppose we ought to rejoin the others."

"In a moment." The viscount turned toward her with a

gaze as blue and breathtaking as the wide Cotswold sky. "First I have something particular to ask you."

Something particular? That usually implied a delicate matter, often romantic in nature. Surely Lord Benedict could not intend to declare some feelings for her…could he? After all, they'd just met the other day and theirs would be a far more unequal match than his brother's, to which he objected so strongly.

Though Rebecca reminded herself of those things, her heart began to beat far too fast, and her voice caught in her tightened throat when she replied, "By all means, your lordship. I am at your service."

She deliberately tried to emphasize with her words the vast gulf between her position and his.

But the viscount refused to take heed. "I do not mean to issue orders or condescend to you, Miss Beaton. I respect you too much for that. In many important ways, I believe we are very much equal. Our great concern for those we care about, for instance."

As Lord Benedict spoke, his deep voice grew softer and mellower in timbre. It might have coaxed a sigh from Rebecca, if she had not been on her guard to avoid any such slip.

"Since I wish to address you as an equal in that regard," he continued, "please feel free to call me by my given name—Sebastian."

His suggestion eroded Rebecca's resolve to keep her hopes in check. She wasn't certain she could bring herself to speak his first name aloud, but from that moment, she would always think of him as Sebastian.

"Would it be too great a liberty for me to call you Rebecca…in private at least?" His penetrating gaze softened until it seemed to caress her face. "It is a fine name—so proud and strong, yet lovely too. It seems a shame not to use it."

To hear her name on his lips provoked an unsettling mixture of pleasure and trepidation. No one had called her anything but Miss Beaton in such a long time it was almost as if they were two different people. "Miss Beaton" would never consent to such familiarity of address from a man she barely knew. But "Rebecca" felt quite well acquainted with Sebastian. Though not as well as she would have liked.

"You may call me what you wish." She resisted the urge to bow her head and cast a glance upward at Sebastian through her lashes. She had seen giddy girls behave that way around their admirers when she'd accompanied Hermione to the Assembly Rooms in Avoncross. She was far too old to flirt, even if she'd had the temperament for it. "Was that all you wanted to ask me?"

Sebastian hesitated a moment as if he'd been so lost in contemplation of her that he'd forgotten what he meant to say. "Yes…er…no! It was another matter entirely."

He inhaled a deep breath, then plunged ahead. "Though we have known each other a very short time, my dear Rebecca, I must tell you how much I have come to admire your sincerity and good sense."

He *was* making a romantic declaration! Forcing herself to keep breathing, Rebecca gave her leg a discreet pinch to wake her if she was dreaming.

"Y-you are too kind." She still could not bring herself to call him by his Christian name. Perhaps when she gave him her answer…

Sebastian's husky, rueful chuckle was even sweeter music to her ears than the gurgle of the fountain. "That is something else I have never been accused of before."

Instinctively, she rose to his defense again. "Then your acquaintances must be blind to your true character."

"Or perhaps," he suggested, "I am a better man when you are around."

What finer compliment could he possibly pay her? "It would make me very happy to think so."

"Then let me return to my question…my request."

"Of course." The prospect of a stable future stretched before Rebecca, as inviting as the verdant Vale of Avoncross. Security of situation and affection was something she'd always craved. Now, just when she'd begun to despair of ever gaining it, her dream seemed poised to come true.

"I need you," Sebastian murmured, "to become my ally."

"Ally?" That was an unusual term for a wife. Though perhaps, given Sebastian's preoccupation with military matters, it should not be too surprising.

"Precisely!" Sebastian made it sound as if the suggestion had come from her. "My ally in the effort to end my brother's imprudent betrothal. I want you to use your influence to persuade Miss Leonard to break it off."

Even as she chided herself for imagining he could ever want anything else from her, Rebecca felt as if Sebastian had pushed her over the edge of this serene terrace garden to hurtle down the steep cliff.

Chapter Four

What had come over Rebecca?

As his request hung in the air, unanswered, Sebastian tried to fathom the sudden change he sensed in her. A moment ago, she had seemed so amenable, as if she knew what he meant to ask before he uttered a word. Then an invisible door had slammed shut between them.

Had she expected him to say something different? Sebastian could not imagine what. He thought he had signaled his intentions quite clearly.

Rebecca stepped back and turned away from him, directing her gaze toward the pastoral beauty of the view. "You expect *me* to persuade Hermione to break her engagement to your brother?"

"I *hope* you will agree to assist me." An undercurrent of aversion beneath her words made Sebastian reconsider his plan. At the moment, it was all he had. And after what he'd seen of Hermione Leonard, he was more determined than ever to prevent his brother from having to go through with this marriage. "You are too prudent not to see that a union between my brother and Miss Leonard is likely to fail."

"Why?" Rebecca turned her striking hazel eyes upon him

again. "Because he is impetuous and inconstant and she does not meet your exacting standards? Those were the reasons you gave me when we first met. They did not sway me then nor do they now. I think more highly of Hermione and Mr. Stanhope than you appear to. I reckon he truly cares for her, and she for him. I believe they can be happy together."

She did not raise her voice or pound on anything, as his brother would have done. Instead she simply stated her position with firm sincerity that Sebastian found much more difficult to dismiss. "Does that mean 'no'?"

Rebecca nodded. "You have praised my sense and sincerity, but those mean nothing to me without loyalty. You also observed that we are alike in our concern for those we care about. How can you suppose I would do anything to cause Hermione a moment's grief? She is very dear to me and I will not advise her against a course of action that I believe provides her best chance of continued happiness."

Much as it disappointed Sebastian to see his promising plan go awry, he found himself equally troubled to lose the opportunity for continued contact with Rebecca.

"You must despise me for even suggesting such a thing." He tried to make light of it, only to discover how much the prospect of her bad opinion troubled him. "At least now I can count you among those who regard me as arrogant, stubborn and ruthless."

Sebastian turned sharply on his heel so she would not glimpse any look in his eyes that might betray his true feelings. "Since that is settled, perhaps we had better be getting back."

He'd only taken two long strides when she called after him. "I do not despise you, Sebastian."

Her words halted him in his tracks, especially the sweetness of hearing her melodious voice caress his name so warmly. He did not dare to face her, however, until he regained control of the emotions she had stirred.

Behind him he heard the faint rustle of her footsteps in the grass and her voice drawing nearer. "You are convinced this marriage will make your brother unhappy. How can I not admire your loyalty and your willingness to take any action necessary to prevent him from making what you perceive as a mistake?"

He had thought his opinion of Rebecca Beaton could scarcely improve. Now it rose to quite alarming heights. "That is an unusually magnanimous attitude. When I first entered Parliament, I knew men capable of pursuing their policies vigorously in the House, yet remaining on terms of warmest respect with those who opposed them most forcefully. I fear such fair-minded tolerance is dying out."

As he spoke, Sebastian slowly turned toward her, relieved by the assurance that he would not lose her esteem over their difference of opinion, no matter how great.

If he'd been fool enough to doubt her sincerity for even a moment, the look in her eyes would have convinced him she meant every word. "It is easier to tolerate opposition when we understand and respect the motive behind it. I know you care about your brother at least as much as I do Hermione. I only wish I could persuade you what a good wife I am certain she will make for Mr. Stanhope. If I could, I trust a fair-minded man like you would withdraw your objections and give their engagement your blessing."

Her words gave Sebastian a promising idea.

"You may be right, though I cannot conceive how you would change my opinion so completely." Smiling down at Rebecca, he offered her his arm and they began to climb the brickwork path back up the hillside. "Is it possible the reverse might also hold true? If I could persuade you of all the reasons I believe a marriage between my brother and Miss Leonard will make them both miserable, would you then endeavor to advise her against the match?"

"Are you suggesting we wage a debate?" Glints of interest and amusement sparkled in her eyes. "The kind you have in Parliament?"

"I expect it will be far more engaging than the dull business of government." As they passed beneath a trellis, Sebastian plucked a rosebud and offered it to her. "But I hope it will give us both an opportunity to consider aspects of the matter we may not have done previously. If we endeavor to keep open minds, perhaps we can reach a decision that will benefit all concerned."

Rebecca lifted the pale pink blossom to her nose and inhaled its fragrance. Sebastian could not help notice how perfectly it matched the color of her lips.

"Is that how our system of government works?" she inquired with an arch of her eyebrow that conveyed astute insight.

"Sometimes," Sebastian admitted with a chuckle. "Let us say, that's how it is *intended* to work."

"But would you not have an advantage over me?" She wagged the rosebud at him like a scolding finger. "After all, you are a veteran of many Parliamentary debates, against some of the greatest orators of our time. I am not even permitted to vote, let alone serve in government."

Though she laughed at the absurdity of her suggestion, Sebastian did not find it so outrageous to imagine a woman of her integrity and judgment enacting laws for the good of the country.

"Depend upon it, my dear, you have a greater advantage than you may realize." His growing regard for her, to begin with. His reluctance to contradict her. His desire to listen to the sound of her voice. "I would fancy my chances better against any member of the House of Lords."

They strolled through the intimate, hedge-walled garden. Since Claude and Miss Leonard had already moved on, they did not linger. Sebastian did not trust himself alone with Rebecca in such a place. Not in his present mood.

"Very well, then," she agreed after silently mulling over his proposal…his *suggestion* for several minutes. "I fear you are only flattering me to win my cooperation, but I believe this represents my best opportunity to help Hermione. Besides, I owe it to her to consider whether there is a possibility this marriage might not be in her best interest after all."

"What about *your* interests? Have you never given them any thought?" During his career in Parliament, Sebastian had learned the surest means to enlist support from anyone was to appeal to their self-interest.

Rebecca shook her head. "I don't understand. Miss Leonard's engagement has nothing to do with me."

"It will affect you, though, will it not? Once Miss Leonard is married, she will no longer require a companion. You will be obliged to find a new position."

Rebecca gave a sharp little intake of breath, as if he had jabbed her in the stomach. Necessity urged Sebastian to exploit the weakness he had exposed. Anything that elicited this kind of response clearly mattered a great deal to her and could be turned to his advantage. But he was distracted by a deep pang of concern. That last thing he wanted was to cause her distress.

But before he could muster an apology, she answered in that disarmingly honest way of hers. "What you say is true. I cannot pretend I am looking forward to leaving behind the life I have made for myself in this idyllic part of the country. Nor am I eager to go elsewhere and begin all over again. I know there are many who would relish such a change, perhaps even regard it as an adventure."

As she spoke, her voice grew softer and huskier until it died away altogether. Sebastian knew what she meant to say next. "But you are not one of those people?"

Rebecca shook her head. "I cherish everything familiar. I long for stability and security the way some people long for fame or fortune."

As direct and open as she was, Sebastian sensed this was not something she would tell just anyone, not even Miss Leonard. He felt honored and deeply moved that she had chosen to confide in him.

She glanced toward the house. "I envy you this place, though not because it is so grand and elegant. I only think how pleasant it must be to walk the halls where your ancestors once walked, to use the rooms they furnished, to look upon scenes they once beheld. To know that, however far you go or how long you remain away, you always have this home waiting for your return. I would feel the same if it were a manor house like the Leonards' or even a snug little cottage."

He'd never thought of the old place in that way before, Sebastian realized. He had taken for granted that it would always be here, never much changed. How would he feel if he were obliged to leave it, not knowing if he would ever return? What if he'd never had a place to call home?

"Rebecca…" He stopped and turned toward her, possessed by an irresistible urge to offer her a comforting embrace.

Fortunately, she still had some grasp of propriety, which had suddenly deserted him. "I beg your pardon, Lord Benedict! I should not have spoken so unguardedly. Pay no heed to my ramblings."

Abruptly she released his arm and rushed ahead toward the main garden, talking even faster than she walked. "Moving from one position to another is a natural part of my profession. When children grow up, their governess must seek a new situation. I have been unusually fortunate to remain as Miss Leonard's companion even after she out-grew the need for a governess. It would be cruelly selfish of me to desire that the dear girl should never marry so I could continue indefinitely in my position. I would rather go elsewhere, knowing she will have the companionship of a devoted husband."

By the time she finished, Rebecca was gasping for breath.

"Please wait," Sebastian entreated her, but she hurried on.

He could have reached out and restrained her but that seemed wrong somehow. Instead, he strode past her and ducked around the final trellis to block her path.

She gave a start when he suddenly appeared in front of her, coming to an abrupt halt.

"Please excuse me," he begged. "I never meant to imply you would put your own interests ahead of your friend's. On the contrary, I admire your wish to see Miss Leonard happy even if it means an unwelcome change for you."

"Think no more of it, sir." Rebecca's gaze darted as if seeking a way around him. "You could not know I had such strong feelings on the subject."

"I share your desire for security and stability," Sebastian admitted. "Though having a fixed home, no matter how grand, does not always ensure those blessings."

What on earth had made him say that? It was a subject he had never broached with anyone—not even his brother.

When Rebecca cast him a questioning glance, he feared

he might be tempted to say more. Before she could draw him out, he stepped back to let her pass. "The clouds are gathering. I expect you and Miss Leonard will want to be on your way before it rains."

Even as he suggested it, Sebastian was torn between a desire to maintain his privacy and the urge to remain in Rebecca's company.

For a moment she seemed poised to question him, then appeared to reconsider. "You are right, Lord Benedict. It *is* time we returned to Rose Grange."

They walked side by side in uneasy silence for several steps, then she spoke again. "I fear our debate has not persuaded either of us to alter our opinions. If anything, mine are more deeply entrenched than ever."

Sebastian could not deny that. Yet the prospect of further discussions and further meetings with Rebecca Beaton appealed to him. "Never fear. This debate of ours is far from over."

"Thank goodness *that's* over!" As the carriage drove away from Stanhope Court, Hermione sank back in her seat with a dramatic flourish. "I have never been so thoroughly cowed in all my life. I find it hard to believe Claude and Lord Benedict are even *half* brothers, they are so little alike."

"Half brothers?" Rebecca mused. "I had no idea. There is a resemblance in looks, though very little in character."

Though Claude Stanhope was a boyishly handsome young man with a most engaging manner, Rebecca could not deny she found Sebastian even more attractive on both counts. In spite of his prejudice against Hermione, he was a fine man who cared about his brother and his country and treated her as his equal.

"So tell me," urged Hermione in the tone of a gleeful

conspirator, "do you still deny you can charm Lord Benedict? If he liked me even half as well as he likes you, I
should not have a moment's worry of him turning Claude
against me."

"I'm certain he would never do that." Rebecca sprang to
Sebastian's defense again, then recalled how he had tried to
enlist her to break up the match. "And I am even more certain he thinks nothing of me except as your companion."

Rebecca cringed to recall how easily she had deluded herself into hoping otherwise. What could have possessed her
to imagine Viscount Benedict had been about to propose to
her? Fortunately the notion had been so far from his true
intentions that he'd had no idea of her foolish false hopes. If
he ever guessed, she would be thoroughly mortified.

Now she knew the truth. He had only cultivated her acquaintance as a means of ending his brother's engagement.
She could not bring herself to tell Hermione. The poor girl
was intimidated enough by the viscount already. If, as Rebecca hoped, the marriage went ahead, she did not want the
knowledge of Sebastian's machinations to create animosity
between him and his sister-in-law.

Hermione shook her head with a doubtful frown. "If his
lordship only thought of you in connection to me, he should
loathe you. Surely you do not think he loathes you?"

"Hardly." Rebecca turned to gaze out the carriage window
at the green hills and hedgerows. They reminded her of the
enchanting tiered gardens at Stanhope Court. "His lordship
was most courteous."

Though she knew part of it might have been a calculated
bid to gain her assistance, she sensed Sebastian genuinely
liked her. What was more, he seemed to value those aspects
of her character that others might consider flaws.

Hermione chuckled to herself as if at some secret jest. "It

is clear your opinion of him has not altered for the worse. To hear the two of you talk, one would think you were old friends."

Rebecca could not dispute that observation, though she knew Hermione did not understand, or entirely approve of her liking for Lord Benedict. She had never felt so much at ease with anyone she'd known such a short time. Usually it took a while for her to warm to new acquaintances and begin to trust them. Yet, on only their third meeting, she had confided some of her most private feelings to Sebastian, not to mention agreeing to the familiarity of first names. Part of her regretted being so unguarded, but another part welcomed such unaccustomed closeness.

"Did you have any opportunity to recommend me to his lordship?" Hermione's question jarred Rebecca from her musing. "Or were you too busy enjoying his gardens and his company?"

"The gardens are marvelous aren't they?" Rebecca hoped she might have the opportunity to see them again, though she doubted she would enjoy them quite so much without the stimulation of Sebastian's company. "Lord Benedict and I talked a little about you and his brother. Though our opinions on your suitability for one another are entirely opposite, that did not prevent us from having a polite exchange of views. I believe he hopes to change my mind as I hope to change his."

Hermione straightened abruptly and leaned toward Rebecca. "You won't let him do that, will you? I don't know what I should do if I lost your support."

"Never fear." Rebecca cast her dear young friend a reassuring smile. "Though I may seem quiet and placid, I am stubborn in clinging to my beliefs. It will take much more formidable persuasion to budge me than Lord Benedict can bring to bear."

"It is not his formidable persuasion that worries me," Hermione replied. "I am afraid he may charm you over to his way of thinking."

Rebecca had to admit, at least to herself, that was the more likely possibility.

Chapter Five

"Come along now," Sebastian chivied his brother a few days after the ladies had visited Stanhope Court. "You don't want to be late, do you? If you're so much in love, you should be chomping at the bit to see your sweetheart again."

"Of course I'm anxious to see Hermione." Claude took one more minute to survey his appearance in the looking glass and adjust his neck linen. "But why are *you* so eager to get to Rose Grange? Have you come to your senses and realized what a wonderful wife she will make me?"

"Hardly." Sebastian jammed on his hat. The more time he spent in the company of Hermione Leonard, the more opposed he became to his brother's hasty betrothal. "I still believe she is too green and countrified to take her place in Society. I don't want a repeat of the past and neither should you, if you have any sense."

"Rubbish!" Claude swept past him out the door. "Hermione is nothing like Lydia and I am constantly reminded that I am not at all like you."

He clambered down the stairs and climbed into the waiting gig, grabbing the reins. Sebastian followed at a more deliberate pace.

Why did his brother sound so slighted by what must obviously be a compliment? And why could Claude not see that he was on the brink of making the very same mistake his brother had made? If there was anything to be gained from a painful past, surely it was the warning it provided for the future.

Sebastian had barely settled beside his brother when Claude snapped the reins and the gig shot off down the steep, winding lane at reckless speed.

Before Sebastian could protest, his brother raised his voice above the rumble of the horse's hooves and the rattle of the wheels. "What gall you have, sneering at Hermione's background when you are so obviously smitten with a mere governess!"

"I...smitten..." Sebastian sputtered "...with Rebecca? Ridiculous!"

"Rebecca?" cried Claude in a tone that was at once triumphant and accusing. "You are clearly on very familiar terms with the woman, which proves my charge cannot be so ridiculous after all."

"It doesn't mean what you think," Sebastian protested. "I was only trying to put Miss Beaton at ease."

That *was* all he'd meant by it, he assured himself, so the lady might be more inclined to use her influence with Hermione Leonard. He could not deny he found Rebecca...Miss Beaton...an attractive woman with many fine qualities he particularly prized. That did not mean he was *smitten* with her!

They were only briefly acquainted, after all, and her background was far different from his...at least he assumed it was. Out of the blue, Sebastian found his thoughts consumed by a desperate curiosity about Rebecca's family and her past.

Confound it all! Could Claude be right? Had his plan to debate the merits of his brother's engagement been nothing more than a convenient excuse to spend more time in Rebecca's company? What troubled Sebastian most was that he could have deceived himself so easily.

Well, no more. Now that he recognized what was happening to him, he would soon put a stop to it. He must win the debate, free his brother from the snare of his engagement and get them both far away from the dangerously romantic atmosphere of the Cotswolds.

As he had warned his brother, when it came to matters of the heart, he did not want the past to repeat itself.

"Please try to hold still, Hermione." Rebecca cast a critical frown at her sketching paper. "How am I ever to capture a good likeness if you are always changing position?"

Since it was rather a cool, dull day, the two of them had taken refuge in the sitting room and seized the opportunity to begin her commission for Mr. Stanhope.

"I'll try," Hermione sighed, "but it isn't easy to stay still with nothing to do. I'd rather keep busy so I don't have too much time to think."

"Think about what?" Rebecca concentrated on reproducing the graceful line of Hermione's neck. The pensive expression on her face was not at all suited to the kind of sketch Claude Stanhope wanted.

"About getting married, of course." Hermione changed position yet again, propping her chin upon her raised hand.

"Why?" Rebecca strove to keep her inquiry casual as she flicked her pencil this way and that to suggest Hermione's unruly cascade of curls. "Are you having second thoughts about accepting Mr. Stanhope's proposal?"

Could Sebastian be right, after all, in his reservations about the young couple's betrothal? She'd been so delighted at the prospect of Hermione making such a fine match, might she have ignored signs of discord?

Forgetting Rebecca's plea to stay still, Hermione shook her head. "Not about my feelings for him, if that is what you mean. Though he is the brother of a viscount, he's not at all proud. He is always so kind and agreeable and…"

"And?" Rebecca's pencil flew as she strove to catch the fond expression in Hermione's dark eyes.

"…and I feel he needs someone to love him. His parents died when he was quite young so he's only had his brother…"

Rebecca was pleased she'd captured that sweet, elusive look before a chill of aversion crept into Hermione's gaze. "Whatever your differences with Lord Benedict, I do believe he cares for his brother very much."

There she went, defending him again.

It was true, though. If Sebastian cared less about his brother's happiness, he would not be trying so hard to break up a match he deemed unsuitable.

"That may be." Hermione's pretty mouth pursed in a doubtful look that quite spoiled its shape. "But his lordship is not very good at expressing those kinds of feelings."

Again Rebecca was tempted to disagree. The other evening in the terrace garden at Stanhope Court, Sebastian had shown considerable warmth. Then again, she recalled, he had not been on the point of proposing to her as she'd so foolishly assumed. Had she mistaken him in other matters as well?

"Perhaps their parents' deaths affected Lord Benedict, too." The instant that notion occurred to her, Rebecca sensed it might be true.

She felt an even deeper kinship to the man for having endured the same kind of early bereavement she had. His title and fortune could not have compensated for that. Might it be the reason for his staunch support of British troops—because he wanted to see fewer casualties, leaving fewer young orphans of war?

The sudden appearance of the Leonard's housemaid distracted Rebecca and Hermione from their conversation. "Two gentlemen come to call on you, Miss Leonard. Viscount Benedict and the Honorable Mr. Stanhope."

"Show our guests in at once, Mary. Then go fetch us tea, please." Hermione leaped from her chair and smoothed her skirts in a manner that looked both eager and anxious.

Rebecca felt only the former. The mere mention of Sebastian's name had set her heart aflutter. When he strode into the room a moment later, he seemed to bring a rush of fresh spring air with him.

After an initial flurry of greetings, Claude Stanhope and Hermione retired to the window seat to converse in hushed tones.

If Sebastian resented being ignored, he did not show it, but approached Rebecca and examined her sketch. "An excellent likeness, indeed. You have succeeded in capturing Miss Leonard's air of winsome youth."

"How do you manage it?" Rebecca gave an indulgent chuckle.

"Manage what?" he inquired warily.

"To make that sound like a compliment to my sketch," she lowered her voice to a furtive whisper, "but not to Hermione."

She feared Sebastian might be offended by her impertinence, but instead a gush of hearty laughter burst from his lips. "That refreshing honesty again." His laughter muted to a mellow chuckle. "Perhaps that is the unique quality you bring to your sketching. Too many fashionable portrait painters work so hard to flatter their subjects that they lose any sense of life and truth. I have never been satisfied with any portrait of me. Though, I daresay they are all a good deal better looking than their subject."

"I cannot imagine that." Rebecca's gaze traced the contours of his features as if committing a sketch of him to her memory.

When she reached his eyes, she gave a guilty start, fearing what he would make of her blatant admiration. But he seemed not to notice.

"Would you be willing to make a sketch of me?" he asked.

Much as she would welcome the opportunity to stare at him to her heart's content, Rebecca replied in a murmur not meant to reach the ears of Hermione and Mr. Stanhope. "Confess, what you truly want is an excuse to spend time with me so you can expound all your arguments against your brother's engagement."

He seemed about to deny it, then appeared to sense that she would accept nothing less than the unvarnished truth.

"Perhaps I am looking for an excuse." Sebastian gave a rueful shrug. "But I would like to have at least one portrait of myself, to pass down to future generations of Stanhopes, that honestly shows the kind of man I am. Please say you will accept my commission."

Her deeply ingrained discretion warned Rebecca she should politely refuse. Her liking for Sebastian was growing dangerously deep even though she knew there was no hope of him returning her feelings. And she could not afford to risk the least suspicion of impropriety or it might ruin her chances of finding a good position in the future.

But how could she deny his request when he fixed her with that beseeching gaze? Besides, if she obliged him, it might put Sebastian in a more receptive mood to hear her arguments in Hermione's favor.

"Very well, then, if you're so set on it." She picked up her sketching pencil and pointed toward the chair Hermione had vacated. "We can start now, if you are willing."

"Entirely." Sebastian seated himself, then called to his brother. "See here, Claude, Miss Beaton has agreed to draw my picture. What manner of pose should I assume?" He struck one exaggerated attitude, then another, making them all laugh…even Hermione.

"Not at all if you want a true likeness," Rebecca advised him. "Just sit still and talk about something that interests you. That will give your features animation."

Mr. Stanhope nodded toward the sitting room window. "I believe I see a ray of sunshine. Shall we take a turn around your garden, Hermione, so we do not disturb the artist or her sitter?"

With an eager nod, Hermione took his arm. "Try not to move about if you can help it," she warned Sebastian, "or Miss Beaton will get vexed with you."

Though Rebecca sensed the young pair were more interested in their privacy than her sketch of Sebastian, she waved them on their way.

Once they had gone, Rebecca took the sketch of Hermione from her easel and carefully rolled it up. Then she replaced it with a piece of fresh paper. "I was going to suggest you tell me more about your efforts to muster support for the troops. But now I think we should resume our debate."

"My thought precisely," Sebastian agreed.

Rebecca began to outline the shape of his face with careful strokes. "Tell me, then, what other objections do you have to your brother's engagement?"

He thought for a moment, as if mentally checking his list for a persuasive argument. "Here is one you are too prudent to dispute—they have not been acquainted long enough. I sent Claude here after Christmas and now it is only May. How can they possibly have come to know each other well enough to enter into a lifelong union? How can they know their own feelings are deep and lasting enough to stay the course?"

Rebecca's hand trembled a little, making her pencil wobble over the curve of his left ear. A week ago, she would have agreed with Sebastian wholeheartedly. But lately she'd discovered how quickly feelings for one special person could take root in the heart.

"I will concede that Hermione and your brother have not known each other long." Rebecca's pencil made a soft scratching sound as it moved over the paper.

Somehow Sebastian knew her sketch would depict him in a way he could appreciate. She seemed to see him more clearly than anyone else did.

"You'll do what?" He had been so absorbed in watching her work that he'd scarcely heeded what she was saying. "Concede? Does that mean…?"

"Does it mean I will admit defeat?" Rebecca completed his sentence with the very words he'd intended to speak. "And advise Hermione to break the engagement? No, indeed. Though I have little experience of such matters, I believe it is possible for two people to quickly recognize they share a special…connection."

Her words trailed off as she became more absorbed in her task. Sebastian wondered what she had meant by "little experience." Little did not mean none at all. Could there have been a young man in her past who'd caught her fancy? Someone she wished had proposed or whom she regretted not accepting? Though he knew it was foolish, Sebastian could not quell a spasm of envy toward the lad who might have once held her hand or stolen a kiss.

Unable to prevent himself from inquiring, he strove to mask the depth of his curiosity with a casual tone. "Have you ever felt that sort of connection with someone you'd only known a short while?"

Rebecca ducked behind her easel, busily adding to her sketch. "There was a group of girls I met at school. We had not known each other long before I felt a strong bond of mutual sympathy. Though we are all scattered throughout the kingdom now, I still think of them frequently with great affection. We exchange letters as often as we are able, but I would dearly love to see them all again."

The wistful note in her voice made Sebastian long to whisk her away in his carriage to visit every one of her friends. It elated him to discover she had not been alluding to a past love, and yet it saddened him too. Rebecca Beaton was meant to be cherished and cared for, not to spend her whole life moving from family to family, educating their pampered daughters until they had no further need of her services.

"Have *you* ever felt that sort of immediate connection?" Her question turned the tables on Sebastian. Caught in her deft ambush, he nearly blurted the truth. Fortunately, hard-won experience came to his rescue. Was Rebecca leading him on, seeking to win him over with her arts of attraction as he sought to win her with his powers of debate?

"I reckon I did feel that sort of instant attraction once." His fingers dug into the arms of the chair and his voice grew cold and harsh. "To my grief, I later discovered I was deceived."

Rebecca's flying pencil fell silent, and her face reappeared from behind the easel. "I am sorry for that, Sebastian. You are a fine man and you deserve better."

Her sincere sympathy and the sweet sound of his name on her lips were like balm on an old, ulcerated wound. If only Rebecca had stopped there...

"I know you must be anxious to prevent your brother from being deceived as you were. But you need have no such fears of Hermione, I promise you. She would never harm a soul, least of all a man she cares for as she does your brother."

Sebastian found himself dangerously tempted to believe her, but he had been protecting Claude for so long. Sometimes he'd been so busy watching out for his brother that he hadn't thought to watch out for himself. He could not stop now.

"Perhaps she would not *mean* to hurt him." Forgetting he was supposed to be posing for the sketch, Sebastian sprang from his chair and began to pace the sitting room. "But they are both so young, her especially. You can vouch for her kind heart, but what of her judgment, her constancy?"

As he passed the window, he gestured toward the garden where the young couple were walking arm-in-arm, talking and laughing. They looked deliriously happy.

Sebastian reminded himself that delirium was a kind of madness brought on by fever. When he glanced toward Rebecca, he feared the fever might be catching.

Chapter Six

A mixture of pride and hopeless yearning welled up in Rebecca's heart as she stared at her sketch of Sebastian, which still needed a little work to complete. She marveled that her hands had managed to produce such a good likeness of him while so much of her thoughts had been occupied with defending Hermione.

Though it might not be as accurate a portrait as a professional artist could render, she flattered herself that it captured his dynamic spirit. About the mouth, she'd managed to convey the self-deprecating wit behind which he hid his basic goodness and concern for others. And in those guarded eyes of his, she'd revealed a secret shadow that had puzzled her...until he'd spoken of being deceived.

Then she'd understood—in part, at least. She could not entirely fathom his feelings, having never before experienced the pain of love rejected or betrayed. Perhaps that was why her awkward effort to comfort him had misfired so badly.

Instead of being soothed by her overture, Sebastian had bolted from his chair to stride around the room, firing off questions about Hermione's judgment and faithfulness. Much as Rebecca wanted to defend the dear girl against his charges, she could not forget the reservations Hermione had expressed about marriage before the gentlemen arrived.

Coming to an abrupt halt near the window, Sebastian flicked a glance toward the young couple strolling in the garden. Then he turned to fix Rebecca with a reproachful glare. "How do we know she accepted his proposal because she truly cares for him and not just because she considers him a *good catch*."

The question troubled Rebecca. If a man with a comfortable home and a good income ever asked for her hand, would she accept, even if she felt no particular affection for him? Would it be such a terrible sin if she did, her practical nature demanded.

Stung by Sebastian's tone and the conflicting feelings he'd stirred in her, Rebecca was sorely tempted to let fly with a scathing retort. Then she glimpsed that shadow in his eyes that had found its way into her sketch. She realized his question had not been meant to accuse or offend her. It sprang from his private pain. Just as she could not fully comprehend the anguish of being deceived, Sebastian did not understand the pressures young women faced.

"I believe Hermione does love your brother." Rebecca set down her pencil and stepped out from behind her easel. "You might see it too if you would look beyond your prejudice against her. I wish you could have heard her singing Mr. Stanhope's praises just before you arrived."

"But?" Sebastian voiced the word she had stifled.

Rebecca hesitated, torn between her loyal inclination to see Hermione well wed and a reluctance to let an impetuous young couple make a mistake they might regret for the rest of their lives. "Hermione said she was *not* having second thoughts about her feelings for your brother."

"But she *is* having second thoughts?" Sebastian seized

upon the damaging implication eagerly. "Did she tell you what aspect of the match troubles her?"

"No!" Rebecca wanted to clap a hand over her mouth, though she knew it was too late. Had she betrayed a confidence that Lord Benedict might use as a wedge between Hermione and Mr. Stanhope? "But I can hazard a guess what it might be."

"By all means," Sebastian urged her, "hazard away."

Could she make up for her earlier lapse or would she only compound it?

Either way, she could not keep silent. "Perhaps Hermione worries that proud people like you will look down on her because her fortune and connections are not as lofty as yours. Perhaps she fears they will make her feel unwelcome in their society. She may even wonder if they will seek to turn Mr. Stanhope against her and make him regret having married her."

She had not meant to go on at such length or for her tone to grow so sharp. Sebastian was a fine man and she had come to like him very much. Lately she feared that liking had strayed into more dangerous territory. For all that, she was becoming impatient with his stubborn antipathy toward the girl she loved as a sister.

To her surprise, Sebastian seemed to recoil from her outburst. "By *they* I presume you mean *me*. Do you share these fears you attribute to Miss Leonard? Do you believe me capable of sowing discord between her and Claude if they wed?"

The shadow in his eyes darkened further. He seemed quite wounded that she could entertain such a notion of him. But why on earth should it matter what someone in her position thought of him?

Torn between her confused feelings for him and loyalty

to Hermione, Rebecca was compelled to speak the truth—though she softened her tone in an effort to spare his feelings. "I do not *want* to believe you would ever do such things. But given your coldness toward Miss Leonard and the effort you have made to break the engagement, I cannot be certain what you might do if she and your brother wed against your wishes."

Sebastian took a step toward her, bringing him closer than was proper for a gentleman to approach an unattached lady. Discretion warned Rebecca to put a more seemly distance between them. But she could not bring herself to back down when she was right. Besides, she liked being close to him, even when he bristled with annoyance.

"I am very disappointed that you could have formed such a vile opinion of me, Rebecca." His slate-blue gaze bored into hers. "I thought you knew me better than that."

His nostrils flared and his firm jaw clenched into even grimmer severity. Yet his whole aspect radiated more injury than anger.

Though Rebecca tried to resist, his response stirred her to the very core. She pressed her lips together, reluctant to speak, for fear she would relent out of sympathy for him, rather than because it was the right thing to do.

Sebastian must have taken that look as a sign she had hardened her heart against him. "I swear I would never do any of the things you have suggested! I admit that before the knot is tied, I will do everything in my power to prevent it. But if my brother does wed Miss Leonard, I will do my utmost to insure their marriage is a success. You do believe me, don't you?"

Rebecca longed to give him the assurance he seemed to crave, but could she? If only her mother's family had taken the approach Sebastian vowed he would, how differently her life might have turned out. Instead, they'd borne a grudge that persisted even beyond the grave.

"I am certain you are capable of magnanimous behavior if you set your mind to it." Her fingertips tingled with the yearning to reach up and give his cheek a reassuring caress, but she did not dare take such a liberty. "But I also know it is not as easy as you imagine to put aside the past and behave contrary to your previous inclinations."

He leaned closer to her. Did he intend to whisper a secret in her ear? Rebecca knew what she wished he would do. Her lips ached with longing for one kiss from him, however meaningless, however fleeting.

The sound of approaching voices broke upon the shimmering intensity of that moment like a splash of cold water. With a guilty start, they both jumped back, leaving a discreet distance between them that gaped like an unbridgeable chasm.

An instant later, Hermione and her fiancé breezed in.

"How is the sketch coming?" Claude Stanhope strode toward Rebecca's easel. "Done, I presume, if Miss Beaton is no longer working on it."

"I still have some finishing touches to add." Rebecca flew to intercept him. What if her sketch somehow betrayed her feelings for Sebastian? "But I can complete those later, without needing Lord Benedict on hand to pose."

She was grateful the younger couple had interrupted before any greater intimacy developed between her and Sebastian. Yet in the wake of her relief came a chilling ripple of regret that spread in ever-widening circles through the still, deep waters of her heart.

Another minute and he would have kissed Rebecca.

That certainty troubled Sebastian over the next several

days, making him avoid Avoncross like the plague, even though it meant letting his brother call on Miss Leonard, unaccompanied.

What truly bothered him, as much as his unmanageable feelings for Rebecca, was the fear that she believed him capable of trying to wreck Claude's marriage, if he wed Miss Leonard. Sebastian would rather Rebecca's sketch of him had turned into a grotesque caricature than fall short of her best estimation of him.

He hated to admit how much her opinion of him had come to matter. Her reluctant suspicions and gentle reproaches stung him worse than he'd been hurt in a long while. Sebastian had vowed he would never again allow a woman that kind of power over him. How had Rebecca Beaton breached all his defenses to strike so deep?

"There you are." Claude strode into the library of Stanhope Court, where Sebastian had been pretending to read for the past two hours. "Miss Leonard and Miss Beaton send their regards and hope you are not indisposed. I assured them you were in the pink of health though rather vexed in spirit."

"Indeed." Sebastian scowled at his brother's heartless levity.

"Oh, yes." Claude grinned as if he found Sebastian's scowl more amusing than intimidating. "That is why I have brought something to show you. I hope it will improve your mood."

From behind his back, he produced a large sheet of rolled paper, tied with a string. Undoing the latter, he let the paper unfurl to reveal Rebecca's completed sketch of Hermione Leonard.

"Lovely, isn't it?" Claude beamed as if he'd drawn the picture himself. "Even you must admit that, Sebastian."

"I have never questioned the lady's good looks," Sebastian snapped. "Nor am I surprised to find Miss Beaton has produced a flattering likeness of her."

The sketch was more than that, he grudgingly admitted to himself. Rebecca had brought out a soft glow of sweetness in Hermione Leonard's dark eyes. The depiction of her lips suggested patience and generosity. Sebastian felt as if he were looking at an entirely different woman. He could not help wondering which of them saw his brother's fiancée more clearly.

"*Miss Beaton* now, is it?" Claude's eyes danced with impudence. "No longer *Rebecca?* I thought the two of you would be on more familiar terms after the other day, not less."

Sebastian bolstered his scowl with a frosty glare. Together, they did a better job of cowing his brother.

Claude ducked his head and began to roll the paper back up with infinite care. "I mean to take this to London tomorrow to have it framed properly. Miss Beaton has finished yours, too, whenever you choose to collect it. I would have brought it with me but I did not want to deprive you of an excuse to call on the lady."

"I do not need an excuse to call on Miss Beaton." Sebastian dropped his heavy book to the floor and surged up from his chair. "Nor do I want one. I am amazed you can tear yourself away from Miss Leonard long enough to go to London. Are you growing tired of her at last?"

"Not in the least." Claude did not look up as he retied the rolled-up sketch. "Hermione and her father are going to pay a short visit to an aunt of hers. I thought I might as well go to London as mope around here until she returns."

"Whereabouts is this aunt of hers?" Sebastian demanded. "I suppose Miss Beaton will accompany them."

He tried to sound barely interested, though that was far from true. Even while he had gone out of his way to avoid Rebecca of late, there had been something comforting about the knowledge that she was not far away if he chose to call on her.

Claude shook his head. "There wasn't room to take both Hermione's maid and Miss Beaton, so she has stayed behind at Rose Grange. I believe she means to use the time to make inquiries about a new position. Do we know anyone who might need a governess? Lord and Lady Rayleigh have daughters, don't they?"

"A pack of young hoydens." Sebastian shuddered. "They need a wild animal tamer more than a governess."

He had no doubt Rebecca would be equal to the challenge of civilizing the Rayleigh girls if she put her mind to it. But it grieved him to think what an uphill battle it would be for her. Not to mention the Rayleighs' estate was off in the northern wilds of Cumberland. It would be quite a change from the Cotswolds, especially for Rebecca, who cherished familiarity.

"A companion, then?" suggested Claude. "Perhaps to the Dowager Lady Stevenage?"

"That sour-tempered, cheese-paring harridan?" Sebastian strode away. "Not if I have any say in the matter!"

"You *don't* have any say in the matter," Claude called after him. "Why on earth should you?"

Why on earth, indeed, Sebastian's reason demanded as he marched off to the stables. Rebecca's future employment was none of his concern. Then why did he feel so desperately anxious about it, his heart countered, and about her well-being in general?

Perhaps it was the same reason that put him in good spirits when he was with her and made him restless when he was not. He had tried to ignore it, and even now he could not bear to give that complicated jumble of feelings its true name.

The moment his horse was saddled, Sebastian set off for Rose Grange at the break-neck pace his brother might have ridden. He tried to convince himself he was only going to take possession of the sketch he'd commissioned. But he knew better than to believe such a lame excuse. What he really wanted was to talk to Rebecca again to convince her he was not as heartless and vengeful as she'd implied.

Even that was only part of the truth, he conceded at last. He simply needed to see her again, to hear her voice and, if he was very fortunate, to catch a glimpse of her smile or a trill of her laughter.

Rebecca did not smile when she entered the sitting room where Sebastian had been asked to wait for her. Instead, she appeared surprised by his unexpected visit—even a bit wary. "If you have come looking for your brother, he left some time ago. The Leonards departed not long after. They have gone—"

"To visit her aunt." A sense of peace stole over Sebastian the moment he laid eyes on Rebecca again. "Claude informed me when he returned home. It is you I have come to see…about my portrait."

He hoped Rebecca would believe that excuse more than he had.

"Then why did you not accompany your brother when he collected the sketch of Hermione?" Her direct gaze demanded the truth.

"Because…I wasn't certain I could face you, knowing what you think of me." Sebastian could scarcely believe he had made such a frank admission of weakness.

Rebecca seemed taken aback as well. "I thought you did not give a fig for anyone's opinion of you. You seemed to take pride in being considered stubborn, arrogant and ruthless."

"In a good cause," he reminded her.

"Ah." She began walking toward the easel. "And you realize that trying to break your brother's engagement is not such a good cause after all?"

"No." The denial rose to his lips instinctively, before he had an opportunity to give it much thought. "But I am certain meddling in his marriage would be. It grieves me that you believe I would do such a thing."

"I do not wish to grieve you. Quite the contrary, in fact." Rebecca caught her full lower lip between her teeth, as if to prevent herself from saying any more on the topic. After a long pause, she turned to a safer subject. "Since you are here and my sketch of you is finished, you might as well take it, if it meets with your approval."

Sebastian moved toward the easel, as much because he welcomed any excuse to draw nearer to Rebecca as because of any eagerness to see his portrait. Indeed, now that the moment was at hand, he found himself a trifle nervous to see how she had depicted him.

Steeling himself, he glanced at the paper. A breath of relief gusted out of him.

"Do you like it?" The anxious tone of Rebecca's question made it clear that, in this instance, she cared as much about his opinion as he did about hers.

He gave a slow nod. "It is very well done."

The likeness was a flattering one, without softening his bold features too much. There was also a sense of vitality about it that he appreciated. One part of the sketch unsettled him, however—a glimpse of unexpected vulnerability in the eyes. It was obvious that Rebecca saw him far more clearly than most people. Perhaps too clearly for his comfort. Was it possible that after such a brief acquaintance she already knew him better than he knew himself? Considering the actions of which she believed him capable, Sebastian hoped not.

He nodded toward the sketch. "Perhaps we should have settled on your fee at the outset, but I believe this is worth whatever price you might ask."

"Nonsense." Rebecca rushed past him and removed his portrait from the easel. "I am not a professional artist and I would never think of charging you a fee. I agreed to sketch your portrait as a favor for a friend. Your appreciation is the only fee I require."

"I do not mean to offend you." Sebastian wished she would look at him, but she kept her attention fixed on the task of rolling and tying the paper. "I merely wish to demonstrate the value I place upon the time and skill you have put into this sketch."

"Do you only value what you pay for?" Rebecca slapped the rolled-up paper into his hand. "In that case you may burn it or throw it away or whatever you wish because I will not accept a penny for it. It was a labor of…that is, I will not cheapen my efforts by taking your money. Now, if you will excuse me, Lord Benedict, since my employers are not at home, I'm sure you can have no further business with a mere servant."

"Please, don't go!" Fumbling the sketch, he managed to catch her by the hand before she hurried away. "You must know I do not think of you in that way. If you insist on making me such a generous gift, then I will accept it and offer you only my gratitude in return."

She did not turn back to face him, but neither did she pull away, as she might if she were determined to flee.

It was possible she might have stayed even if Sebastian released her hand, but he did not want to take any chances. "Please assure me you know I do not think of you as a *mere servant*."

"What else should I presume to think?" she countered in a wistful murmur shaded with bitterness. "It is clear your chief objection to Hermione is that she lacks the proper rank and fortune to move in your circles. Compared to her, I am not of the slightest consequence to someone like you."

Rebecca finally made an effort to extract her hand from his grip. Much as Sebastian longed to maintain that contact between them, he would not do it by force. He must find some other way to keep her there to hear him out.

"I do have my reservations about Miss Leonard's suitability for my brother on account of their difference in rank and fortune." His words tripped over one another in his haste to get them out. "But not for the reason you suppose."

In the time it took him to blurt all that out, Rebecca had taken several steps toward the door. Now she stopped and turned back to face him again. Clearly he had succeeded in rousing her curiosity. "What other reason can there be but that you judge the worth of people based on titles and income?"

"I hope nothing in my manner toward you has given you cause to believe that."

"N-no," she admitted, much to Sebastian's relief. "But I have known people of rank and fortune who despise anyone they consider beneath them."

Which people, he wondered. And what harm had they done to her? But this was an opportunity for him to explain, not ply her with questions. "Well, I have known people, beautiful women in particular, who use their wiles to prey upon wealthy and titled men in order to advance themselves."

"How did you know such women?"

He tried to toss off his reply in a tone of indifference, even though it felt as if he had ripped it from the very flesh of his heart. "I had the misfortune of marrying one."

Chapter Seven

"You are married?" A clammy wave of shame broke over Rebecca when she contemplated the tender feelings she'd secretly harbored toward Sebastian.

"*Was* married," he corrected her. "Some years ago when I was even younger and more foolish than my brother."

"You divorced your wife?" Though she had no right in the world, Rebecca could not help feeling slighted that he had once given his heart to another woman.

"Divorced?" Sebastian wrinkled his strong, jutting nose as if at some distasteful odor. "I might have had grounds, but I could not have borne the humiliation of having all that dragged out before my colleagues in Parliament."

After a moment of uneasy silence, he continued, "Lydia died after two years spent making my life miserable."

Hearing the pain and bitterness in his voice, Rebecca knew at last what was responsible for that shadow in his eyes.

"I'm sorry," she murmured, knowing she was not offering Sebastian the customary consolation on the loss of his wife. "Why did you not tell me before?"

The question had scarcely left her lips when she realized

how little right she had to ask it. She had concealed far more important information from him. Besides, it was none of her business whether or not he'd ever been married.

To her surprise, Sebastian did not bring up either of those reasons against her. "It is not something I care to talk about. Indeed, I try to think of Lydia as little as possible. Though my brother's betrothal has stirred up all manner of unpleasant memories."

"Perhaps it would help to talk about them." Rebecca was not certain what prompted her to make such a suggestion—especially since she had never shared *her* unpleasant memories with anyone else.

She'd sometimes wondered if it might ease the heartache of those recollections, if she could unburden herself to someone close and caring. If she could persuade Sebastian to confide in her, it might help dispel the weight of his past. Then perhaps he would recognize that Hermione was nothing like the wife who'd deceived him.

Sebastian did not respond to her offer right away. Rebecca sensed a struggle taking place within him over whether to accept or decline.

"What good would it do?" he demanded at last, with almost savage intensity. "The past is done and nothing can change it. All I can do is learn from my mistakes and make certain neither I nor my brother repeat them."

It grieved her to see him hurt so badly over something that had happened years ago. She knew how it felt to bear the scars of the old wounds.

"It is true we cannot change the past." Groping for the right words, Rebecca raised a silent prayer for guidance. "But I believe people *can* change if they are open and willing. You changed your opinion of me, not because my character had altered, but because you came to know and understand me better."

The grim severity of Sebastian's expression eased as she spoke. Slowly, he sank onto the settee.

"You reckon I can alter my perception of the past by trying to understand it better?" He sounded doubtful but not altogether resistant to the possibility.

"Surely it is worth a try." With careful, deliberate movements, Rebecca took a seat on the nearest chair.

It was some distance away from Sebastian and not directly opposite him. Instinct, or perhaps inspiration, warned her that he needed to maintain wider physical boundaries if he was to breach the defenses around his heart.

Expecting to encounter further objections or reluctance, she could barely contain her surprise at his next words. "I met Lydia during my first Season in London, when I came to take up my seat in the House of Lords. I was a callow young fool who'd been buried in the Cotswolds trying to raise my younger brother after our father's death. I was not prepared for the stimulation of Society, the feminine portion in particular."

As he spoke, Rebecca fancied his features looking more like his brother's. She could easily picture the young man he'd been—inexperienced, trusting and hungry for someone to love him.

"It was Lydia's second Season." Sebastian stared toward the window. The colors of the flowers outside looked even more vivid in contrast to the overcast sky. "When I was first introduced to her, I had never beheld such a glamorous creature. It was as if she had stepped out of a fine painting or the pages of a novel."

A stab of self-doubt pierced Rebecca. No wonder Sebastian had been willing to give her a second chance and take her into his confidence. Her plain looks and lack of style would have raised no unwelcome reminders of his late, un-lamented wife. She possessed none of the charms that might have placed his heart in peril.

She could not be sorry for anything that had allowed her to draw close to him. And yet…part of her wished she had the appeal to make Sebastian as attached to her as she was to him.

Stifling that foolish regret, she focused her attention on Sebastian's next words. "When that fascinating creature en-couraged my attentions, I was beside myself with delight. Before I knew what was happening, I found myself be-trothed, then married to a woman with whom I was barely acquainted. Only once the knot was securely tied did my lovely bride begin to show her true character. I soon dis-covered it was a hangman's knot in the noose around my neck."

He reached up to loosen his neck linen as if he could still feel the rope tightening around his throat. "I'd known Lydia had no money to speak of, but I was too unworldly and be-sotted to care about such matters. After we were married she began wanting more and more from me—jewels, ac-counts at all the best shops, a small fortune in pin money. As if her demands were not enough, her grasping relations came crawling out of the woodwork until I feared they would ruin me. When I protested that I could not support them all, she grew cold toward me and threatened to find a man who could give her and her family everything they wanted."

As Rebecca listened, a sense of outrage began to simmer within her, quickly intensifying to a full boil. Just as she had defended Sebastian against Hermione's angry comments, she now wished she could take up arms on his behalf against his manipulative wife and her pack of greedy relatives. But even if she could go back in time, she would be powerless to stop them. Any help she could give Sebastian must be here and now.

She doubted that offering him a sympathetic ear would be enough. But it was all she had.

"I tried to placate her at first." Sebastian rested his forehead on the palm of his hand. "Because I thought I loved her and I could not bear to lose her love. In the end I came to realize there was nothing to lose. She did not love me and never had, any more than a greedy sow loves a brimming trough of swill."

The bitterness of his words was so caustic Rebecca fancied they might blister his mouth. "All that saved me was the discovery that I had never truly loved her either. I had been infatuated with a pretty mask. The person behind it was a stranger to me. Worse than a stranger—a loathsome parasite!"

That could be true, and the belief might have spared Sebastian worse heartbreak. Yet Rebecca sensed his feelings for his late wife had been deeper than he could bring himself to admit. The way Lydia deceived and used him had cut deep. Perhaps he'd succeeded in burying those memories and the feelings they provoked until recently, but they had festered all that time, ready to flare up more venomous than ever.

"I felt trapped in a marriage that was destroying me." Sebastian's voice had gradually grown quieter until Rebecca had to strain to make out what he was saying. "I hated the man I had become. One night she threatened, yet again, to leave me if I did not give in to her insatiable demands. I told her not to raise my hopes with false promises. She flounced off, and I heard nothing more from her until she was found dead of a fever a few months later. When I received the news, I felt nothing but relief."

Somehow Rebecca knew that was not the whole truth. Relief might have been his chief reaction, but not the only one. Perhaps he'd been tormented by guilt or grief for the marriage he'd hoped to have when he first fell in love with the beautiful debutante.

"Now you know the whole sordid story." Sebastian rose from the settee with an air of deep weariness. "I wish I could claim it helped to speak of it, but that would not be true. I only hope it has helped you understand why I am driven to protect my brother from repeating my mistake and why I so deeply mistrust marriages of unequal fortune."

"I *do* understand." Rebecca got to her feet. "But that does not mean I agree. I know Hermione Leonard better than almost anyone. I promise you, she is nothing like…that woman."

His face might have been hewn from granite and his eyes from slate. It was clear he would not, or could not, heed her. "Everything about that girl reminds me of Lydia when I first met her—all the sweetness and smiles, whispery voice and girlish giggles. The way Claude gushes on about her—he spouts all the same drivel as I used to, sometimes word for word."

"You made a mistake committing your life to a woman without truly knowing her." Rebecca strove to reach him. "Do not make the mistake of condemning Hermione before you truly know *her*."

For a moment, she thought she'd succeeded.

Then Sebastian struck back. "Can you honestly assure me Hermione Leonard would have consented to wed my brother if he were poor?"

"I…" Loyalty to Hermione urged her to swear it was true.

If she did, there was a chance Sebastian might believe her. But the truth was more complicated than that. With the painful memories he'd confided fresh in her mind, Rebecca could not truthfully claim that Hermione had given no thought to the advantages of wedding a man with a secure income and bright expectations.

Her hesitation appeared to give Sebastian the answer he'd sought and expected. "I thought not."

He headed for the door. "In that case, I reckon we should cease our debate. We are each too firmly convinced of our own positions. Nothing would come of continuing now except bad feeling between us. I should regret that."

"So should I." Was this the last time she would see him? "Sebastian, wait!"

He turned back toward her with one dark brow raised.

She ached at the prospect of parting from him forever without giving some indication of her feelings for him. But how could she? A woman like her had no business caring for a man so far beyond her reach. Everything he had told her about his marriage made her more deeply attached to him, yet his revelations had also made it impossible to betray a hint of her feelings. If he ever guessed that she cared for him, he would only despise her as another fortune hunter.

Stifling a sob of frustration, she seized upon a convenient excuse for delaying him. "You forgot your sketch."

Retrieving it from the settee, she brought it to him. Hard as she tried to prevent her hand from touching his, it did. A swift brush of fingertips, searing yet oh so sweet.

Then he was gone.

He must not go back to Avoncross, Sebastian struggled to convince himself.

If there was one harsh lesson his marriage had taught

him, it was to know when to cut his losses. He'd told Rebecca neither of them could hope to sway the other. But that had only been half right. Even after all she'd compelled him to reveal about his past, she remained as stubbornly loyal to Hermione Leonard as ever. Meanwhile, she had come dangerously close to persuading him, with her clear-sighted reason and appealing sincerity, even though he knew he was right.

Reliving the misery of his marriage had made him more committed than ever to protecting his brother. He must abandon his plan to enlist Rebecca's help and figure out some other way to free Claude from his hasty betrothal…before it was too late.

"Are you coming or not, Sebastian?" Claude glanced toward the mantel clock in the dining room, then back at his brother. "Do make up your mind. The service starts in half an hour and I plan to be there, with or without you."

Once again, Sebastian warned himself he should stay away from Avoncross. Only…he was not certain he dared let Claude go there by himself.

His brother had returned from London the previous day with the handsomely framed sketch of his fiancée and a ring to seal their betrothal. What if Miss Leonard persuaded the besotted young fool to whisk her off to Scotland for one of those scandalous *anvil marriages?* Sebastian dared not take that chance.

"Of course I'm coming." He took one last swig of coffee, then rose and followed his brother.

Though Claude drove at his usual headlong pace, they only managed to slip into the sanctuary as the service was about to start. For the next hour, Sebastian followed the liturgy as if his life depended on it. Every time his gaze strayed toward Rebecca Beaton, he forced it back to the pages of his prayer book. Whenever he found himself listening for her voice during a hymn, he sang louder to drown her out.

Unfortunately the Old Testament lesson was no help at all in keeping his mind off her. *"Who can find a virtuous woman? For her price is far above rubies. The heart of her husband doth safely trust in her, so that he shall have no need of spoil. She will do him good and not evil all the days of her life."*

It seemed to Sebastian as if the writer of that ancient proverb was mocking him. He had not been able to find a virtuous woman—quite the contrary. Though he had once given Lydia a present of rubies, his heart had never been able to safely trust in her.

And yet, the Scripture held out the promise of another kind of woman—strong, productive, wise and honorable. An appealing image rose in his mind of Rebecca as a woman of ancient Israel, clad in a flowing robe and veil. He could picture her spinning wool, baking bread, tucking a child in for the night. That vision provided healing balm to his heart, raw from the painful memories he had gouged out of it.

The moment the service concluded, Claude sprang forward to speak to Miss Leonard and her father. Sebastian hung back, not wanting to get caught up in their exchange of meaningless pleasantries. He was not prepared for Rebecca to take up a position at the end of his pew and wait patiently for him to venture out.

"Miss Beaton." He acknowledged her with a respectful bow, hoping she would not guess the kind of thoughts he'd been having about her. "I hope you are well."

"Well enough." She cast him a hesitant smile, as if she was not certain whether it would be welcome. "I wondered if I might claim a small favor of you?"

Could he refuse any favor she chose to ask of him?

Sebastian feared he might be powerless to. "Do you wish to claim payment for sketching my portrait? Would it not have been simpler to accept my offer of money?"

Her smile disappeared, leaving Sebastian to reproach himself for having chased it away. "I am not seeking an exchange. The sketch is yours to keep whether or not you oblige my request."

"What is this favor, then?" He tried not to feel suspicious, but where women were concerned, it had become second nature.

"Would you consent to walk with me back to Rose Grange? I assume you and Mr. Stanhope came here in your gig. I believe he might like to offer Hermione a drive home."

Sebastian was far from certain he could trust his brother not to make a dash for Gretna Green. Still, he could not keep from offering Rebecca his arm. "It is no favor you request, Miss Beaton, but one you confer. I would be honored to escort you home."

They exchanged a few words with his brother and Miss Leonard on the way out, just enough to acquaint the younger couple with their intentions.

"Capital." Claude looked like a schoolboy who'd just been given a treat. "We'll meet you back at Rose Grange, then."

Once the others were out of earshot, Sebastian grasped for some harmless topic of conversation.

But the lady appeared to have other ideas. "I must confess I did not ask you to walk me home only for Hermione's sake. I have been thinking a great deal about our conversation the other day and I felt I must speak to you."

Despite his best effort to remain impassive, Sebastian flinched. "Must we spoil a nice walk by dredging up all that unpleasantness again?"

It was pleasant to walk beside Rebecca, adjusting his gait to hers, savoring the subtle pressure of her hand on his arm, drinking in the mellow music of her voice. If only she would talk about something else.

Apparently that was too much to ask. "I appreciate you taking me into your confidence and I do not wish to distress you. But for the sake of Hermione and your brother, and most of all for your sake, I feel I must."

Perhaps reluctant to let him reply in case he might protest further, she hurried on. "I believe it is vital for you to forgive your late wife."

Her suggestion fell like a fresh blow on an unhealed wound.

"Forgive Lydia?" He nearly gagged on those words. "She must answer to a far higher power. My blame or forgiveness will not matter now."

"Not to her perhaps," Rebecca persisted with well-meaning stubbornness. "But to you and those around you. The bitterness you still harbor toward her is casting a blight upon an otherwise fine character. Though what happened is in the past, it still affects your actions to this day."

"You mean my opposition to Claude's engagement. I thought we agreed to cease any further discussion of that rather than risk bad feeling between us."

"I shall be sorry if you think ill of me for raising this matter. But it is a risk I must take *because* I think so highly of you."

Sebastian could not resist the warmth of her concern. It touched him more deeply than he was comfortable being touched, yet somehow it soothed the very feelings it inflamed. "What you ask is impossible. Lydia used me. She broke my heart and put me through two years of torment.

Even if it would do any good, I would not know how to begin."

Rebecca seemed encouraged by his response, which was quite the opposite of what he'd intended. "Understanding is always a worthwhile place to start. If you cannot understand Lydia, at least try to have a little sympathy for Hermione... and me."

He already had far too much sympathy for her. "I don't see what you have in common with them."

"When we last met, you asked if I could swear Hermione would wed your brother if he were poor. When I could not, you assumed I meant she does not truly care for him. That is not what I meant at all. You see, it is not possible for a person of limited means to approach marriage in the same way as one with a comfortable, secure income. A woman especially, since she has few opportunities to earn more than a pittance."

Sebastian seized the opening she'd provided. "That is precisely why I feel marriages of equal fortune are preferable."

Rebecca shook her head. "Just because a woman must consider her future does not mean she would wed *only* for fortune. Since we met you have often commended my prudence and good sense. If I had an opportunity to wed, would I be prudent to marry a man who could not provide for me?"

"Of course not!" The notion of Rebecca wed to another man tore at him, especially if the match would doom her to a life of hardship.

"But that is the only kind of man who would be of equal fortune to me," she reminded him. "Now consider another possibility. If I were to receive a proposal from a man who could provide well for me, giving me a home of my own at last and allowing me to raise my children rather than always other people's, would you condemn me for accepting him?"

Though he still shrank from the thought of her as another man's wife, how could he blame her for pursuing a union that would give her the kind of life he wanted for her? "I hope you do not doubt my answer to that. I could not be so severe."

"Thank you." She gave his arm a squeeze, as if he had done her some great favor rather than simply responding to a "what if…?" "Yet it would be an unequal match. I have only my small salary and very little saved."

"I know where you are leading with this," Sebastian grumbled. "I will admit there may be times when such matches might be acceptable, as long as fortune was not the only consideration. Still I do not see how this has any bearing on Lydia and my…*forgiving* her."

"Imagine I had a family who'd fallen on hard times and relied on me to assist them," Rebecca urged him. "What if I were young and beautiful, capable of attracting the ardor of a wealthy man? Perhaps I would be too foolish and immature to love this man as he deserved. I might care for another whose lack of fortune would make him unacceptable to my family. What would you advise me then? Should I please myself at the expense of my family or be a dutiful daughter by wedding a man I did not love?"

"No!" Sebastian came to an abrupt halt. "I cannot have you compare yourself to Lydia, even in fancy. You are nothing like her!"

Except in the pull she exerted upon his heart. "If you had been in the situation you describe, I know you'd have found some way that would not have deceived and hurt…the man who cared for you. You would have told him frankly of your circumstances and your true feelings, then let him choose whether to walk away or try to win your love. You would not have led him on to milk him for every farthing you could get."

Rebecca sighed. "I hope I would act with such integrity, but I cannot be certain. Hurt, fear and desperation make people do terrible things. We cannot condone their actions, but surely we can try to have compassion for their motives. It becomes easier if we ask ourselves what we would do in their place. I believe *that* is the beginning of forgiveness."

As usual, she was making arguments Sebastian could not altogether refute. But the possibility that he might come to pity Lydia after everything she had put him through was like the cold barrel of a cocked pistol biting into his belly.

He began walking again as if fleeing pursuit. "I know the Bible bids us to forgive, but the best I can do is try to forget. Even that is not easy when I fear my brother is about to fall into the same trap."

"Can you not see?" Rebecca gasped as she exerted herself to keep up with his brisk stride. "That is how your bitterness is hurting you and others. When we first met, you told me you would never wed or sire a family. You also said you had *saved* your brother from past romantic entanglements. Even if you manage to part him from Hermione, I fear he might never find a wife who would meet with your approval. In the end, he might come to resent your interference as much as you resent Lydia."

That sounded like a threat—one with a terrifying ring of truth. Was it possible he might alienate his brother and end up a bitter old man, entirely alone?

His fear provoked Sebastian to lash out. "What gives you the right to lecture me on this subject? I am not one of your pupils, learning proper deportment or whatever it is you teach them. What do you know about suffering and bitterness? Shut away from life, training young girls in all the arts and graces they need to snare well-to-do husbands."

Rebecca let go of his arm and shrank from his outburst. In her wide, changeable eyes, he glimpsed the sharp sting his words had inflicted. It made him thoroughly despise himself. She was the last person who deserved his censure and the very last he wanted to hurt.

He reached for her. "Rebecca, I didn't mean…Please, forgi—"

How did he dare ask her forgiveness when he had spent the last quarter hour railing against it?

She stumbled back as if she feared he might strike her if she let him get within reach.

Suddenly Sebastian realized they had reached Rose Grange.

He opened his mouth once more to apologize. But before he could force any words out, he heard the distinctive rattle of the gig behind him.

"Sebastian! Miss Beaton!" cried Claude. "Wish us joy! After you left, we spoke to the vicar and set the date for our wedding. The first reading of the banns will take place next Sunday!"

Sebastian's first reaction was alarm that he had less than a month to rescue his brother. Then Rebecca's warning echoed through his mind, and he found himself questioning whether that would be the right thing to do after all.

Chapter Eight

"Isn't it the loveliest ring, Miss Beaton?" Hermione dropped the pillowcase she'd been embroidering and fluttered her fingers in front of Rebecca, showing off the engagement token Mr. Stanhope had brought her from London. "He said being away from me for even a few days made him all the more determined to marry me, no matter how much his brother objects."

In the middle of writing a letter, Rebecca nodded absently. She found it difficult to concentrate on either her letter or Hermione's conversation as Sebastian's accusations gnawed at her. All the previous night, she'd tossed and turned, wrestling with them. Hard as she tried to persuade herself he was wrong, deep in her soul she knew the truth when she heard it. She had no right to lecture him or anyone else about forgiveness. Not because, as he believed, she had never been wronged or mistreated but because she *had*.

To this day, she still held a grudge against her mother's family. Never once, since she'd gone away to school, had she made any effort to contact them. Never once in her prayers had she mentioned them. Like Sebastian with his late wife, she tried to think of them as little as possible. When that could not be avoided, she'd dwelt on the wrongs they'd done her. Never had she tried to do what she'd so glibly advised Sebastian—considered the events of the past from their perspective, honestly seeking to understand why they might have acted as they had.

Hermione heaved a sigh. "Dearest Claude says his brother will give us no peace until we are either parted or united irrevocably. Since we cannot bear to be parted, we must be married as soon as possible. He assured me that once we are man and wife, Lord Benedict will accept the situation."

Raising her hand to her lips, she bit her thumbnail, a nervous habit of which Rebecca had spent several years trying to break her. "I only wish I could be certain Claude is right about his brother. The viscount is so disapproving I hate to think what he might do if we wed against his wishes."

"I agree with Mr. Stanhope." Rebecca recalled Sebastian's fierce denial when she had raised that possibility. "Once you are wed, his lordship will accept you as his sister-in-law with as much grace as he can muster. I only wish you would not let his opposition push you into marrying before you are both quite ready. Remember the old saying, 'Marry in haste, repent at leisure.'"

"I shall never repent marrying Claude!" Hermione protested…a bit too much, Rebecca thought. "I hope you have not let Lord Benedict turn you to his way of thinking just because he is so attentive to you."

"Of course not." Rebecca tried to grasp her young friend's hand, but Hermione rose from her seat and backed away. "I only want you to be very sure of your feelings and Mr. Stanhope's before you commit yourself to him for the rest of your life."

"I *am* sure of two things." Hermione edged toward the door. "Sure that Claude Stanhope is the man I want to marry and sure that you have been heeding his brother. For shame! How could you let that horrid man turn you against me?"

Before Rebecca could insist upon her innocence once more, Hermione stormed off, shutting the door hard behind her.

Rebecca rubbed her temples in an effort to ease the crushing headache her worries and regrets had spawned. She had tried not to heed Sebastian's misgivings about the engagement, but she had to admit a few of them had merit. What a cruel irony it would be if his antagonism brought about a hasty marriage the young couple might later repent. She knew he would take no pleasure in being proven right if they ended up unhappy together.

She must warn him! Once the first banns were read, there would be all manner of speculation and gossip if the wedding was postponed. Now, it would only take a quiet word with the vicar to allow Hermione and Mr. Stanhope the time they needed to become better acquainted and banish any second thoughts.

Rebecca packed away her writing materials, then hurried off to change clothes. Once she was properly attired to pay a call on Stanhope Court, she sought out Squire Leonard to ask for the use of one of the horses.

"Why of course, my dear." The squire's kind, weathered face betrayed surprise at her request. "You are welcome to take the carriage if you wish."

Rebecca smiled and shook her head. "A horse will be less trouble for everyone. Besides, I am not going far and the day is fair and calm."

"Suit yourself then. By the by, Miss Beaton, I hope this whim of Hermione and her young man to wed so soon will not create any difficulty for you, finding a new position and so on. We shall miss you around Rose Grange after all these years."

"Thank you, sir." Rebecca's throat tightened. She had always liked Hermione's father, who kept busy with his small estate and his duties as local magistrate. He had trusted her to teach and raise his daughter and seemed pleased with the result. "I shall miss you as well. But I mean to write to Hermione often and hope to hear all the news of Avoncross."

She dodged his question about finding a new position, because her inquiries so far had met with no success. She'd written to all her school friends. But none of them had heard of any opportunities for her. Unless she could persuade Sebastian not to push his brother into a hasty marriage, she would have very little time to find new employment.

Could that be why she was suddenly giving more credence to his doubts about Hermione and Mr. Stanhope, Rebecca asked herself as she thanked Squire Leonard for the use of the horse and headed away.

On her ride to Stanhope Court, she thought it over and satisfied herself that Hermione's future happiness was her prime concern, not her own convenience. Yet she would miss Avoncross and the comfortable life she'd made for herself at Rose Grange. As she rode out of the village into the countryside, her gaze lingered on the green hills and hedgerows with the wistful appreciation of one who must soon leave them.

Almost before she knew it, she found herself turning off the road onto the winding, wooded lane that led up to Stanhope Court. As she rounded the first bend in the lane, she startled at the sight of Sebastian riding toward her.

He seemed equally surprised to see her. His horse whinnied and reared slightly when he reined it to an abrupt halt.

"Miss Beaton." The viscount swept off his hat and bent

low in his saddle. "You must have divined my thoughts. I was on my way to call on you and give you…these."

Juggling the reins and his hat, he freed one hand to extend a colorful nosegay of garden flowers. "And to offer my apology for the rude manner in which I rebuffed your kindly meant advice yesterday."

Rebecca leaned forward to accept the flowers. It was impossible to negotiate the transfer without her gloved hand brushing against Sebastian's. Even with the double barrier of leather between them, a sweet whisper of sensation fluttered up her arm when they made contact. Much as she would miss the Cotswold and Rose Grange, she feared she would miss the viscount's stimulating companionship even more.

She had fought her growing feelings for him, knowing nothing could come of them but disappointment and fruitless yearning. Yet her heart had refused to heed reason. Every time they parted company, she felt a deepening void in her life. Every time they met again, a powerful rush of joy engulfed her. She knew there was no longer any sense hoping for a poor curate or a kindly widower to make her an offer of marriage. She could not wed any other man when her heart belonged to one she could never have.

"They're beautiful, thank you." She lifted the flowers to inhale their fresh, sweet fragrance…and to hide her eyes so Sebastian would not glimpse the ache of longing in them and guess her feelings. "But you owe me no apology. What you said was true. I have no right to lecture you or anyone else about forgiveness."

"Perhaps not." Sebastian turned his horse and urged it forward at a leisurely walk, while Rebecca's mount fell in step. "But I know you meant well and some of what you said made an impression on me. Even if it had not, I had no call to speak to you as I did. My only defense is that anything to do with my marriage is a very sore subject with me."

"I understand." Pleasant as it was to ride at his side, Rebecca wished they were on foot so she might cling to his arm.

Sebastian gave a wry chuckle. "And that is the beginning of forgiveness?"

She risked a glance at him and a smile. "I believe so. You understand that I meant well, which made it easier to excuse me for meddling where I had no right."

"Was that why you came here?" An unaccustomed glint of levity twinkled in his eyes. "So we might argue over who was more to blame?"

"Not entirely." Rebecca recalled the reason for her visit. "I also came to warn you that your opposition to their engagement is what has put Hermione and your brother in such haste to wed."

She repeated what Claude Stanhope had told Hermione. "I believe it is vital that they not rush into marriage. They need more time for the bond between them to ripen before they are joined for a lifetime."

"Does this mean you and I are on the same side now?" Reining his horse to a stop in front of the house, Sebastian swiftly dismounted then came to help Rebecca down. "We make much better allies than we do opponents."

She gave a little gasp when he clasped her carefully around the waist and lowered her to the ground with effortless strength. "I think we have always been allies in desiring the happiness of those we hold dear."

For a quiet, drawn-out moment, they stood with his hands around her waist and hers raised to his shoulders. It would have taken only the slightest adjustment for their present stance to melt into an embrace.

Then a lad came running from the stables to take the horses.

Rebecca and Sebastian sprang apart. But after an awkward moment, he gallantly offered her his arm and returned to their conversation. "If we are agreed that Miss Leonard and my brother should not rush into marriage, what can be done to prevent them? Do you think they might listen if we sat them down and talked to them, presenting a united front?"

Much as the notion appealed to her, Rebecca felt bound to express her reservations. "I am afraid that would only serve to make them unite against us, which is the last thing we want."

Sebastian gave a dispirited nod. "What do you suggest then?"

She hesitated, loathe to spoil this moment of closeness between them, as she knew her suggestion would. But she could not refrain from answering indefinitely, and she could see only one solution. "I think you must tell them you will withdraw your objections to their engagement."

"Withdraw my—?" Sebastian stared at Rebecca, wondering how his treasured ally had suddenly turned traitor. "You know I cannot do that. Is this some new stratagem you have contrived with them to get around me?"

"I would not do that," she insisted with a ring of sincerity he found impossible to doubt. "I hope you know me well enough to believe I never would."

His accusing stare softened, and he allowed one corner of his lips to arch slightly. "I suppose I do. I apologize for my suspicions but my answer remains the same. I cannot pretend to accept this engagement when—"

Rebecca interrupted to finish his sentence. "—when every time you look at Hermione you are reminded of Lydia?"

"I was going to say, 'when I believe it would be a grave mistake.' But your suggestion is not untrue."

They entered the house, walking down the main gallery. Absorbed in their conversation and Rebecca's company, Sebastian had little conscious idea where he was headed. He could take his lovely guest into the sitting room and call for tea. But that would require her to let go of his arm, a deprivation he could not bear. So he walked past the sitting room…the dining room…the library, out into the gardens.

Rebecca seemed not to notice where they were going as she concentrated on trying to persuade him. "I must have rehearsed half a dozen arguments on my way here, but now I see it is no use appealing to reason. It is your heart and soul I must win over so you will be free to do the right thing."

Win his heart? It felt as if she had been doing that from the moment they met.

"You think I do not understand how hard it is to forgive," Rebecca continued, "because I have never been hurt. But that is not true. Indeed, before coming to Rose Grange, I was more accustomed to neglect and mistreatment than kindness."

The thought of someone hurting her made every muscle in Sebastian's body tense. "Who mistreated you, your parents?"

His father had been cursed with a volatile temper of which he'd occasionally borne the brunt. Perhaps that was what made him seek to control his anger. One of the things he'd most detested about Lydia was how close she'd come to making him lash out.

Rebecca shook her head. "Never my parents. What little I recall of them was always gentle and loving. I believe the early foundation of their affection may have been what carried me through all that came after."

So she had lost her parents at a young age, too. Sebastian scarcely remembered his mother, who had died when he was a small child. The loss of Claude's mother had been much harder to bear. She had been as devoted to him as to her own little son, and it was partly for her sake that he'd always tried to look out for his brother.

"What came after?" As they walked, he could not keep himself from drawing closer to her.

Rebecca kept her eyes downcast, watching the path as if she feared some obstacle might spring up to trip her. "They died of diphtheria the winter before I turned five. Papa was a poor clergyman with no family, so I was sent to live with my mother's relatives. They were wealthy and titled and they had never forgiven Mama for marrying beneath her."

A great many things suddenly became clear to Sebastian, including why she'd been so indignant at his opposition to marriages of unequal fortune.

"Did they harm you?" Instinctively his fists clenched. He wanted to thrash anyone who had dared lay a hand on her.

"Beat me, you mean?" Rebecca shook her head. "They were far too well bred to stoop to that sort of thing. But they could use words to inflict injuries as painful as any blow and far longer lasting. I was never allowed to forget that I was an embarrassing, inconvenient burden to them. They passed me from one to another like a hot potato no one wanted to be left holding. No sooner would I begin to find my way around a new household, learn people's names and become accustomed to the routine than I would be sent somewhere new to begin all over again."

"No wonder you prize familiarity," Sebastian mused, recalling the first time she'd confided in him.

They'd been in the same place then—the Fountain Garden his grandfather had hewn out of this hillside. There was a mysterious air of peace about this secluded garden that seemed to invite disclosure.

"Finally, when I was nine," Rebecca continued, staring out over the tranquil Cotswold countryside, "they decided I should be sent away to school. So off I went."

"Was that the school where you met those friends of yours?" Sebastian tried to recall if she'd told him any more than that about the place.

She nodded. "The Pendergast Charity School for Orphaned Daughters of the Clergy. It is a shame the place did not live up to its impressive name. It was the most wretched institution—cold, damp, ill-staffed and ill-provisioned. For all that, I preferred it to the fine houses of my relatives where I had been infinitely better fed and clothed. At least there I had friends who cared for me, and I was able to stay long enough to become accustomed to it."

Words continued to trickle out of her as if a dam had been breached. She told him more about the harsh deprivations of her years at the school and the forlorn confusion of being shuffled from one uncaring relative to another. His chest ached with a mixture of sympathy, grief and rage over what she had endured. He could not bear to think of her wanting for anything ever again, or going away to yet another new place.

"So you see," she murmured at last, "I do know how it feels to be hurt and to carry the bitterness of it around with you always."

She turned toward him then, tilting her head to meet his gaze. As he stared into her eyes, Sebastian thought he might get lost in them and found he welcomed the opportunity. They were Cotswold eyes—the warm golden brown of local stone, blended with the vibrant green of the rolling hills. This was where she belonged.

"I know how difficult it is to forgive those who have hurt you," she continued, "because I have never truly forgiven my relatives. As you said, the best I have been able to do is try to forget them."

"Do not trouble yourself over it." He clasped her hands between his. They felt small and cold, desperately in need of his strength and warmth. "Those people do not deserve your forgiveness."

She considered for a moment, then replied, "How many people do you suppose would ever be forgiven if they had to deserve it? I'm not certain I would."

"Nonsense," he growled, compelled to protect her, even from her own self-doubts. "What have you ever done that would need forgiveness?"

"What a short memory you have." She flashed him a rueful grin that faded all too quickly. "The first time we met, I misjudged you and misled you. Most recently I have been a hypocrite, urging you to do what I could not do myself."

A fine mist rose in her eyes.

"Don't fret about any of that!" He released her hand and gathered her into his arms. "I don't blame you. I understand."

Wasn't that what she had advised him to do for Lydia?

His effort to comfort Rebecca failed miserably. Or perhaps the anguish of all the painful memories she'd unearthed overcame her. A shudder went through her and then another as she began to weep in his arms. Even after she grew quiet, Sebastian found he could not let her go. It felt so right and natural to hold her like this.

And when she tilted her face toward him, it felt right and natural to lean forward…

Before prudence or wariness intervened to prevent him, he gave her a kiss that seemed to have been lurking on his lips all this time, awaiting just such an opportunity. To his relief and delight, Rebecca did not shrink from it but kissed him back.

It was just the sort of kiss he expected from her—sincere and generous with a refreshing air of innocence. Like a long-lost key, her kiss slipped into his heart, unlocking all the tender feelings he had resisted and denied. Out they poured, washing away painful memories, filling the arid, empty spaces within him, overwhelming every other thought but those of her…and *them*.

He could have stayed there forever, holding and kissing her.

But too soon, Rebecca stirred, tensed and drew back from him. "I'm so sorry, Sebastian…Lord Benedict! I did not mean to take advantage of your kindness like this. I must go!"

He caught her hand. "Stay with me, Rebecca! Not just now, but always. Marry me, please! Say you will be my wife."

No sooner had those words left his mouth than dark doubts assailed him. How long had he known Rebecca Beaton, after all? Not much longer than he'd known Lydia when he proposed to her. And Rebecca had even more mercenary reasons to accept him than Lydia had—she'd told him so herself.

His heart sprang to her defense, insisting that Rebecca was nothing like his late wife. She was sincere, kind and understanding—a compound of all the best virtues!

But that argument only made his reason all the more suspicious. The intoxicating ardor he felt for her was all too familiar, though even more intense than he remembered from the last time. By allowing himself to care so much more for Rebecca, he had given her infinitely more power to make him happy...or miserable.

All those thoughts flashed through his mind while his proposal seemed to tremble in the fragrant air between them. Part of him yearned desperately for Rebecca to accept, while another part grew sick with fear that she might. In any case, it was out of his hands now. He'd blurted out the fateful words that had placed him in her power, and he could not take them back.

"I..." She searched his gaze for some reassurance that this was what he truly wanted. "I..."

As he steeled himself for her answer, equally fearful of either, she cried, "I *must* go!"

Wrenching her hand from his, Rebecca spun away and ran up the path as if her darkest terrors were snarling and snapping at her heels.

He wanted to go after her, but the tyranny of bitter memories kept him frozen there. In that moment, he realized the only thing worse than either of the answers Rebecca might give him was no answer at all.

Chapter Nine

What answer would she give Sebastian to his unexpected proposal?

After several days spent thinking of little else, Rebecca was no closer to a conclusion than she'd been when she fled the romantic tranquility of the Fountain Garden.

With all her heart, she longed to accept, for so many reasons. The most important of those was that she had come to care for Sebastian in a way she'd never expected to feel for any man. She admired his protectiveness, his concern for others and his willingness to use his high position to do some good. Yet he was no tiresome model of virtue. His company was well spiced with wry wit and informative, entertaining conversation. Besides that, she felt a deep connection to him on account of the losses and hurts they'd both suffered and tried to overcome.

Then there was his fine house and comfortable fortune. She wished she could claim they did not matter to her, but that would be untrue. For someone like her, who had moved so often and felt the humiliating deprivations of living on charity, the security of a home like Stanhope Court and freedom from the grim shadow of want would be cherished blessings indeed.

Another blessing was that she would never have to be parted from Hermione. They would be even more like sisters than they had been, connected by family ties rather than terms of employment. If she agreed to wed Sebastian, Rebecca knew he could have no grounds to continue opposing his brother's engagement to Hermione.

The thought of Hermione made Rebecca glance toward the pianoforte, where her young friend was practicing a romantic but rather melancholy air. It occurred to her that Hermione had been very subdued these past few days. She chided herself for being so preoccupied with Sebastian's proposal that she had not noticed until now. Was Hermione having more second thoughts about marrying Claude Stanhope so soon? Was she worried about how her future brother-in-law might treat her?

Vowing to broach the subject as soon as Hermione finished playing, Rebecca fell prey to all manner of doubts about the wisdom of accepting Sebastian's proposal. If only she could be certain that he cared for her the way she had come to care for him. But the manner of his asking made it clear he'd been motivated by pity rather than love. Though he tried to pretend otherwise, she knew he was a man of deep compassion. He must have been moved by her tale of woe and wanted to spare her any further insecurity or deprivation.

Considering the depth of her feelings for him, could she be satisfied with a marriage that promised comfort, security and companionship, but not love? And what of Sebastian— would he soon come to regret a second marriage he'd made in haste, out of kindness? Might he be as miserable with her as he had been with his first wife, though for different reasons?

She could not forget the look in his eyes when he'd realized he had proposed to her—a deadly mixture of panic, regret and dread. Yet she'd sensed very different feelings from him when he'd held her in his arms and kissed her. If he did not love her yet, she believed he was capable of loving her…if only he could banish the shadows of his past.

The final notes of the music Hermione had been playing faded away. Its tone had matched Rebecca's yearning, pensive mood.

"That was lovely, my dear." She applauded softly. "I don't believe I've ever heard you play it before. What's it called?"

Hermione started at the sound of Rebecca's voice, as if she'd forgotten she was not alone in the room. "It's a 'Division' by Jenkins, a sweet melody but rather sad."

Rebecca nodded. "Just what I was thinking. I wonder what the composer had in mind when he wrote it?"

Rising from the pianoforte, Hermione walked over and sank down on the far end of the settee. The troubled look on her delicate features mirrored the beautiful, plaintive music she'd been playing.

"Is something the matter?" Rebecca slid closer to her on the settee. "You don't seem your usual, cheerful self of late."

A qualm of remorse gripped her for having neglected her young friend in recent days.

"Oh, Miss Beaton." Hermione's lower lip trembled. "Are you still angry with me after the way I spoke to you the other day? I know you would never let Lord Benedict turn you against me, but I've been so anxious and confused. I'm sorry I took it out on you! Can you ever forgive me?"

"Dearest girl!" Her throat tightened at the realization of how Hermione had misinterpreted her preoccupation. "I cannot *still* be angry, for I never was to begin with."

When Rebecca opened her arms, Hermione dove into her embrace. "As for forgiving you, I would, of course, but there is nothing to forgive. I knew you could not mean what you said about me taking Seb—Lord Benedict's side."

"I was certain I m-must have offended you." Hermione did not sound entirely convinced by Rebecca's reassurance. "You've hardly spoken a word to me since then."

"Nor to anybody else." Rebecca smoothed back the hair that had tumbled over Hermione's forehead. "I've had a great deal on my mind of late. Nothing to do with our talk the other day. I'm sorry I've been so distracted."

"What have you been thinking about? Finding a new position and going away?"

"Partly." Rebecca hesitated, uncertain how much to tell her young friend. But she needed to confide in someone, and this might make Hermione think more critically about her engagement. "The fact is, Lord Benedict…has asked me to marry him."

The news jolted Hermione upright. "Lord Benedict? Are you joking? I know he's been very attentive to you, but I thought it was only so you would use your influence on me. I don't understand how he can want you for a wife when he claims I am not a suitable bride for his brother!"

Rebecca shook her head. "This is not something I would joke about. As for the other, I wish I knew how to reconcile that contradiction, but I am at a loss."

"What answer did you give him?" Hermione demanded. "I know you have a far better opinion of him than I do and it would be a brilliant match. But do not forget the advice you gave me. Marriage means committing the rest of your life to this man."

"That's what frightens me." Heaving a sigh, Rebecca rose from the settee and crossed to the window overlooking the garden. "That is why I have not given him my answer yet. I have been thinking of almost nothing else ever since."

She gazed out at the garden where she and Sebastian had first met. Some of the flowers then in bloom had gone to seed, while new ones had blossomed to take their places. She marveled at how far their acquaintance had ripened in such a short time. What if those feelings faded just as quickly? "I know you have not seen the side of him that I have. But I believe I would never regret marrying *him* if I could be certain he would not regret marrying *me*."

"If he were any other man," Hermione muttered, "I could assure you with complete confidence that would never happen."

Her young friend had hit upon the difficulty, Rebecca mused. Sebastian—Lord Benedict—was unlike any other man she'd ever met. While she admired and treasured his uniqueness, it was not without its dark side.

Just then the Leonards' housemaid appeared bearing a message. "A footman brought this from Stanhope Court, miss."

"Thank you, Mary." Hermione bounded up from the settee with her hand extended to receive the note.

"No, miss." The girl held the folded, sealed paper out toward Rebecca. "I was told to deliver it to Miss Beaton."

"Me? Are you certain?" Taking the note gingerly, as if it might grow teeth at any moment, Rebecca confirmed it was indeed addressed to her.

As she broke the seal and began to read, Hermione

dismissed Mary, who looked frankly curious. "What does it say?"

"We are summoned to Stanhope Court." Rebecca labored to read Sebastian's spiky scrawl for the first time. "Lord Benedict will send his carriage to collect us."

Turning the note over in her hand, she murmured, "He must have gotten tired of waiting for my answer."

That did not explain why he wanted both of them to come.

"Have you decided what you'll tell him?" asked Hermione.

Rebecca shook her head. "I shall soon have to make up my mind."

A chill snaked down her spine. Whichever choice she made, she was afraid she might end up regretting it for as long as she lived.

"The ladies will be here soon." Sebastian glanced from the mantel clock to the housemaid. "You know what to do?"

"'Course, sir." She pursed her lips in a suggestive smirk that turned his stomach. "Not a hard task, is it?"

"I'm sure you've had plenty of practice." Sebastian strove to conceal the worst of his aversion.

He needed this creature's assistance, though he wished there'd been some other way. Unfortunately, time was fast running out for his brother, and several sleepless nights had left his mind too muddled to devise a better plan.

"Practice?" She laughed the way women did when they wanted to flatter a man when they found him witty. "Why, you and me could have a dress rehearsal right now if you like."

"That will not be necessary." His lip curled. "Your part

may not be difficult but proper timing is essential. So keep your wits about you."

"I will, sir." She walked past Sebastian, deliberately brushing against him. "You can count on me."

Pulling a cloth from the pocket of her apron, she pretended to dust the windowsill.

Sebastian turned on his heel and strode away to await the arrival of Rebecca and Miss Leonard. As he neared the entry hall, he caught a passing glimpse of his reflection in a looking glass and scarcely recognized himself. He looked haggard, disheveled and bleary-eyed—almost as bad as during the worst days of his marriage. Rebecca hadn't even accepted his proposal and already she was putting him through the same misery as Lydia had.

Every hour that passed, he grew more certain that asking her to marry him had been as terrible a mistake as his brother proposing to Hermione Leonard. Why had she kept him hanging for days on end, waiting for the ax to fall, when there could be no question she would take advantage of his fatal lapse in judgment? His fortune and the security it provided would be too great a temptation. Marriage to a viscount would also raise her rank, perhaps higher than her relatives. She would be free to flaunt her new title in the faces of those who'd once cast her out.

With all that to entice her, why had she fled from him in the garden, then? And why was she taking so long to give him her answer? Could it be that she did not care for him and shrank from spending the rest of her life with him?

He welcomed the sight of his carriage coming up the lane, for it distracted him from the vicious spiral of doubt that had plagued him ever since he blurted out that blasted proposal.

A few moments later, he bowed over the ladies' hands

when they'd alighted from the carriage. "Miss Leonard, Miss Beaton, thank you for accepting my invitation on such short notice. Shall we go join my brother for tea?"

Though habit and inclination urged him to offer Rebecca his arm, Sebastian resisted. Thrusting his hands behind his back, he strode off, leaving the ladies to follow.

"Lord Benedict?" Rebecca's voice rang with a note of tender concern. "Are you ill? You do not look well."

"I am no worse than usual, I assure you." He raised his voice to alert his accomplice of their approach. She was one woman who had better not betray him.

As they reached the door to the sitting room, Sebastian stood back to let the ladies enter first. It was more than simple courtesy. This way, they would have an unobstructed view of the proceedings.

A sharp gasp from one and a shrill cry from the other assured him the housemaid's timing had been flawless. Perhaps she would find success on the London stage as she so desperately desired.

Sebastian entered the room to find Claude blathering on about how the servant had suddenly thrown herself at him and kissed him.

"It's not how it looks, Hermione. I can explain. Well, perhaps not explain, but…" From his wild gestures and frantic tone, it was clear he knew there was no hope of his fiancée believing such an improbable story.

"Away you go!" Sebastian growled at the housemaid. "I'll deal with you later."

The girl sidled off, still smirking.

In the brittle silence that descended upon the room, Sebastian waited for Miss Leonard's reaction. She had said nothing since her first squeal of dismay. Was that a good sign or a bad one?

Protective as ever, Rebecca moved closer and put her arm around her young friend. But she did not speak. Like Claude and Sebastian, she seemed to hold her breath waiting to hear what Hermione would say.

For a long moment Hermione locked gazes with Claude, who appeared to offer a silent plea for understanding. Then she turned those enormous, childlike eyes in Sebastian's direction. In them he read a question and a wrenching depth of innocent pain he could not bear to witness.

Her whispery voice shattered the expectant hush. "I believe you, Claude."

The young man's bated breath exploded in a gasp and sob. The question that rose to his lips was the same one that echoed through his brother's mind. "You do?"

She did? Where was the outrage he'd expected, the possessive hysteria?

Hermione gave a shaky nod. "I know you are a good, honorable man. I am certain you would never betray my trust."

He should have known, a persuasive little voice in the back of Sebastian's mind sneered. The girl must be so greedy for the advantages she would gain by wedding his brother that she was willing to turn a blind eye to flagrant evidence of betrayal.

"Thank heaven!" Claude stumbled toward her, his hand pressed to his chest. "And thank *you* for being so sweet and trusting. I was so afraid this would make you change your mind about marrying me."

When he reached for her, Hermione retreated into the shelter of Rebecca's arms. "I'm afraid…it has."

Claude flinched. "But you just said you trust me. I don't understand."

"Perhaps you should ask your brother."

"My brother?" He glanced toward Sebastian. "What has he got to do with…? Oh, no. Sebastian. Tell me you didn't do this!"

"I had to. You forced my hand. After the banns are read tomorrow, there would have been no going back. I know you're upset now, but you'll soon forget. You always do."

"Forget?" With a feral cry, Claude lunged toward Sebastian, his fist raised.

Sebastian stood unflinching before his brother's attack, not out of courage or resolution but because he was concentrating so hard on Rebecca. The sharp intake of her breath was followed by a faint, wounded whimper. In her gaze he glimpsed a desperate yearning to deny that he was capable of such a thing.

At the last instant, Claude stayed his blow. Instead, he hurled words that injured Sebastian far worse. "Forget her? Never! And I will never forgive you for what you've done."

He turned to Hermione. "Please don't punish me for my brother's malicious mischief!"

"I do not believe he acted out of malice," she replied. "He only wanted to protect you."

"I am not an infant!" Claude cried. "I do not need his protection, especially not from you! You are the best thing that has ever happened to me."

"You think that now." Hermione's voice broke. "But if we were to wed against your brother's wishes, it would create a breach between you that might never heal. One day, you might come to blame me for it and wish you had not married me after all. I could not bear that."

As Claude begged her to reconsider, Sebastian felt his mind was about to burst trying to reconcile two entirely contrary ideas. Hermione Leonard was not clinging desperately to her engagement after all. Nor was she breaking it in a fit of jealous rage, but out of concern for his brother's future happiness and hers…and perhaps even his. Could he have misjudged her so horribly?

The harder Claude pleaded, the more gently implacable Hermione grew, like a slender sapling bending before a gale, but never breaking. When her eyes began to glitter with unshed tears, she turned and buried her face in Rebecca's shoulder.

"Not now," Rebecca advised Claude. "Perhaps later."

But it was clear from her tone that she doubted the passage of time would change Hermione's mind. Casting Sebastian a final look that mingled pity and disgust, she led her young friend from the room.

When the ladies had gone, Claude rounded on his brother again. "You have no idea, have you, of the harm you've done—of what you've cost me?"

After what he'd just witnessed, Sebastian was beginning to grasp the devastating consequences of his actions. But he could only repeat the rote excuse that sounded feeble, even to him. "I was trying to pro—"

"Protect me?" Claude bellowed. "Or punish me for finding the kind of love you have never known and never will? All these years, you've been more than a brother to me— mother and father and friend all in one. But today, I am ashamed of you."

With that final swipe, his handsome young features crumpled, and he fled.

Sebastian reeled from Claude's accusations. He would never seek to punish his brother for finding happiness and knowing love! Would he? Until today he would never have believed it. Now he was not so sure.

And could he be so riddled with bitterness that he would rather throw away his best chance of happiness than admit he might have been wrong? That appalling thought sent him flying down the main gallery, praying he would not be too late to catch Rebecca. Though after what he'd done, he feared he had no right to pray for anything.

But when he clambered down the steep stairs from the portico, he saw his carriage still parked at the head of the lane. Rebecca was helping Hermione into the vehicle with the tender solicitude she might have shown an ailing or elderly person.

When he called for her to wait, she turned on him, her eyes flashing with righteous wrath. "Are you proud of yourself, Lord Benedict?"

Proud? Sebastian shook his head. He had never been more ashamed of his actions.

Rebecca raised her brows. "I thought you would be elated after accomplishing what you set out to do from the beginning. Arrogant, stubborn and ruthless, indeed. Only do not claim you acted in a worthy cause. We both know that would be a lie."

"Please, Rebecca." He teetered on the brink of a black pit of guilt and despair, and only she had the power to drag him back from the edge.

"Who were you really trying to save today?" she demanded. "Your brother or yourself?"

"Myself?" What could she mean?

"Yourself," she repeated, "from marriage to me. You knew I could never wed a man who would stoop to something so vile."

He wished he could deny it, if not to her, at least to himself. But her charge had a sickening ring of truth.

Rebecca shook her head slowly and sadly, as if she could not fathom anything so offensive. "You needn't have gone to all this trouble, you know. I'd already made up my mind to refuse your proposal, in spite of how much I'd let myself care for you."

"You had?" Why would she reject such a fine match if she cared for him?

"I knew you didn't really want me." Her gaze flitted away, but not before he glimpsed a bleak mist in her eyes. "I'm accustomed to that. I learned long ago that it's best to leave without making a fuss."

Before he could say another word, she turned and scrambled into the carriage.

The kindest thing he could do for her, he realized, was to fold up the step, close the door and watch in silence as *his* carriage bore her away.

Out of his life.

Forever.

Chapter Ten

A month after Rebecca and Hermione had driven away from Stanhope Court for the last time, life at Rose Grange was finally settling back into its familiar pattern.

She should have been happy about that, Rebecca told herself, or at least content. Instead she felt restless, often sad and sometimes angry. There were days when the only thing that induced her to get out of bed was the need to look after Hermione and try to cheer her a little.

That was proving a challenge. Hermione spent far too much time in her room with the excuse of headaches or indigestion. Why she would have indigestion, Rebecca could not fathom for she hardly touched her food. She was growing alarmingly thin and pale, with dark hollows under her eyes.

It might have helped if she'd been willing to talk about what was clearly on her mind. But since that day she had refused to speak of Mr. Stanhope or his brother. Was Hermione trying to forget what she could not forgive? Rebecca knew from experience how futile, even dangerous, that could be.

Now, as Hermione sat at the pianoforte, listlessly picking

out yet another slow, doleful melody, Rebecca could stand it no more.

"Enough of this." She surged up from her chair and dragged Hermione to her feet. "We are going to pay a call on some poor soul who is unable to get out and enjoy the fine summer weather."

Hermione tried to resist. "What if we meet someone on the way? I know the whole village must be gossiping about my broken engagement."

They'd heard that Claude Stanhope had departed for parts unknown. Lord Benedict was said to be in seclusion at Stanhope Court, seeing no one.

"Nonsense!" Rebecca tugged her through the door. "I'm certain everyone has tired of the subject and moved on to some fresher local scandal by now."

She knew she must sound heartless, but this was the first spark of spirit she had seen from Hermione in days.

Still, she was quite surprised when her young friend gave a wan smile. "Perhaps you're right. I have spent too long wallowing in my misery. It will do me good to remember people with worse troubles. Let's visit Mrs. Rollins. She is such a dear soul and I have neglected her of late."

To Rebecca's immense relief, they had a very pleasant visit with Mrs. Rollins—only a little subdued on Hermione's part. The few people they met on their walk through the village were all kind and tactful. It gave Rebecca hope that it would be even easier to coax Hermione out the next time.

As they strolled home, arm in arm, Hermione glanced toward the church. Rebecca realized they were passing the spot where Sebastian had often parked his gig on Sunday mornings.

"How could he do something so heartless to me?" Hermione asked in a small voice, as if thinking aloud. "I never would have done anything to hurt him, or...his brother."

"Of course you wouldn't." Rebecca slipped a comforting arm around Hermione's shoulders. "But someone did hurt him very badly and he has never gotten over it. Bitterness warped his protective feelings for his brother into something hurtful."

"Can you still defend him," Hermione cried, "after what he did?"

"I do not condone his actions in the least, but I do have a little compassion for what made him act as he did. I hope someday you can, too. Otherwise I am afraid you could end up the same way. That would be a great pity indeed."

She felt on firmer ground talking about forgiveness these days. One good thing to come out of all this was that she'd taken the first small step toward making peace with the hurts of her past. She had written a letter to her Aunt Charlotte, not asking anything, but opening the door for further contact. Of course, that had been almost three weeks ago, and she'd received no reply. Perhaps her aunt wanted nothing more to do with her than she had when Rebecca was a child.

But at least she had tried. Somehow, making the overture had lifted a burden from her soul.

Hermione gave a choked little sob. "I'm afraid I may be more like him than I care to admit. I made noble-sounding excuses for breaking my engagement, and I did mean them. But some spiteful part of me knew it might turn Claude against his brother. It felt like the only way I had to strike back at him. For that, I hurt the man I claimed to love and threw away my only chance for happiness!"

The tears Hermione had locked tightly inside her now

began to flow. Rebecca sensed they were not so much for the injury Lord Benedict had inflicted upon her, but remorse for *her* actions.

"I'm certain you will have many more chances for happiness." Rebecca produced a handkerchief and handed it to her young friend. "Indeed, I think we both will."

Did remorse for one's own failings and compassion for the flaws of others breed hope, Rebecca wondered. Suddenly she felt more hopeful than she had, not just in the past weeks, but in many years.

"I wonder what's for dinner?" Hermione asked as they reached Rose Grange. Her tears had dried and she sounded much more like her old self. "Our walk has given me an appetite."

The housemaid met them at the door. "A letter came for you, Miss Beaton."

"Thank you, Mary." Rebecca's stomach tightened as she stared at the elegant, flowing script and realized it must be from her aunt.

Bracing herself for what it might say, she began to read. As she scanned the words, a smile slowly tugged at the corners of her mouth. By the time she finished, she was beaming while blinking back tears.

"It must be good news," Hermione speculated as she removed her bonnet and gloves. "Is it from one of your friends?"

"My Aunt Charlotte," Rebecca murmured, still somewhat bemused. "Lady Atherton. She is widowed now and living in Bath. She would like me to come for a visit."

"That *is* good news." Hermione tried to appear enthusiastic. "You could do with a change of scene."

"I reckon we both could," Rebecca replied. "Would you like to come with me? From the tone of her letter, I am certain Aunt Charlotte would welcome your company. I know I would be grateful to have someone familiar with me."

"Could I?" Hermione did not have to feign her excitement now. "We used to go to Bath when I was a child, but I haven't been in years. I would love to visit there again."

Seizing Rebecca in an impulsive embrace, she whispered, "I believe you were right about having more chances for happiness."

Though she nodded in agreement, Rebecca could not suppress a pang of sorrow for the happiness she might have known with Sebastian. Much as his actions had hurt her and Hermione and his brother, she was certain he'd hurt himself worst of all.

The only thing worse than having his happiness ruined by others was the knowledge that he had done it to himself. During the past three months, Sebastian had discovered that, to his grief and shame. The only good thing that had come out of it was his learning a hard but worthwhile lesson about forgiveness. With that, he had found the first true peace he'd known in a very long time.

Now, as he marched through Bath's Sydney Gardens on an unseasonably warm autumn afternoon, Sebastian feared he might be about to lose that hard won serenity. Coming face to face with Rebecca again would be a brutal reminder of what he had willfully destroyed through his arrogant, stubborn, ruthless actions. He only prayed he had not ruined her happiness, too, by rejecting her love and devotion even more cruelly than her relatives had rejected her as a child.

His prayer was not a mere wish that events might unfold as he desired, but a humble, heartfelt petition lifted to a Higher Power who understood him better than he understood himself. One that could still love and forgive him in spite of what he'd done. The hardest part about learning to trust and embrace that Divine Grace had been recognizing that the Lord also forgave those who'd hurt him.

His steps slowed as he scanned the crowd that had turned out to enjoy the pleasant weather and promenade their fashionable finery. Was it too soon to put his recent enlightenment to the test by facing two of the people he had most deeply wronged? What if Hermione Leonard threw his overture back in his face, as she had every right to do? What if he looked into Rebecca's dear eyes and saw only the corrosive bitterness he had caused? Might he fall back into his old destructive habits and lose the small spark of faith that had been his salvation?

Though that fear terrified him to the darkest depths of his soul, Sebastian knew he could not let it stop him if there was the slightest hope he might put right a tiny part of what he'd so callously shattered.

Just then the twirl of a parasol caught his eye, and he recognized two familiar figures on the main promenade. Yet, they looked different than he remembered, Sebastian realized as he approached them—Rebecca especially. Instead of the plain, dark clothes in which he was accustomed to seeing her, she was decked in a golden yellow walking dress with a smart little brown jacket and cunningly trimmed bonnet that framed her face to perfection. Miss Leonard looked very pretty too, in shades of pink.

It appeared the eligible gentlemen of Bath had taken notice of two such beauties in their midst, for a trio of dashing young bucks had engaged the ladies in spirited conversation. As he hung back, reluctant to interrupt, Sebastian found himself torn between pleasure at seeing Rebecca look so well and a sinking mixture of jealousy and despair. Was he already too late?

Before he could answer that question to his own satisfaction, Miss Leonard glanced his way and gave a violent start of recognition. Did the poor creature think he meant to insult her in front of her new acquaintances and spoil her chance to secure a husband?

When she smiled and called his name, her generosity of spirit humbled him. "Lord Benedict, what a surprise to see you in Bath. Gentlemen, may I present Viscount Benedict. My home in the Cotswolds is near his estate, which has the most beautiful gardens I have ever seen."

Miss Leonard introduced the young beaux, but Sebastian had eyes and ears only for Rebecca. Up close, she looked even lovelier than at a distance. Her complexion had taken on a fresh bloom, making her look nearly as young as her former pupil. Though her eyes held a soft brown shadow of sorrow, they were lightened by a verdant glow of deep joy.

Perhaps awed by Sebastian's title or frightened by his reputation, the young dandies made themselves scarce soon after their introduction. He was not sorry to see them go.

"What brings you to Bath, Lord Benedict?" asked Rebecca. "You are not ill, I hope," she added, referring to the way many people flocked to the fashionable spa to drink and bathe in the local mineral waters.

"I am no worse than ever." He repeated his accustomed wry quip. "I need not ask if you ladies are well for you could not look so lovely unless you were in the very best of health and spirits."

As he spoke, Sebastian intercepted a look between Hermione and Rebecca. It seemed to suggest, as his brother once had, that he sounded far too amiable to be the real Viscount Benedict.

"If I look well," Rebecca replied, "it must be on account of my new clothes. We are presently staying with my aunt, Lady Atherton, who is determined to spoil me with kindness." She glanced about. "Has your brother accompanied you to Bath by any chance? I should so much like to see him again."

The mention of Claude caused Miss Leonard to give a sharp little intake of breath.

Sebastian hoped he did not disappoint her too greatly when he shook his head. "Unlike you, I have not had the happiness of reconciling with my estranged family."

Pleased as he was that her life had taken such a fortunate turn, he could not stifle a pang of regret. Rebecca's aunt was clearly a lady of fortune, perhaps anxious to make up for past neglect by showering her niece with everything her money could buy. Even if he could ever summon the nerve to court Rebecca properly, she no longer had any compelling reason to encourage his attentions.

Thrusting that dispiriting thought to the back of his mind, Sebastian strove to concentrate on what he had come to do. "I have heard my brother is in London where he has found lucrative employment with an insurer of shipping. Though I believe it is his way of declaring independence from his interfering elder brother, I am proud of him."

The ladies nodded in agreement, but afterward Miss Leonard's head remained slightly bowed.

Rebecca appeared concerned for her young friend and perhaps anxious to escape the company of one who had distressed her. "You failed to answer my question, sir. If you are not ill or traveling with your brother, what has brought you to Bath?"

There it was, open and direct as always. "I must admit, I have come in search of Miss Leonard."

"Me?" Hermione squeaked.

Sebastian nodded. "Ever since we last parted company, I have been tormented by the shame of the great wrong I did you. And the terrible harm I caused my brother by depriving him of as fine a wife as he could ever find. I neither expect nor deserve your forgiveness, but I beg you not to make my innocent brother pay for my wicked folly. A single word from you is all it would take to restore his happiness. Anything you would ask of me, I will do and be grateful for the obligation if only you will give my brother reason to hope."

Miss Leonard raised one delicate, gloved hand to still her trembling lips. When she mastered her voice to speak, it was with the blessed whisper of true kindness and generosity. "How can I withhold forgiveness when I am in need of it myself? If your brother can find it in his heart to pardon me the grief I have caused him, it would be the greatest honor and joy of my life to be united with him."

Too moved to stand, Sebastian sank to his knees, seized her hand and pressed it to his lips. "There is nothing in my power I can do to adequately show my gratitude."

She let out a self-conscious giggle that was one of the sweetest sounds Sebastian had ever heard. "You could begin by standing up before you draw any more attention to us. I fear it will be all over Bath by sundown that you have proposed to me. I must write to Claude at once before the gossip spreads to London and he thinks the world has gone mad."

Her quip made Sebastian chuckle past the lump in his throat as he scrambled to his feet. "In that case, I will detain you ladies no longer. If you permit me, I will dispatch my footman to deliver your letter. A fast enough relay of horses might just outstrip the speed of gossip."

Behind his banter, his heart ached at the prospect of

parting from Rebecca, who had blinked back tears as she witnessed his exchange with Hermione.

"I'm afraid that won't do at all." Hermione's radiant smile belied her words. "By all means let your footman take my letter to London. I will have it ready to send in an hour. But as for the gossip, I fear there is only one way to nip it in the bud."

"Indeed?" The glint of sweet mischief in her eyes made Sebastian a trifle wary. "And what is that?"

"You must propose to my friend again, of course." As Rebecca glared at her and tried to protest, Hermione hurried on. "I see your neighbor, Mrs. Goddard. I can walk home with her so you two may talk in private."

She glanced around at everyone staring at them. "At least as private as you're likely to get in the middle of Sydney Gardens."

She breezed away, calling out to Mrs. Goddard, while Rebecca remained behind, looking thoroughly rattled. "I cannot imagine who raised that girl to be so abominably forward! Pray do not feel obliged to propose to me at her bidding."

But Sebastian sank down again, on one knee this time, for all the gawkers to see. "I would say you brought her up very well. I only wish I had not been too blind to appreciate her many merits until now. She is sweet-natured, forbearing, clever and witty. Not to mention very perceptive to bid me do the one thing I wished to with all my heart. I would say she will make my brother the best wife in the world, but that might not be quite true. If you will consent to marry me, dearest Rebecca, then even such a paragon as Hermione can only come second. I have no right to ask, let along hope that you will accept. But if you do, my happiness will be assured."

The whole park seemed to hold its breath with him as he waited for Rebecca's answer.

Instead she replied with a question of her own. "You've found a way to forgive Lydia, haven't you?"

"Not without a struggle," he confessed. "But I have. After hurting those I loved, I found I could begin to understand her, as you advised me. Forgiving your family must have taken far more goodness than I could muster, but it does not surprise me that you were able to. I am delighted to see how happy it has made you.

"Prosperous, too," he added. "I fear I no longer have anything to tempt you to marry me. Except my heart, and you know better than anyone what sorry condition it is in. But whether you choose to claim it or not, it belongs to you and always will."

"I would not have dared wed a man who could not forgive." Rebecca seemed to have forgotten their audience. "And I could not have been a proper wife until I had learned. Now, I believe we can be happy together. And I would rather have your battered heart for my treasure than all the gold and titles in the world."

This was better than good fortune, Sebastian realized as he surged to his feet. It was pure, sweet grace, precious and unfathomable.

"Go ahead and kiss the lady!" called someone from the crowd, of which Sebastian and Rebecca were suddenly aware again. "You cannot make tongues wag any harder than they will already!"

As the onlookers erupted in laughter, Sebastian and Rebecca laughed too, as they fell into each other's arms. Their lips met in a kiss of such tender intensity that neither heard a sound as the crowd broke into loud applause.

Except the pulse of their two hearts, healed and united by the power of love.

Epilogue

The Cotswolds
June 1815

"United at last!" Sebastian's voice rang with a note of sweet triumph as he and his bride rushed from the church to their waiting carriage under a shower of rice and rose petals. "I was beginning to wonder if this day would ever come."

A gurgle of joyful laughter welled up from the depths of Rebecca's heart as he helped her into the carriage for the drive back to Stanhope Court for the wedding breakfast. "Eight months is not such a long engagement. To hear you and your brother complain of late, one would think Hermione and I had made you wait eight *years!*"

She turned and waved to her new brother and sister-in-law, who were presently running the gauntlet of rice to the carriage behind theirs. It was her hope and prayer that they would enjoy many more moments as happy as this one in the years ahead.

Climbing into the carriage beside her, Sebastian caught her hand and raised it to his lips. "I suppose you are going to remind me that I was the one who objected to couples rushing into marriage before they were very well acquainted."

"Why should I remind you?" She raised her forefinger to give his nose a gentle tweak. "You seem perfectly well aware of your position. I must confess, though I've enjoyed getting to know you better these past eight months, I have been growing impatient to begin our life together."

She and Hermione had insisted that if either of the gentlemen wished to withdraw from their engagement at any time, they would be free to do so without reproach. As a result, both brides could now bask in the happy certainty that their new husbands were as eager as they to be wed at last.

"I reckon these nuptials will long be remembered in Avoncross." Sebastian did his best to insure that by producing a pouch full of coins which he proceeded to toss among the throng of local children. "Not only was it a double wedding for the House of Stanhope to the two most beautiful and accomplished ladies of the parish, but coming so soon after the great victory at Waterloo, all of Britain can rejoice. Mark my words, Bonaparte is finished for good this time!"

"That is certainly cause for rejoicing." Rebecca's happy smile faltered a little. "Though it grieves me to think how many women have lost husbands in that dreadful war while I have been blessed to gain such a fine one."

Having emptied his coin pouch, Sebastian signaled his coachman to drive on while he took Rebecca's hand once again. "Your compassion for others is one of the qualities I love most about you, my dearest girl. We will find a way to help those women, I promise you. That will be my new mission in Parliament—to see that our troops and their families are properly looked after now that the war they won is over. But I hope your concern for them will not dim your happiness of *our* special day."

She gazed into his eyes. "Nothing could do that, I assure you. Today is a celebration of our love. I was pleased to see how many of my relatives came to the wedding. Aunt Charlotte must have soaked three handkerchiefs during the ceremony. I only wish…"

"What?" Sebastian prompted her, eager as ever that she should have anything her heart desired.

One day he would understand that all she needed to make her happy was his abiding love. "It would have been so nice if some of my school friends could have come to the wedding. But they are all so far away and have obligations to their employers."

She could not help wondering if they had also stayed away for fear of looking poor and dowdy at such a grand occasion.

Before that thought could dampen her spirits, Sebastian spoke. "I was planning to take you to Vienna or Italy for a glittering honeymoon. But if you would rather, we could make a tour of our own country, stopping to visit with each of your friends on our way. Would you like that?"

"I would indeed!" Rebecca hesitated for an instant, then remembered that they were married at last. On her wedding day, surely a bride could be forgiven an ardent impulse. Throwing her arms around Sebastian's neck, she pressed a warm kiss upon his cheek. "My friends were such a great comfort and support to me during dark times. I pray they may one day find the kind of happiness I have found with you."

* * * * *

Dear Reader,

Sebastian and Rebecca's story was a gift to me in so many ways. I had submitted a proposal to Love Inspired Historical for a novel set in England during the Regency era, but didn't have very high hopes that the editors would buy it. When I received a call asking me for that book and a second, plus a bridal-themed novella, it was the answer to a prayer.

The only catch was that the novella needed to be written quite quickly, and I had no idea what to write! That weekend, my husband and I took a road trip with the Celtic choir to which we belong to provide special music for a church in rural Nova Scotia. While we drove, I jotted down ideas that I hoped might work for the novella. Seeking inspiration from my favorite stories, I thought of Shakespeare's play *Much Ado About Nothing* and found just what I was looking for. By the time we returned home, I had fleshed out a story that I couldn't wait to write.

Through the summer I sat out on our back deck for several hours each day, enjoying the sunshine, birdsong and the smell of freshly mown grass while I visited England's scenic Cotswold countryside in my imagination. As the story unfolded, I felt a renewed joy in my work that had gotten a bit lost over the years. Now, I would like to offer this story, that was such a blessed gift to me, as a gift to you. I hope it will touch your heart and stir your soul.

Deborah Hale

QUESTIONS FOR DISCUSSION

1. At the beginning of the story, when Rebecca allows Sebastian to assume she is Hermione, she doesn't actually lie, yet her conscience bothers her. What would you have done in her place and why?

2. Sebastian's marriage left him bitter. Have you known anyone who's been burned by love? How did they learn to let go of their bitterness?

3. Though the earl and the governess are very different in rank and fortune, what values do you feel they share that help create a bond between them?

4. When Sebastian hears the proverb about a good woman's value being far above rubies, it reminds him of Rebecca. Do you have a favorite proverb from Scripture? What is it about those ancient, wise words that still speaks to you thousands of years later?

5. Rebecca wonders if remorse for our own failings and compassion for the flaws of others breeds hope. What do you think about that?

6. Have you ever experienced "pure sweet grace, precious and unfathomable," as Sebastian does when Rebecca accepts his second proposal? How did it make you feel?

7. There is a French proverb: "To understand all is to forgive all." How do you think this applies to Rebecca and Sebastian? How does it apply to your life?

THE GENTLEMAN
TAKES A BRIDE

Louise M. Gouge

This book is dedicated to my beloved husband, David, who has stood by my side through my entire writing career. I would also like to thank my wonderful agent, Wendy Lawton, who works so hard on my behalf. I'm proud to be your client. I'm also proud to be a Love Inspired Historical author. This is the most delightful "job" I've ever had! Thank you, Melissa!

But seek ye first the kingdom of God,
and His righteousness; and all these things
shall be added unto you.
—*Matthew* 6:33

Chapter One

Hampshire, England
June 1810

"I will not settle for an untitled husband." Lady Diana Moberly lifted her pretty little nose and sniffed. "I shall find a peer to marry, or I'll not marry at all."

Seated beside her cousin in St. Andrew's Church, Miss Elizabeth Moberly listened with rapt attention. After all, Di had just returned from her first London Season and knew everything about courtship and marriage. And in a few minutes, the wedding ceremony would begin, and Di's older sister would marry a handsome gentleman she had met at Almack's only two months ago. An *untitled* gentleman. Di insisted she would do better.

Before Elizabeth could voice agreement, her other cousin, Miss Prudence Moberly, squeezed Elizabeth's hand and leaned around her to address Di.

"But what if the Lord wills for you to marry a good Christian gentleman without a title?"

Elizabeth swung her attention from Pru back to Di.

Di sniffed again. "La, such a question, Pru, but just what

I would expect from you. Haven't I told you? The Almighty and I have an understanding about such things." She gazed down her nose at Pru.

Elizabeth released a quiet sigh. She and her two cousins had been born within months of each other eighteen years ago. The youngest daughters of three brothers, they looked almost like triplets, with blond hair, blue eyes and ivory complexions. They had enjoyed a merry childhood together, yet these days their views on most everything were different. Di was always ready with an opinion on any topic and brooked no contradiction. Pru was the sweetest soul, but she never backed down from differences with their titled cousin, especially on spiritual matters. Elizabeth vacillated between the two, but these days she tended to follow Di, who always seemed to have more fun.

Still, Elizabeth could not deny the peace she felt in this small stone church, which her family had attended for over two centuries. Countless relatives had been baptized here, and many lay buried in the ancient graveyard outside. Whenever she came here, it seemed to enfold her in sheltering arms, encouraging her always to seek God's will, whatever she might undertake in life.

Perhaps she could take the advice of both cousins. She would ask the Lord to send her a *titled* Christian husband.

But this was Sophia's day, and Elizabeth wished her great happiness with Mr. Whitson. Today, all things seemed to smile upon the bride. The sun shone brightly, and no one in their vast family had succumbed to illness to spoil the celebration. Flowers from Aunt Bennington's garden and bright green and white ribbons bedecked the altar and the pew ends, filling the air with the heady fragrance of roses.

The rustling of ladies' gowns and the shuffling of leather shoes on the wooden floor caught Elizabeth's attention, and she glanced over her shoulder. Across the aisle, several people had moved down so a tall young man of perhaps three and twenty years could slide into the pew.

Goodness, he was handsome, if a bit untidy. His wavy black hair appeared to have been arranged by the wind, and his black coat, while quite the mode, had a leaf caught under one lapel and perhaps a stray burr or two clinging to the sleeves. His lean, strong jaw was clenched, and his blue eyes gleamed with the look of a man set on accomplishing an important task. The gentleman must have ridden post-haste to arrive in such a condition. At the sight of him, Elizabeth's heart seemed to hiccough.

Or perhaps it was Pru's elbow in her ribs. "Tst," her proper cousin admonished. "You shouldn't stare."

"Humph." Di's ever-uplifted nose punctuated her disapproval of the latecomer.

Wishing to please her cousins, Elizabeth stared ahead. The bride's mother, Aunt Bennington, sat in the front row with her eldest son, the viscount, his viscountess and her two eldest daughters and their husbands. In the second row, Elizabeth's parents, Captain and Mrs. Moberly, sat with one of her brothers. Pru's parents, who lived outside of London, had sent her to represent the family for this happy affair.

Soon the door beside the altar opened, and the vicar, Mr. Smythe-Wyndham, entered, followed by Uncle Bennington, the bride Lady Sophia and Mr. Whitson.

Elizabeth's resolve about titles wavered when she saw the groom. Tall, with broad shoulders and blond hair that curled around his well-shaped face, Mr. Whitson's appearance more than made up in form what he lacked in rank. Elizabeth could not deny cousin Lady Sophia had found a handsome man, even though Elizabeth preferred darker features.

As if driven by her own thoughts, she turned toward the

dark-featured stranger across the aisle. Seeing the stormy expression on his face, she drew in a quiet gasp. His strong, high cheeks were pinched with…anger? Dark stubble shaded his clenched, sun-bronzed jaw. His black eyebrows met in a frown over his straight nose, which pointed like an arrow toward the wedding couple, while his blue eyes shot flashing daggers.

Alarm spread through Elizabeth, but she had no time to think or act.

"Dearly beloved, we are gathered together here in the sight of God and in the face of this congregation to join together this man and this woman in holy matrimony." Mr. Smythe-Wyndham intoned the opening words of the solemn rite in his rich baritone. He read of God's purpose for marriage, then moved on to charge the couple to confess it now if there existed any impediment to their union.

Suspicion shot through Elizabeth, and her gaze again slid across the aisle to the dark-browed stranger. His face exhibited a controlled rage much like her father's when indignation filled him over some serious matter. The man edged toward the front of his seat, like a lion about to spring upon its prey.

"If any man do allege and declare any impediment," the minister read, "why they may not be coupled together in Matrimony, by God's Law, or the Laws of this Realm—"

The stranger shot to his feet, holding high a folded sheet of vellum. "Indeed, sir, I do declare an impediment."

Chapter Two

Philip could hear the waver in his own voice and could barely control his trembling arm as he held up the condemning contract. It was no small thing, even a dangerous enterprise, to thwart the plans of an aristocrat as powerful as Lord Bennington. Yet honor demanded that Philip must attempt it.

The moment he spoke—shouted, actually—the couple before the altar turned. Philip felt a surge of satisfaction when Whitson went pale and his jaw dropped. But the horror and fear in the bride's plain face stung Philip's heart just as his sister's tears had done when she learned of her fiancé's treachery. Every person in the rows ahead of Philip turned to stare or gape or glare at him.

"How dare you?" The short, portly, gray-haired man standing beside the bride, no doubt Lord Bennington, sent Philip a haughty glower that should have flattened him. "What's this all about?" What he lacked in stature, he made up for with his commanding voice and presence.

At least he didn't dismiss Philip out of hand. Nor did the youthful minister, who closed his prayer book and watched the proceedings with a troubled frown.

"Sir." Philip gulped down his anger and nervousness. "I have here a signed marriage contract between one Gregory Whitson of Surrey and myself on behalf of my sister, Miss Lucy Lindsey of Gloucestershire."

Her mouth agape, the bride nonetheless stared up at Whitson with confusion. "Mr. Whitson?" Her voice shook.

Philip took some satisfaction that she, too, didn't immediately dismiss his claim.

Whitson tugged at his ruffled collar but didn't look at Philip. Instead, he bent down and whispered something to Lord Bennington. The earl stiffened, shot another glare at Philip, then gave the bride a softer gaze and squeezed her hand. The gesture imparted an odd reassurance to Philip. The man loved his daughter and would see to the matter. Just as Bennington was known for his arrogance, he also had a reputation for honesty and integrity.

"My lord." The brown-haired minister appeared concerned, but didn't cower before the earl. "Shall we adjourn to the sacristy?"

Bennington replied with a curt nod, gave Philip a brusque summoning gesture with a bejeweled hand and ushered his now-tearful daughter toward the side door.

Philip could only partly attribute the buzzing in his ears to the murmuring congregation. Nerves tight with anxiety, he moved into the aisle, glancing briefly at three look-alike sisters in the third row on the other side. No, not look-alike. One blonde miss openly sneered at him while the other two sent more kindly gazes his way. The young lady in the middle, whose face was a model of perfection, gave him the tiniest nod. He couldn't guess what it meant. Perhaps nothing at all. Perhaps his nerves were playing tricks on him.

One thing that played no trick on his senses was the image in the window above the altar. With morning sun shining through the stained glass, the likeness of Christ the Good Shepherd glowed as a symbol of Truth, and Philip's quivering heart quieted. God had sent him on this mission of honor, and He would see it through to the end. With that assurance, Philip straightened his shoulders and strode toward the front of the sanctuary for the imminent confrontation.

Like Daniel marching into the lion's den.

"Well, of all the ridiculous things." Di waved her lace fan languidly. "Poor Sophie." Her amused tone suggested anything but sympathy for her elder sister.

"Di, how can you be so cruel?" Elizabeth shuddered, not knowing where to place her own emotions. While she loved Sophie and wished her happy, the young man had displayed great sincerity during his protest. But then, Mr. Whitson also presented a sincere demeanor. Whom could one believe? With everyone in the room all aflutter, Elizabeth could tell others were asking the same question.

"We must pray for them." Pru did not wait for agreement but bowed her head and mouthed her petition.

Elizabeth followed her example, beseeching the Lord on behalf of all concerned. At a touch on her hand, she looked up to see Papa reaching over the back of his pew. His troubled gaze told her exactly what he was thinking. Unlike the rest of the family, he'd not cared much for Mr. Whitson. As a former captain in His Majesty's Royal Navy, Papa never failed to correctly determine a man's character. But Uncle Bennington never denied any of his eight children their whims and desires, and so the engagement had proceeded.

The door opened, and Mr. Smythe-Wyndham beckoned to Papa. Papa traded a look with Mama, then rose and exited the sanctuary. Elizabeth found it significant that Uncle Bennington was seeking Papa's counsel.

Aunt Bennington had been fanning herself furiously for some time. Now she stood and followed Papa from the room. Returning within minutes, she appeared to have regained her composure. Always the perfect hostess, she gazed around the sanctuary and tapped her folded fan on her opposite hand. A hush fell over the room.

"Ladies and gentlemen, I am certain this will all be resolved soon. In the meantime, I should like to invite you to our...hmm, what shall I call it? Not our *wedding* breakfast." She faltered briefly.

Elizabeth heard Di gasp beside her. Aunt Bennington never faltered.

"To breakfast." Aunt's voice had regained its strength. "Mustn't waste all that fine food. You cannot imagine how busy the cook has been these past weeks." She beckoned to her eldest son George, Viscount Bampton, who hastened to offer his arm. Then, pointing her fan toward the back of the church, she strode down the aisle, head held high. "Shall we go?"

In order of precedence, the viscountess followed on a brother-in-law's arm, then the other brothers and sisters and their spouses. After them, Elizabeth's family filed out. Although Di belonged with her sisters, in these country settings, she always begged permission to be with Elizabeth and Pru. Among her sisters, she held the least rank. Among her cousins, she was first.

As Elizabeth awaited her turn, she saw Uncle Bennington and Papa return, along with Sophia, Mr. Whitson and Mr.... was it Lindsey? Sophie's eyes were red, but she still clung to Mr. Whitson's arm. The departing guests made way for them to leave the church. Mr. Lindsey, however, hung back and sagged into an empty pew. No one spoke to him. In fact, he might have had the plague for the way people cleared the area around him.

Elizabeth's heart ached when she saw him kneel in the pew, his shoulders slumped forward as if in defeat. He must have received a verbal beating from Uncle Bennington. But Uncle did not recall the guests so that the wedding might proceed, and the vicar did not reemerge from the sacristy. There must be some validity to the man's claim.

With Di and Pru tugging on her arms, Elizabeth cast one last glance at the handsome, *brave* young man before she took her place in the line of departing guests. A twinge of guilt struck her as she realized she would far rather meet him than attend Aunt Bennington's breakfast.

Chapter Three

Philip finished his prayer and sat back in the pew, wondering where he would find the energy to ride down to Southampton to take a room. He'd ridden hard for five days to get here, and his horse needed tending. But at least he'd achieved his purpose. Lord Bennington had declared he would summon his solicitors to examine the marriage contract Philip had presented to him. Whitson wouldn't get away with taking Lucy's ten thousand pound dowry and using it to court an earl's daughter.

At the thought, an unpleasant sensation began to rise from Philip's stomach to his throat, and he swallowed hard. He hadn't eaten breakfast this morning but pushed his poor horse at top speed after a short night's rest in an inn. He shuddered to think of how matters would have been complicated had the wedding been completed. As it was, he planned to fully prosecute Whitson for his treachery.

Philip gazed at the comforting image in the window over the altar, knowing it held no power but was merely a reminder of God's mercy. Still, he couldn't deny that the reminder had given him confidence to face a powerful earl and his influential brother. But with the confrontation over, weariness was closing in.

Now his stomach rumbled in earnest. Before he could stand, a hand clamped down on his shoulder, and he looked up into the lined face and icy blue eyes of Captain Thomas Moberly. The gentleman's black hair was shot through with silver, giving him a distinguished look that surpassed his titled brother's appearance.

"Hungry?" The captain gave him a quirked smile inviting…friendship?

Philip coughed out a laugh as he rose to his feet. "I hardly think Lady Bennington wants me to join the party for breakfast."

The captain shrugged. "Probably not. But you are welcome to stay in my home until this matter is settled. Bennington's solicitors should be here in a few days."

Philip stepped back and bumped into the pew. "Do you mean it, sir?" He felt like a schoolboy invited into a secret society.

The captain's gaze narrowed. "I never lightly offer my hospitality." His voice held a warning edge, and Philip could imagine many a midshipman cowering before the man.

"N-no, sir." Philip wanted to salute, but he'd never been in the navy, so the gesture would look ridiculous. "Thank you. I accept."

The captain tilted his head toward the door. "Come along, then. You have a horse?" The man's light tone encouraged Philip.

"Yes, sir. I've ridden fairly hard these past days, switching out horses at inns along the way."

"Ah. Then you can ride in the carriage with my family, and my groom will see to the beast."

Outside the picturesque stone church, Captain Moberly presented Philip to his pretty American wife, his lovely daughter Miss Elizabeth and his equally appealing niece Miss Prudence. Philip settled into the landau across from the three ladies and beside the captain, hoping he wouldn't have to make conversation. After all, what could he say to this family whose peace he'd just shattered?

Good manners dictated that Elizabeth pay attention to their guest, and in truth she had no difficulty doing so. Before Di had been swept away by her mother, she had whispered that Mr. Lindsey seemed dreadfully common, but Elizabeth disagreed in the extreme with that assessment. His conduct was unreservedly proper, even charming, if one could call shyness in a gentleman charming. She felt her own measure of shyness as he tried to give Mama his full attention, but his gaze kept returning to her. And she had difficulty restraining herself from sneaking glances at his handsome though unshaven face.

No, no. She must not do this. She must not encourage his glances. Must guard her heart, must not squander it on an untitled gentleman, however nice he might be.

"Tell us of Gloucestershire, Mr. Lindsey." Mama always mispronounced such county names, insisting upon including every syllable, as Americans were wont to do.

Mr. Lindsey seemed not to notice. "It is quite beautiful, ma'am. We have a fine cathedral and many charming parish churches. The River Severn runs past our land, and we've a view of the Cotswolds to the east, with the Forest of Dean and the Malvern Hills on the north."

Elizabeth hid a smile at his rote recitation, which revealed his nervousness as nothing else could.

"We've a busy seaport, and our main export is wool." He clamped his lips shut, and his eyes grew round, as if he thought he'd spoken too much.

Mama hummed with interest. "What a lovely, concise tour you've given us. Just the right information to inspire my interest in traveling there."

Mr. Lindsey's charming grin beamed his gratitude for Mama's graciousness. But then his expression grew serious, and he looked across the landscape thoughtfully.

Papa caught Elizabeth's gaze and tilted his head toward their guest. She knew what he wanted. At home she always quizzed their guests and showed great curiosity about their homes, especially if they were from London. But she did not wish to know about Gloucestershire, for it was in the opposite direction from London and far too provincial to capture her interest. Nor did she wish to know more about this courageous man, despite the fact that he had risked much for his sister's sake.

She sent Papa a tiny frown, but he narrowed his eyes, giving her a steely, warning look. His "captain look," as she and her brothers and sisters called it. She huffed out a quiet sigh and searched for a suitable question to ask their guest.

"Tell us about your sister, Mr. Lindsey."

The gentleman's troubled gaze returned to her, and he smiled. "I fear I am the wrong man to ask, for I can speak of her only in superlatives."

Elizabeth's heart tried to do a merry country dance over his delightful comment, but she silenced the music. "Humph. You speak very prettily about her. You should give lessons to my three brothers, for they insist I am still the pest they *claim* I was in childhood."

The gentleman laughed, and his blue eyes twinkled. "Miss Elizabeth, I'd be happy to school your brothers in how fortunate they are to have such a charming sister."

Her gaze strayed to Papa, whose eyes now were lit with merriment, his "I told you so" look.

But Elizabeth could think only of how dangerous this man was…to her heart.

Chapter Four

Philip forced his eyes away from the young miss whose merry glances at her father suggested a warm relationship between them. Unless Philip was mistaken, that bode well for his mission. He had limited experience outside of Gloucestershire, but the calm spirit he observed in this family gave him hope. He raised a silent prayer of thanks for God's provision in sending him a supporter in Captain Moberly, although he mustn't assume anything.

He risked another look at the two young ladies. They were equally pretty, each in her own way. Both possessed thick golden curls and lively blue eyes, but the configuration of their countenances varied slightly in nose and chin and cheekbones. A small dimple graced Miss Elizabeth's left cheek near her lips when she smiled. A natural beauty mark kissed Miss Prudence's right cheek near her eye. Given a choice, a man would have difficulty deciding which young lady was the more beautiful.

What was he thinking? He hadn't come here to admire the local females.

An unnerving suspicion crept into his mind. Surely the captain didn't plan to divert Philip from his quest for justice by this offer of hospitality. *Surely* Moberly and Bennington hadn't found time to conspire against him in those few moments outside the church.

No, he must not think this way. His mind was too scattered by this matter and the two other distressing situations at home.

Lord, these are large burdens for my inexperienced shoulders. Please give me wisdom. As before, the answer seemed to be *Trust Me and deal with one problem at a time.*

"Ah, here we are." Captain Moberly stared off to the right. "I never tire of the view when we come home to Devon Hall."

Philip followed his gaze. Across a vast green lawn planted with numerous flowerbeds stood a magnificent three-story house, its gray stone Palladian architecture sparkling in the sunshine. A long, tree-lined drive shot from the main road directly to the front door, and soon the carriage reached its destination.

Servants poured from the house, along with more dogs and children than Philip could count. He managed to follow the captain from the carriage and lend his hand to the young ladies without mishap while the captain assisted his wife. Philip then stood back to await instructions from his host... and to observe the chaos.

While the spaniels barked and jumped, two tiny boys clung to the captain's legs and begged to be picked up, and a pretty miss of perhaps six years attached herself to Mrs. Moberly. A dark-haired young lady emerged, followed by a shy girl of perhaps ten or twelve.

As he attempted to sort it out—somewhat—Philip could barely keep from laughing at the merry madness. The captain and his wife employed no such restraint, for both doled out generous kisses and hugs and laughter, making certain no child was missed. One would think they'd been separated from their grandchildren for a month instead of just a few hours. And the young ladies participated in the melee with equal enthusiasm.

"Belay that!" The captain's laughing voice boomed above the bedlam.

Everyone stopped. The children giggled.

"Mr. Lindsey." Moberly beckoned to Philip.

Philip stepped through the crowd. "Yes, sir?"

The captain proceeded to make introductions and explanations. He and Mrs. Moberly had six children, three of whom were married, and these were a few of the grandchildren, staying here while their parents traveled. The dark-haired lady was the governess. Philip noticed with admiration that the captain announced each child's name as if he or she had just won the derby. Philip had never met anyone who introduced his small children to guests. Other families kept them in the nursery and schoolroom until they were presented to society.

Surely such a warm-hearted family man could be trusted to do the right thing, even for a stranger.

Elizabeth watched their guest with interest. He had not appeared the slightest discomfited by the children or the dogs. An admirable trait, to be sure. Few young men who had courted her older sisters had looked as comfortable amidst the Moberly mayhem.

The children were sent back to the nursery, Papa ordered his valet to assist Mr. Lindsey and Mama instructed Cook to prepare a breakfast. With everything completed, the adults gathered in the drawing room.

Mr. Lindsey's former calm now disappeared as he sat forward and clasped the carved oak arms of his chair, and his dark eyebrows bent into a frown.

"Miss Prudence, Miss Elizabeth, it just occurred to me. I am the cause of your missing Lady Bennington's breakfast." His sincere tone underscored the sorrow written in his eyes.

Elizabeth traded a look with Pru. "Never mind, Mr. Lindsey. We see our cousins all the time."

"And there will be other parties this summer," Pru added.

Papa sent an approving nod their way. "Indeed. The roads are deeply rutted between here and Bennington Manor."

It seemed to Elizabeth that Mr. Lindsey's sun-browned cheeks deepened in color, but with the morning light streaming through the windows in his direction, she could not be certain. She did observe that his anxious expression softened.

"You are most kind, ladies, Captain Moberly." He relaxed into his chair. Almost slumped, in fact. How tired he must be.

Breakfast was announced, and they proceeded to the morning room and helped themselves from the buffet.

Elizabeth's mouth watered at the mingled aromas of coffee, eggs, sausages and fresh bread. Seated across from Mr. Lindsey, she noted his flawless manners, as fine as any she had observed among her titled relatives and their guests. Papa's valet must have shaved him, for his black stubble had disappeared.

Once again, she noticed his well-made clothing, but also the calluses on his hands. Not too conspicuous, just enough to show he performed some sort of work. But then, Papa and her brothers also had calluses because Papa insisted they must make themselves useful around the property. So it was not necessarily a sign he wasn't a true gentleman. And his hair, now combed, appeared recently trimmed.

Oh, stop it!

Such musings were ridiculous. She really must cease thinking about him. Once the matter with Mr. Whitson was settled, Mr. Lindsey would return home to Gloucestershire. Which, she reminded herself, lay in the opposite direction from London, where she fully intended to go next spring. Papa might not see any value in his daughters having a Season, but where else could she find a titled husband? Rare was the occasion when an unattached peer of the Realm visited their neighborhood.

As she frequently did, Elizabeth rehearsed the reasons for her quest. Children born into the aristocracy were sheltered from many of life's troubles. They received the best education and had access to the best physicians when they were ill. Titled men sat in Parliament and made important decisions affecting the entire world, even history itself. Their wives owned the responsibility of supporting charitable institutions, as her step-grandmama, the late Dowager Lady Bennington, had so generously done. With a titled husband, Elizabeth would be able to provide for her children and benefit her country. Surely no one could find fault in her reasoning.

Then why did she feel so drawn to Mr. Lindsey, who could give her none of those things? *No.* She tore her traitorous gaze from him once more. She *must* resolve to wed only a peer. But she had a feeling she would have to post a heavy guard around her heart while in the gentleman's presence. Her future—and that of any children she might have—depended upon it.

Chapter Five

Philip resisted the urge to tug at his cravat or shift in his chair. But he did cast a wary eye at the family seated around the long oak table. During the entire time the captain's valet had shaved him and freshened his clothing, Philip had tried to discern exactly how much influence Moberly might possess. He appeared to have a comfortable relationship with Bennington, but he'd also deferred to his elder brother, the bride's father, in their brief conversation at the church. Should the earl set his mind against Philip...but he wouldn't think of that. Lord willing, justice would prevail against Whitson.

As Philip had descended the staircase, he'd heard the musical laughter of Miss Elizabeth and Miss Prudence coming from the morning room. Now seated across the table from the young ladies, however, he sensed a reluctance on the part of Miss Elizabeth to engage in conversation. He shouldn't expect anything more, should turn his attention to the more amiable Miss Prudence, who joined Captain and Mrs. Moberly in extending the kindest hospitality to him in conversation. But he was forced to admit it was the reticent young lady who stirred his interest.

"And so, Mr. Lindsey," Captain Moberly said, "you trust your younger brother to attend to matters at home? How old is this lad?"

"Yes, sir, I do trust him." Philip recalled with a smile Charles's intense concentration as he'd listened to his parting instructions. "He's eighteen but quite competent."

The captain nodded his understanding. "I have commanded midshipmen of eighteen who could master their responsibilities capably."

This bit of comradeship boosted Philip's confidence in Moberly. While he couldn't grasp why the man would befriend him, he'd accept this as a gift from the Lord. Cautiously accept it. Perhaps the captain was merely keeping an eye on him until the matter was settled.

The atmosphere of this sunny room bolstered his spirits, as did the aromatic coffee and delicious breakfast fare. Recalling the proverb that warned against gluttony in the presence of a king, Philip didn't surrender to his ravenous appetite but slowly ate his tasty sausage and eggs.

"Tell us more about your sister, Mr. Lindsey." Mrs. Moberly's placid smile seemed at odds with her probing gaze.

Philip swallowed a bite and sipped his coffee, stalling to keep himself from blurting out that Lucy didn't deserve the ill treatment Whitson had shown her. That she deserved a true-hearted man. That if Philip were not a Christian, he'd call the man out, no matter the laws against dueling, an option he still might consider. But he wouldn't confess it here. Mrs. Moberly was not at fault for Whitson's treachery, and Philip wouldn't unleash his anger or threats upon her.

"My sister is a gentle girl, ma'am." Unexpected emotion

rose in his throat, and he downed another gulp of coffee. "Too trusting, I fear." Knowing he must stop before he said too much, Philip glanced around the table.

The eyes of each lady held sympathy and glistened with a hint of tears. Captain Moberly glowered. For a moment Philip feared he'd angered the man.

"It's insupportable." The captain fisted one hand on the table. "I will not rest until…" He pursed his lips. "This afternoon Bennington will send to London for his solicitors. If you wish to engage your own man, now is the time." One eyebrow rose. "I would not embarrass you, sir, but if you require assistance—"

"Ah. No, but I thank you, sir." Philip withheld a laugh. "I can manage." No sense in telling the man how far off the mark that offer was. "I'd be most grateful if you would pray for my sister and myself."

Now the captain's eyebrows arched. In the corner of his eye, Philip noticed a movement across the table and turned to see Miss Prudence give Miss Elizabeth a playful grin.

"Yes, of course." Moberly sent him a sober nod. "That goes without saying."

"Yes, indeed," Mrs. Moberly said.

Miss Prudence nudged her cousin.

Philip couldn't quite gauge the expression on Miss Elizabeth's face. The slight smile on her perfectly formed lips indicated her approval, and the appearance of her dimple sent a pleasant tickle through his chest. But those lovely blue eyes held…puzzlement? A hint of sorrow?

What on earth could be distressing this lovely young lady? Protectiveness surged up in his chest, and he longed to help her. Perhaps in these next few days before the solicitors arrived, he could befriend her and discover the cause of her unhappiness. With the house full of people and countless chaperones available, surely no one would consider the gesture improper.

Elizabeth's heart sank even as her esteem for Mr. Lindsey rose. She must, must, must not be attracted to this man, this truly remarkable man. She could see the pain written across his face for his sister and his determination to set things to right, just as Elizabeth's father and brothers would should she be treated so shabbily. But his request for prayer, something she never heard outside her immediate family, firmly established Mr. Lindsey's character in her mind. And Pru's teasing grin did not help Elizabeth's attempts to stave off her soaring admiration for the gentleman.

Even now, his kindly gaze in her direction stirred her feelings and sent warmth up her neck into her cheeks. She surrendered to a smile but could think of nothing to say.

The morning room's side door swung open, and Elizabeth's brother James strode in and walked directly to the buffet. "I say—" He popped a bite of sausage into his mouth before filling his plate. "—what a morning. That fellow who stopped the wedding certainly provided a smashing bit of entertainment. Poor Sophie wept all the way home. Nobody said a word at Auntie Bennington's breakfast and—"

"Ahem." Papa's voice boomed across the room, accompanied by Mama's "James!"

"Jamie!" Elizabeth's cheeks flamed with mortification for Mr. Lindsey.

"What?" Jamie turned around, and his eyes settled on Mr. Lindsey, whose face had reddened beneath its sun-browned surface. "Oh." Jamie's boyish grimace resembled that of a child caught stealing a cake. Then he shrugged. "Sorry, old man." He walked around the table and put his plate down at the setting beside Mr. Lindsey's, then reached out to him. "Do forgive."

Mr. Lindsey stood and shook his hand, the picture of graciousness. "No harm done." His wry grin added to his charm. "Philip Lindsey."

"James Moberly. Jamie, to my friends." He tilted his head toward Papa and grinned. "A bother to the captain."

"Sit down, boy," Papa said, "or you'll be swabbing the deck for the next forty years."

Jamie gave him a mock salute, sat down and dug into his breakfast.

The family banter must have soothed whatever offense Jamie caused, for Mr. Lindsey relaxed back into his chair.

To Elizabeth's relief, Jamie and Papa engaged their guest in discussions of horses and fencing and their tailors, relieving her of any obligation to join the conversation. Which, of course, gave her the opportunity to further observe the man. But much to her chagrin, she could not find one fault in his speech or deportment or opinions. And it did not help her cause to see Mama watching the gentleman with rapt attention, that sly smile etched across her lips which Elizabeth had not seen since her older sister met the man who was now her fiancé.

Chapter Six

"Some say one horse is as good as another." Jamie Moberly waved his fork in the air for emphasis before shoving a bite of egg into his mouth. "But I've got a gallant colt I want to run in the derby." He glanced at his father.

"We'll see." The twinkle in the captain's eyes even as his dark eyebrows bent into a frown caused Philip to long for the days when his own father had gently prodded him toward manhood.

"I say, Lindsey." Jamie nudged Philip. "How about a ride? We can take the girls and go out to the Roman ruins. What do you say?"

Philip had spent the last few days riding hard to get here, and the last thing he wanted was to get back on a horse. But both young ladies voiced their agreement, and all eyes fell on him. Once again, he felt this family's warmth reaching out to include him.

"Sounds like just the thing." He could hardly reject an opportunity to spend more time with Miss Elizabeth.

"I'll tell Cook to prepare a picnic." Mrs. Moberly seemed oddly eager about the event, for she smiled most charmingly at Philip. "You can go ahead and take your ride, and I'll send the basket out to the ruins in the early afternoon."

With all in accord, they had only to dress for the outing. While the ladies scurried away to don their riding dresses, Jamie offered Philip his older, taller brother's clothes. Never one for fashion, Philip generally left all to his valet. But until Wilkes arrived in a day or two, he must make do with the generosity of his hosts for fresh clothing.

The cutaway black coat fit him well, but the buckskin breeches felt rather snug, indicating they'd been recently purchased. Philip hoped Jamie was right when he said his brother Richard wouldn't mind his wearing them, for leather clothes once stretched couldn't be shrunk without being ruined.

Properly dressed, the party met outside the front door. Miss Elizabeth made a pretty picture in her rose wool habit adorned with gold and black embroidery. Her matching beaver hat, perched atop her shiny golden curls, sported a small spray of black feathers held fast by a gold broach with a pink tourmaline at its center.

Miss Prudence wore a similar habit of moss green, but it was a bit frayed at the edges. Philip surmised she was a poorer relation, yet her cousins' courtesy toward her gave no hint of a lower status. Such behavior elevated them all in Philip's estimation. This truly was an extraordinary family. Although he couldn't entirely let down his defenses, his earlier wariness was slipping away as he spent more time with this merry little band.

Two grooms brought around four excellent beasts that seemed as ready for an excursion as their riders. They nickered and pranced around as if impatient to begin.

"Jamie, will you help me?" Miss Prudence beckoned to her cousin.

"Of course." He proceeded to lift her into the saddle.

With the grooms busy steadying the horses, Philip realized where his duty lay.

"May I assist you, Miss Elizabeth?"

She appeared somewhat startled, and her cheeks took on a pink shade that matched her dress. "Why, yes. I thank you, sir."

The instant Philip gripped her waist and lifted her, the scent of her rose perfume reached his nose, and his pulse quickened. The two of them easily managed the maneuver, like a well-executed dance they'd performed together a hundred times before.

Seated upon her sidesaddle, she looped one leg over the pommel and gripped the reins with tanned gloves. Taking her left black half boot in hand, Philip settled her foot in its stirrup. A mild shock bolted up his arm at the contact, and he quickly withdrew his hand, appalled at his own reaction. Yes, the lady was attractive, but this was not the time to notice such things, not when Lucy's case remained unsettled.

"I thank you," she repeated, this time rather breathlessly, and gave him a nod to confirm she was seated comfortably. Indeed, the lady presented the very image of an accomplished rider.

His admiration for her growing, Philip forced his gaze away from the vision before he made a ninny of himself.

As Elizabeth guided Juno along the woodland path, she felt Mr. Lindsey's gaze on her. A quick glance behind her confirmed it, and warmth crept into her cheeks. This simply would not do. Should he continue to show such interest and good manners, her resolve might weaken.

When he'd helped her onto the horse, his grip on her waist

had been all that was proper, yet her spine had tingled pleasantly. Even now, the echo of that sensation skittered across her shoulders. If only she could find something else to focus on. The familiar landscape provided just the answer.

Sunlight filtered through the trees and sparkled on the remaining drops of last night's rain still clinging to shadowed leaves. The narrow stream beside the path rushed over rocks and branches, whispering its secrets to the passersby. The breeze carried the fragrance of rich soil and growing things from the field beyond the woods, mingling with the smell of horseflesh and leather, a perfume to Elizabeth.

When Jamie had suggested this excursion, her love of riding had betrayed her resolution to avoid Mr. Lindsey. Elizabeth found nothing quite so diverting as wandering the countryside on horseback in the summer—not even dancing. If she loved anything as much as riding, it was exploring Roman ruins, even the familiar ones on Bennington lands, for the workers there continued to excavate and find more artifacts. She'd heard of Roman sites in Gloucestershire, large settlements and buildings left by those ancient conquerors of Britain. What a delight it would be to see them. Surely Mr. Lindsey knew all about them. She was certain he would be an excellent guide.

Oh, my. There I go again.

If a true distraction did not come across her path soon, the gentleman might take up residence in the part of her brainbox that engendered attraction. Oh, how she must guard her heart against this man's charms, his *unconscious* charms. For surely he had done nothing overt to draw her interest.

She glanced back and saw Mr. Lindsey leaning over to speak to Pru, who rode beside him. They both laughed. An odd twinge tickled Elizabeth's insides, but she dismissed it. Pru was thoroughly smitten with another worthy gentleman, one who had no objections to her small dowry. One whom Elizabeth longed to prompt to begin his suit before someone else snatched her beloved cousin away.

She dismissed her matchmaking thoughts, for ahead lay their destination and her favorite view of the countryside.

"Ah, here we are." Jamie, riding at the front, waved his crop toward the upcoming clearing. "Looks like someone else had the same idea."

As they rode out into the opening, Elizabeth stifled a gasp but not because of the view. There on the stone remnants of a Roman wall sat Di with two young gentlemen. Beyond them, under a canopy, three servants tended a long table laden with picnic fare.

A quick perusal of the area revealed that Sophie and Mr. Whitson were not among those present, and Elizabeth relaxed. She recognized one gentlemen as Di's cousin on her mother's side. Although it had been some years since she had seen Lord Chiselton, she could not be more pleased. He was exactly what she needed to take her mind off Mr. Lindsey. At ten, she had vowed to marry the viscount, who was five years her senior and possessed the title in his own right. It was not too late to revive her girlish dream.

"Beth! Pru! James!" Di stood and waved. "Do join us."

Mr. Lindsey drew his horse up between Jamie and Elizabeth. "Perhaps I should return to Devon Hall." His frown conveyed regret but no hostility.

"Nonsense." Jamie dismounted and surrendered his reins to a groom who had come to the site with the other servants. "No one here will be offended by your presence." He chuckled. "I think they'd rather like to meet someone bold enough to interrupt a Bennington wedding."

Mr. Lindsey grimaced in a rueful fashion, and Elizabeth reached out to touch his arm. "Do stay, Mr. Lindsey." Once again she betrayed herself, but more to cover for Jamie's brashness than because she truly wanted Mr. Lindsey here. Well, she did not wish him to leave, but—

Oh, do be quiet, she ordered her silly heart.

"I thank you, Miss Elizabeth. This outing is indeed helpful in keeping my mind occupied." He dismounted and came around her horse to help her down.

Once again, his warm, strong hands on her waist sent a pleasant chill up her back. The ease with which he lifted her down brought forth an unplanned sigh. To cover it, she coughed.

"Are you well, Miss Elizabeth?" His eyebrows dipped into a frown, enhancing his appealing features. An agreeable warmth filled her cheeks.

"I am well, thank you."

No, I am anything but well.

With all the determination she could muster, she turned away from him and strode toward Lord Chiselton.

Chapter Seven

"We will not stand on formalities," Lord Chiselton said after presentations had been made. His smile seemed to invite friendship that transcended rank.

Yet Philip's first assessment of the man hadn't been favorable. Perhaps it was due to the warm welcome extended to the viscount by Miss Elizabeth. A foolish reaction, of course, especially when he learned from their brief conversation that she'd known the man when she was but a child. Thus, her enthusiasm upon seeing him again was understandable. But Philip had noticed an inappropriate stare akin to lechery in Chiselton's eyes as the young ladies first approached him. Even Whitson hadn't shown such impropriety toward Lucy.

The other gentleman, a Mr. Redding, displayed only the most proper manners, a perfect sycophant for the viscount. Philip chided himself for this lack of charity, but he could find no pleasure in being here. If not for Miss Elizabeth's plea, he would have returned to Devon Hall. But after they dismounted, she seemed to prefer the other man's company.

"Today," Chiselton went on, "we are all students of history, gazing into the past amidst these remarkable ruins. Imagine the souls who lived in this place, baking their bread over there." He pointed to the stone remains of what had probably been a large community oven. "Taking shelter from a winter storm in yon dwellings." One hand fisted at his waist, the other raised like an ensign at the front of an expedition, he strutted toward a row of crude foundations that appeared recently excavated. "Ah, how I do love Britain's history."

The others followed him, adding their agreement like so many toadies. Well, not everyone. Jamie rolled his eyes once or twice at Chiselton's remarks. Philip found it comical that the viscount had assumed the role of guide, as if three of his companions hadn't grown up in this place.

Lagging behind, Philip sauntered up to the group just as Miss Elizabeth looked his way.

"Mr. Lindsey, I have heard of Roman ruins near Gloucestershire. What can you tell us about them?"

As all eyes swung in Philip's direction, he felt a pleasant kick under his ribs from the lady's attention. So she would not discount him altogether.

The viscount lifted his aquiline nose and glared at him briefly before softening his expression. "By all means, Lindsey, do tell us."

Philip shrugged. "I fear there's not much to say, Miss Elizabeth. They're like most, I suppose. Some impressive. Some commonplace." He wouldn't be dragged into a competition with this man.

"No doubt." Chiselton's sneering grin, which quickly disappeared, set the man's character firmly in Philip's mind. Like most peers, he exhibited an insufferable arrogance, a sense of privilege precluding any obligation to those less fortunate.

Philip shuddered away his fears about his own future. Could any man wear the mantle of nobility in a truly noble manner?

Disappointed by Mr. Lindsey's response, Elizabeth surmised he was much like Papa. Quiet but not remote, a little taciturn but not truly aloof. She would like to become better acquainted with him, to understand the man hidden behind those deep blue eyes that seemed to miss nothing.

No, no. She would not.

What she truly wanted, or *should* want, was to become better acquainted with Lord Chiselton. The youthful viscount seemed to know everything, from the way the Romans mixed concrete to how they built roads all over the ancient world. Further, he possessed a willingness to share his vast knowledge on a variety of subjects, a virtue, to be sure. Further still, he held the Chiselton title in his own right and had sat in the House of Lords for three years since reaching his majority. Why, he took part in decisions affecting England and all her colonies. Wealthy as a potentate, this young man had an excellent future.

Well formed, moderately handsome and half a head taller than she, he presented an appearance that was quite impressive. His sense of fashion could not be improved, although Elizabeth thought he did wear a rather heavy shaving balm… or was that cologne? And perhaps he could do without a few of those rings on his hands. And maybe the gold cufflinks and ruffled cravat were rather much for a picnic.

On the other hand, the taller Mr. Lindsey wore borrowed clothing and no other jewelry than a simple silver cravat pin, but he did have a quietly distinctive air about him she could not deny.

While the servants set out the repast, the group dispersed.

Jamie strolled away with Mr. Lindsey, while Lord Chiselton wandered toward the food-laden table and began to supervise. Elizabeth and Pru made good use of their fans, waving away the heat of the day.

Pru looped her free arm around Elizabeth's. "Have you noticed Di's interest in Mr. Redding?" Her frown revealed a mild concern.

Elizabeth eyed her other cousin and her companion, who stood facing the downward slope of the hillside. In the small valley below, a flock of sheep grazed on the thick green grass and drank from a small pond. But from the way Di leaned toward the gentleman and gazed up into his well-formed face, Elizabeth doubted the two were discussing that pastoral scene.

She bit back a laugh. "Hmm. Shall we remind her of her vow to marry only a peer? I don't suppose Mr. Redding is heir to a childless relative's title, but one never knows about these things."

"Silly." Pru nudged her. "I'm more concerned about the gentleman's character."

"But surely her cousin would not introduce her to the wrong sort." Elizabeth turned a more critical eye toward Mr. Redding. His fashionable black coat and tan riding breeches appeared new, as did his black beaver hat. His grooming was impeccable. The few remarks he had made during their tour of the ruins indicated he possessed both wit and an education. She rather liked the way his brown hair curled around his slender face. Based on appearances only, she would not mind his inclusion in their family.

"One would hope Lord Chiselton would protect her." Pru's forehead wrinkled. "But that is not what concerns me. Have you ever seen Di look at any gentleman with such rapt attention? And she met Mr. Redding just this morning."

Elizabeth turned toward the ancient Roman oven, where Jamie and Mr. Lindsey stood laughing like old friends. Then she glanced at Lord Chiselton, who was sampling the bread rolls and cold meat slices. "But why is that a cause for concern? At breakfast, were you not attempting to tease me into an attraction to Papa's guest, whom we met *just this morning?*"

"Perhaps I should not have teased you." Pru smoothed the frayed cuff of her riding coat. "Still, Mr. Lindsey's character appears obvious to me. Consider the sense of honor and the *courage* it required to risk Uncle Bennington's wrath to defend his sister's rights. And of course I trust Uncle Moberly's discernment unreservedly, and he clearly likes Mr. Lindsey. Still, we should never choose a husband in haste, for we could spend the rest of our lives regretting it. Think of poor Sophie's hasty decision."

"Indeed. I am convinced Mr. Lindsey has saved her from great sorrow." Elizabeth's heart dipped in sympathy for their cousin, whose sweet but plain face had never attracted the attention of gentlemen. "And to think she met Mr. Whitson at Almack's."

"Whoever sponsored him will be mortified when they learn of his deception." Pru's blond eyebrows dipped into a frown. "It is a cautionary tale for every young lady."

"What are you two gossiping about?" Jamie returned to their company, with Mr. Lindsey following.

Their guest, whom Elizabeth had seen talking enthusiastically with her brother, now appeared taciturn once again.

"More to the point—" she brushed a leaf from Jamie's shoulder to distract him so she would not have to answer his question "—what were you two laughing about? It's poor manners not to share a good story."

Trading a look, the two men chuckled, and an agreeable

sensation swept through Elizabeth's heart. Jamie was a dear but the least practical of her three brothers. If Mr. Lindsey befriended him, perhaps he could be a good influence. After all, the gentleman owned and managed property, which required a certain maturity.

"Very well, then, if you will not tell us—" she grasped Pru's arm "—shall we join Lord Chiselton at the table?"

"Must we?" Jamie wrinkled his nose. "I never cared much for him when we were children, and he hasn't improved with age."

"Tsk." Pru's disapproving cluck did not match the merriment in her eyes.

"Now, Jamie." Elizabeth tapped his arm with her fan. What flaw did her brother and cousin see in Lord Chiselton that she could not? But they were nearing the table, so she could not ask. "Mr. Lindsey, you have not yet told us the cause of your laughter."

"Oh, that." He pulled out a chair for her. "We discovered mutual interests in both horse racing and dogs. We were trying to outdo each other with stories of their antics."

"I see." She sat down and looked over her shoulder into his twinkling blue eyes. "Well then, because I know all of Jamie's stories, you must tell us yours."

"Ah, hounds," Lord Chiselton said. "A subject near to my heart." Seated at the head of the table, he appeared to have once again assumed the duties of a host. Never mind that Elizabeth's mother had arranged this entire meal and sent her own servants out to serve it. For a moment, his presumption nettled her, but she brushed the sting away. As a peer, no doubt he was accustomed to taking charge. There was nothing wrong with that.

While the viscount launched into a saga of ears and tails, Elizabeth studied Mr. Lindsey, who sat across from her. He listened to Lord Chiselton, and occasionally his eyes flickered with interest. At other times they reflected boredom. But the viscount prattled on, apparently oblivious to his audience's response. Despite his loquacity, he did manage to clean his plate.

In the brief intervals between the viscount's discourses, Mr. Lindsey spoke quietly to Pru on his right and Mr. Redding on his left, each of whom responded with interest. Of course Di cut him completely, refusing to answer when Mr. Lindsey spoke to her. Elizabeth chided her cousin with a cross look, but Di lifted her nose and sniffed in her arrogant way. Yet Mr. Lindsey simply breathed out a quiet sigh and resumed his gracious discourse with Pru.

Yet even as she scolded herself for making comparisons between the gentleman and the viscount, she was forced to admit that Chiselton was the less pleasant companion. *But still a peer,* she reminded herself.

And I shall marry a peer.

Chapter Eight

Standing in the corner of Captain Moberly's library, Philip perused the shelves hoping to find a book to hold his interest until supper. Late afternoon sunlight filtered through the west windows, making the titles on the book spines clearly visible and providing adequate light for reading, at least for a while.

The smell of leather and tobacco and old books reminded Philip of his own library, which his father had stocked with every essential work of literature, sparing no expense. From these two walls of books, Philip surmised that Captain Moberly possessed a similar interest in the world of knowledge. He ran his fingers over the titles, as if that would help him make his choice.

Shakespeare always provided an insightful diversion, but he felt the need for something more spiritual in nature. Perhaps Milton could help rid his mind of the afternoon's outing and fill it with interesting information to discuss, should the need arise. Although he couldn't count himself a desired guest, he'd been invited to stay and would offer his share of conversation to help make the evening pass pleasantly. More pleasantly than the day, he hoped.

He'd enjoyed riding with Jamie and the two young ladies, especially Miss Elizabeth, until they'd encountered that other party connected to this vast Moberly family. While Redding possessed an amiable and courteous disposition, both Lady Diana and her cousin the viscount hadn't missed an opportunity to demonstrate their scorn for Philip. Lady Diana had cut him directly, acting as if he weren't present, while Chiselton had kept trying to engage him in a boasting competition, never mind the topic. Dogs, horses, imports, America, even the weather, all were thrown down like gauntlets. Philip's minimal experience with Society made him wonder if this sort of conversation was normal. If so, he hoped never to mingle with such people. Yet the day might come when he had no choice.

Milton's *Paradise Lost* didn't prove to be the hoped for distraction. Satan's complaints against the Almighty sounded much like Whitson's sniveling attempt this morning to justify his breach of contract. Philip shoved the heavy volume back onto the shelf and pulled out the most recent edition of *The Gentleman's Magazine.* He'd not read his own copy yet and wondered what news he would find.

As he expected, along with the usual domestic news, the magazine contained articles regarding the ongoing fears of invasion by France and news that the Prince Regent was facing a clash with the United States. Although Philip disliked the conflicts, he couldn't criticize their causes. Was not every quarrel about money and power? In fact, his very reason for being in Hampshire was to demand material satisfaction from Whitson. Sometimes a country—or a man—had to exact justice, whether for his family or for property, even if it required force to compel another party to do what was right.

His chest burning with renewed anger over Whitson's betrayal of dear Lucy, Philip returned the quarterly to its place. He must settle his emotions before attempting any social interaction with his hosts.

He found *Johnson's Dictionary* and moved a wing chair to face the shelves at an angle so sunlight could illuminate the pages. This was as good a time as any to increase his vocabulary, for he performed poorly at parlor games involving riddles. If his hosts preferred games over conversation, he'd have difficulty keeping up.

Lost in his studies, he barely noticed the click of the library door. But the subsequent girlish laughter thoroughly startled him.

"Sh. Shut the door."

Miss Elizabeth's voice? He couldn't be certain, for the lady spoke in a whisper.

"Now you must tell me everything." This time, Miss Prudence spoke. "What did Lord Chiselton say to you?"

Philip was highly curious to know what the viscount said to Miss Elizabeth, but honor demanded he must not eavesdrop. He stood quickly, dumping *Johnson* on the floor with a thump, and turned to face them. "Good evening, ladies."

Both gasped, then eyed each other with mischievous glances and pressed hands to lips, apparently struggling to cover their laughter. Miss Elizabeth's cheeks flushed pink, and her dimple made an appearance, enhancing her beauty.

Philip felt a jolt beneath his ribs, a strangely pleasant sensation becoming all too familiar in this lady's company. He struggled to suppress it. Until the matter of Lucy's dowry was settled, he had no business looking to his own marriage prospects. No matter how beautifully Miss Elizabeth smiled.

* * *

"Why, Mr. Lindsey, what a surprise." With much difficulty, Elizabeth swallowed her silliness and offered Mr. Lindsey a pleasant and, she hoped, *mature* smile. How dreadful if he thought her a mindless chit given to giggles and gossip. But why should she care about his opinion?

"Yes." He picked up the large book he'd dropped a moment ago and placed it on a shelf. "Captain Moberly granted his permission for me to use his excellent library."

Another laugh escaped Elizabeth. "And you chose to read a dictionary?"

"Yes." He made his way around the chair. "A man should never cease seeking knowledge." No apology or embarrassment colored his tone. Interesting.

"No, he should not." *Unless he believes he already knows everything.* Elizabeth could not imagine Lord Chiselton reading a dictionary.

He stared at her for a moment, then moved toward the door. "If you ladies will excuse me—"

"You needn't leave," Pru said. "We can sit and chat until supper is announced." She waved toward the grouping of upholstered chairs by the windows.

"Or—" Elizabeth sent her cousin a quick frown "—we can join the others in the drawing room."

"Or—" One of Mr. Lindsey's eyebrows quirked in a mischievous expression. "*I* can join the others in the drawing room, and you ladies can finish your discussion of Lord Chiselton." He grimaced. "Forgive me. That was unnecessary."

Elizabeth bit the insides of her cheeks to keep from laughing. She did not dare look at Pru. "There is nothing to forgive, sir. Please, let us all go. I am certain Mama and Papa will wish for our company." She felt a mad impulse to tell him what the viscount had said, but that would be unkind. Best to tell Pru later when they went to bed.

They exited the room, descended the wide front staircase, and made their way to the drawing room. Everyone was there, even the children and their governess. A mild sense of foreboding struck Elizabeth. Surely her family would not engage in their usual antics in front of this stranger. But there was no turning back.

"Ah, there you are." Seated on the blue settee, Mama directed them to their chairs. "Now we can begin. We are about to be entertained by the children."

Elizabeth glanced quickly at Mr. Lindsey, expecting to see boredom. After all, it was not the custom of most families to put forth their children in this fashion. But just as it had this morning when he first arrived at Devon Hall, the gentleman's expression softened as he looked at the little ones.

"Quiet now." Seated in his favorite chair, Papa presented a regal picture, with his handsome, noble visage and full head of graying hair. He gazed fondly at the little troupe of performers. "Helena, you may begin."

Elizabeth's six-year-old niece sat at the pianoforte and laboriously plunked out a Mozart tune, or a vague semblance thereof. When she finished, the adults applauded and voiced their praise. Again Elizabeth noted Mr. Lindsey's generosity, for he clapped his hands along with the others.

"Very fine, my dear," Papa said. "Now, what else do we have?"

The five-year-old twins, Lewis and Guy, stepped forward into the center of the room wearing ragged robes from the attic's costume chest. Guy slumped down on the floor with one leg bent to the side and put on his best pitiable expression.

Eleven-year-old Frances, strangely self-conscious, blushed as she stood up with her Bible.

"We will now present a play from Acts 3, verses one through eleven." She proceeded to read about the disciples Peter and John praying at the temple in Jerusalem for a lame man. Now in costume, Helena played John, and Lewis made an impressive Peter. Guy, always the most dramatic, put on a performance as the cripple that no doubt would have pleased William Shakespeare.

Elizabeth and her brothers and sisters had presented this story to their close relatives several times, but she never failed to get chills up her back when "Peter" extended his hand to the "lame man," who leapt to his feet, danced around and cried, "Praise God!"

Again the adults applauded with much enthusiasm, and Elizabeth saw a look of wonder on Mr. Lindsey's face. More of a glow, actually, as if he had seen the actual miracle instead of a simple portrayal by children. A strange and agreeable sentiment filled her chest at the sight. Like Papa, this gentleman was a man of true faith, a rarity among their acquaintances. A rarity among all the men she had ever met.

But she could not decide whether this was a reason to become better acquainted with him or to avoid him altogether.

Chapter Nine

For his early morning Scripture reading, Philip found the familiar passage in Acts that the children had re-created the night before. Once again, wonder welled up inside him over this remarkable family. Teaching the little ones to perform Bible stories was an extraordinary way to ingrain Scripture into their mental and moral constitutions. So much better than requiring that they endure the droning sermon of a vicar or curate, whose words must be incomprehensible to their young ears. Philip would remember this experience when…*if* the Lord blessed him with offspring.

At the end of his reading, he prayed for the Moberly household, Miss Elizabeth in particular. Last evening, she had appeared as moved as he by the children's performance, but he had no opportunity to speak to her about it. As he'd noticed yesterday over breakfast, she seemed to be struggling with some concern. But after yesterday's outing at the ruins, he realized it wasn't his place to offer assistance when so many caring family members surrounded her.

In his prayers for his own family, he asked that dear Lucy might recover quickly from Whitson's treachery and that

Bennington's solicitors would arrive from London hastily to set matters to right. The sooner this travesty was behind them, the better.

Just as Philip closed his Bible, Captain Moberly's valet, Hinton, arrived with shaving supplies. He brought with him the suit Philip had worn on the ride from Gloucestershire, having refreshed the garments with whatever mysterious method valets employed. Grateful for the assistance, Philip felt like a new man when he went downstairs to the morning room for breakfast, where he met young Moberly.

"Going down to Southampton." Jamie waved a small bun covered with strawberry jam. "Want to ride along?"

"I thank you, sir." Philip gave the idea a moment's consideration, but another day of riding held no appeal. "Permit me to beg off today, and I'll go with you next time."

"Very good." Jamie slapped Philip's shoulder in a brotherly manner and trotted away.

Philip followed the aroma of sausages to the buffet. A footman, the room's sole inhabitant, informed him that the ladies were still sleeping and Captain Moberly was taking his morning tour about the manor grounds.

Now that was a ride Philip wouldn't have minded. He often wondered how other landowners inspected their properties. Father's untimely death six years ago, when Philip was only seventeen, had left several matters unsettled, several responsibilities untaught. Although his loyal steward had done his best, Philip always sensed some important gaps in his education. Perhaps, if invited, he could join the captain another day.

He helped himself to a plateful, once again grateful for the hospitality Moberly had bestowed on him. The fare at any inn couldn't compare to the offerings of a devoted family cook. And the backache he'd developed from tavern mattresses during his journey disappeared after one night in the Moberly guest room's feather bed.

The footman offered both coffee and tea. With a bit of guilt, Philip chose the more expensive tea. He must find a way to repay his host for the expenditure required to keep a guest. Perhaps his steward could advise him on an appropriate gift to send after everything was settled here.

After finishing his breakfast, Philip nodded his appreciation to the footman. "Can you tell me, my good man, where I might occupy myself without disturbing the family?"

The servant must have anticipated his question, for he didn't hesitate. "The conservatory, sir. Captain Moberly has a tropical garden that produces year 'round."

"Ah, very good." Philip took directions from the man and quietly maneuvered his way through the house to the large glassed-in room attached to the rear. He'd noticed it yesterday and wondered what might be growing there. His own hothouse produced a small selection of fruit and herbs, but he'd like to increase its variety and yield.

When he opened the glass door, a warm blast of air swept over him, bringing the scents of lemons and strawberries. A middle-aged gardener and his young apprentice greeted him and continued their labors.

Philip wandered down the rows of plants, finally settling on a stone bench to admire the herbs and vegetables. Through the open back doors, he could see the outside garden soaking up a light rain. For the first time, he noticed the overcast sky, a certain sign of his displacement from the familiar. At home, he always considered the weather before planning his day.

Everywhere he looked, the profusion of greenery heralded

a vibrant newness of life. Strangely, instead of admiration, the sight stirred up a familiar hollow ache just under his ribs. His vicar suggested it was loneliness, possibly an indication that the time had arrived for Philip to marry. But he couldn't begin his quest for a bride until he exacted justice for Lucy. Further, he had no idea how to find an appropriate wife. If the Lord willed for Philip to marry, He would have to bring the right woman into his life.

The inside door swung open, and Miss Elizabeth entered, charmingly dressed in a pale green gown of sprigged muslin whose color reflected in her eyes and turned them the color of a turquoise gemstone. The now familiar jolt under his ribs replaced the ache and brought Philip to his feet.

"Good morning, Miss Elizabeth."

"Oh." Elizabeth blinked. "Good morning, Mr. Lindsey." She had not expected to see him here. "Please sit down, sir." Locating the gardener nearby, she relaxed. The man's presence ensured propriety.

"Will you join me?" Mr. Lindsey waved to the bench where he'd been seated. His blue eyes shone with a look she could not discern but found very attractive.

Having forgotten why she had come to the conservatory— perhaps a sprig of mint for her tea?—she accepted his invitation. "Did you sleep well?"

"Indeed I did, thank you." His gentle smile brought warmth to her cheeks. "I thought never to see you without your charming cousin. Is Miss Prudence well?"

Elizabeth shook her head. "The poor dear has one of her rainy-day headaches." She eyed the hazy windows, which were steamy from the rain. "Perhaps the weather will clear this afternoon, and she will feel better."

"Please give her my regards."

"Yes, of course."

They sat quietly for several minutes until their silence engendered merriment within her.

"And so, Mr. Lindsey." She gave him a playful grin. "With the inclement weather, will you spend your morning in the library reading *Johnson's Dictionary?*"

Mr. Lindsey chuckled, and his eyes reflected good humor. "I was depending upon that for my entertainment, but perhaps you can suggest another activity."

"Hmm." Elizabeth gazed toward the windows again and pasted on a thoughtful expression. She should not have inquired about his plans. But with Jamie on an errand and Papa about his usual business, someone must entertain their guest. Mr. Lindsey deserved that courtesy, even though he was not a peer. And one diversion came to mind. "If you like to sketch or paint, you may join Mama and me in the parlor." As the words came out, she wished them back. "Unless you consider those pastimes only for ladies."

His dark eyebrows arched. "Are they? Then we should tell Mr. Blake he must cease his etchings and devote himself solely to his poetry."

"Oh, you know of William Blake?" She wasn't exactly certain why, but Elizabeth reveled in their mutual knowledge of the obscure artist. "I believe Papa plans to purchase one of his paintings. He is not widely known but quite gifted."

"I agree. Well, then, I'll join you in sketching, though I fear I've not much talent for it."

"Mama can bring out the best in anyone." Elizabeth's pride in Mama's skill vied for preeminence with her present enjoyment of Mr. Lindsey's company. She noticed for the first time the silver flecks in his blue eyes and wondered if she could capture that shade on her palette. Yes, it was just as well that they were joining Mama. Too much private discourse with Mr. Lindsey could be dangerous to her peace of mind.

"I should like to spend time with Mrs. Moberly." Mr. Lindsey's expression brightened. "I had hoped to ask her about America."

"You must permit me to warn you off that topic." Elizabeth gave a mock shudder. "She has been cross with her home country ever since the thirteen colonies rebelled against the Crown and formed their own government."

Mr. Lindsey returned an exaggerated gasp, even as his eyes twinkled. "I thank you, Miss Elizabeth. You've saved me from a grave blunder."

After a shared moment of laughter, their conversation moved to the garden. Elizabeth gave him a tour and stood quietly by as he questioned George, the gardener, about the orange and lemon trees and the variety of herbs. His eagerness to learn impressed her, for here was a man diligent in all his duties, an admirable quality. She could just imagine how well he tended his own property, however large or small it might be.

She confessed to herself she enjoyed the gentleman's company. Last night, he had fit right into this household like an old friend, like the dear people her eldest brother and sister had married. How easy it was to forget why he was here. And to forget her vow to marry only a peer. But somehow she must not forget, must turn her thoughts back to Lord Chiselton.

Last night when she and Pru had retired to their shared bedchamber, her cousin had fallen right to sleep. Thus Elizabeth had had no chance to relate Lord Chiselton's parting words. Yet somehow she felt certain that, despite the viscount's seeming arrogance and self-centeredness, what he'd said to her privately yesterday afternoon could change her entire opinion of him…*and* her future.

Chapter Ten

"You have underestimated your skill, Mr. Lindsey." Elizabeth peered over the gentleman's shoulder at the drawing of Jamie's spaniel. The dog lay in front of the parlor's blazing fireplace staring toward the door in anticipation of his master's return. They had agreed the beast made the perfect subject for their artistic endeavors. While Mr. Lindsey's proportions were somewhat off, his depiction of the dog's winsome black eyes showed promise.

"I thank you, Miss Elizabeth." He set down his charcoal and wiped his fingers on a cloth. "May I return the compliment?" Studying the picture on her easel, he tilted his head, glancing from the spaniel to her drawing, then to his own illustration. "Ah, I see my error. The ears should sit lower."

Smudging the darker lines with the cloth, he picked up the charcoal stick and began making his corrections. As he concentrated on his subject, his countenance took on a most charming and youthful look, like that of an eager student who has just discovered a new principle. He glanced at her and smiled. "The spaniel is devoted to his master, isn't he?"

"Yes, and obedient as well. He'll stay right there until Jamie returns."

Thinking of returns, Elizabeth could not imagine what was keeping Mama. She'd put them both to work on their drawings, then traipsed off to greet Papa when he returned from his morning ride. Now Elizabeth must consider how their being alone in the drawing room might look to an unexpected guest—Lord Chiselton, for instance. Still, a footman stood outside the open parlor door, so she doubted anyone would find the situation improper.

In any event, she felt entirely safe and comfortable in Mr. Lindsey's company. Too comfortable, actually. And despite the long silences between Mr. Lindsey and herself, the longer Mama was absent, the more Elizabeth hoped she would continue to delay her return.

Which was nonsense, of course. She'd met this gentleman only yesterday under the most awkward circumstances for her family. How could she possibly have become so fond of his companionship in such a short time?

"What do you think?" Mr. Lindsey leaned back from his work and frowned.

"I was just thinking—oh." Elizabeth realized his meaning just in time to keep from saying exactly what she'd been thinking. "That you do possess artistic talent."

Despite the rain, Wilkes arrived the next afternoon in Philip's traveling coach, the bold fellow having learned of his location at Bennington Manor. He brought with him clothing, letters and Father's Wogdon and Barton dueling pistols. Fortunately for Philip's standing with the Moberly family, Wilkes had tucked the weapons in his clothes trunk and didn't reveal them until he and Philip were alone in the guest room.

"Just in case, sir." Wilkes wore his usual blank expression, except for the hard glint in his eyes.

An uneasy feeling crept through Philip. "Is Miss Lindsey well?" Lucy had never been given to hysterics, but she'd also never been betrayed by a fiancé. Perhaps a duel would be necessary after all. Christian or not, he couldn't permit her to be utterly crushed. Honor would require that he demand satisfaction from Whitson and prevent him from destroying another young lady's health and future.

"I believe her letter will provide that information, sir." The briefest frown bent Wilkes's eyebrows before his face once again became a mask.

Philip slumped into the desk chair. "Best read it right away." He accepted the letters from his valet, one each from his sister, his brother and his steward.

Apprehension filled his chest as he broke the first seal, but Lucy's news wasn't what he expected. Instead, she wrote that their kinsman, Stratford Lindsey, had died the day Philip had left for Hampshire. This distant cousin had never been in good health, but they'd all prayed he would enjoy a long life. "Perhaps if I had accepted his proposal instead of Mr. Whitson's," Lucy said, "his health would have improved."

Philip must post a letter tomorrow to assure his sister she bore no fault for Stratford's demise. He'd been a man of great faith, and they could rest assured of seeing him in heaven when their own times came.

Although Philip's heart wrenched at the sad news, he also experienced relief that he wouldn't have to be God's instrument in another, less honorable man's demise. For Lucy went on to say she'd resigned herself to Whitson's true character and felt grateful she'd been spared a lifetime with him. Brave girl! He prayed she hadn't written that for his benefit. Of course, her acceptance of the situation didn't absolve Whitson of his duty to return the dowry, but it made Philip far less inclined to demand satisfaction in a duel.

But Stratford's departure now placed another weight upon Philip's shoulders that he could hardly contemplate. Would not contemplate until the final cog in God's machinery fell into place. Perhaps the Almighty, in His great mercy, would grant him a reprieve.

The two-day drizzle grew into a rare summer storm that threatened to delay the arrival of Uncle Bennington's London solicitors. The dismal weather also put into jeopardy Aunt Bennington's summer garden party, a tradition at Bennington Manor for over half a century.

"The event was instituted by our grandfather, the second Lord Bennington," Elizabeth explained to Mr. Lindsey over an afternoon game of whist. "It began as a replacement for the annual Midsummer Eve festival, which of course is pagan in origin. Grandpapa could not countenance such celebrations, yet he and Lady Bennington desired some sort of diversion after the London Season. They decided to hold a large garden party a week or more after Summer Solstice so as to make a distinction. When Parliament lingers, of course, it must sometimes be postponed until July."

Jamie won the trick and gathered his cards. "We have bowling, billiards, dancing, racing, grouse hunting, that sort of thing. It goes on for days until everyone is agreeably exhausted and goes home."

Mr. Lindsey's bemused expression spoke clearly of his disinterest. He would hardly be welcomed at her aunt and uncle's annual party. "Oh, dear. We did not mean to advertise an event that will exclude you." She had noticed his sober demeanor ever since the arrival of his valet, but did not think it her place to inquire about the cause.

"Ah. Of course. Sorry, old man." Jamie gave an apologetic

shrug. "I'm not much for all that myself. I know the girls are expected to attend, but I'd prefer to stay home and read."

"Oh, Jamie, what nonsense." Pru laughed as she dealt the next hand. After a day abed, she'd regained her color and joined them for the afternoon activities.

Mr. Lindsey's eyes and crooked smile exuded lighthearted amusement, and Elizabeth's heart skittered about within her. "You've all been most generous in entertaining me. I believe when the time comes I can manage on my own for a few days."

"Oh, indeed." Jamie covered an artificial yawn with his free hand. "You can spend your time reading *Johnson*."

Mr. Lindsey laughed. "So the ladies told you about that. I don't suppose I'll ever be free of that incident, shall I?"

"Not in this house." Jamie fanned his cards and smirked.

Mr. Lindsey's good humor and graciousness only added to Elizabeth's admiration. Try though she might, she could not find a single fault in the gentleman, despite her attempts to give Lord Chiselton first place in her thoughts. Nor had the viscount done anything to ensure her interest, such as calling upon her. Of course the storm made travel difficult and perhaps even dangerous. Still, the significance of his parting words had begun to fade from importance. Had he been harmlessly flirting with her? Surely not. He was her best hope for the type of marriage she wanted. Where else in her neighborhood was she likely to encounter a peer?

"Are you going to play?" Jamie nudged Elizabeth's arm.

"Oh. Yes." She laid a trump card on the leather-topped table, then snatched it up. "Oops. I have a diamond after all."

Jamie crowed. "And now we all know you have the king of clubs."

Even Mr. Lindsey grimaced at her blunder. "An interesting move, to be sure." But no censure colored his look or tone.

Pru sent her a playful grin. "What were you thinking about, Beth?" The silly way she batted her eyelashes brought heat to Elizabeth's cheeks. Pru knew Elizabeth's thoughts all too well. Knew all her secrets. Even what the viscount had said. And frowned upon every word.

Chapter Eleven

Crouched behind a large cabinet, Philip hid with his back against the wall listening to the giggles coming from the nursery down the corridor. Through the open door across from his position, he could see Miss Elizabeth's skirt draped on the floor behind an upholstered chair. She peered at him around the chair, and he motioned toward her skirt. Nodding her appreciation, she quickly tucked it and herself out of sight.

Jamie was nowhere to be seen, but he owned a reputation for being the best at hiding. Philip felt a strong urge to challenge that reputation, but he didn't know the house well enough and would probably find himself in a room inappropriate for a guest to enter. How easy it was to forget his status among these people who treated him as a family member.

The children finished counting to one hundred, and the governess, Miss Alistair, clapped her hands. "Go on now. Find them."

Philip could hear the children's light steps as they dashed from the nursery. Within moments, they trekked past him, led by eleven-year-old Frances. Philip had no doubt she saw him from the corner of her eye, but she blocked the view from her little cousins and hurried them along, urging them to keep looking.

Philip couldn't decide whether to surprise them or to race to the nursery before they could catch him. Experiences these past days taught him they took particular delight in being startled, so startling won out.

He stood, raised his arms overhead, and bellowed "Roar!" The sound echoed throughout the corridor.

All four children shrieked loudly enough to shatter the windows at the head of the staircase. As they fell into giggles, he lumbered like a bear down the center carpet of the passageway with the children fast on his heels. The two boys latched onto his legs and dragged him down before he reached the safety of the nursery door.

He landed on his belly and, for the briefest moment, saw only black. Shaking his head, he pulled in a lungful of dusty, humid air and rolled over, grabbing one twin and tickling him until the child shrieked again. He couldn't yet tell one from the other, but he thought this was Guy. Lewis, in the meantime, was attacking Philip's head with a small pillow.

"Quarter. Quarter," Philip roared. "I demand quarter." Seated on the floor, he looked up just in time to see Captain Moberly reach the top of the staircase, remove his pipe from between his teeth and stare at Philip as if he were a lunatic.

Philip suddenly remembered himself, and his entire head and body ignited with embarrassment. "Uh, good afternoon, Captain."

The captain's eyes brightened, and he seemed to struggle not to laugh. "Never surrender, Mr. Lindsey. They'll use it against you next time."

"Grandpapa," the twins cried in unison, then left their prey and attacked the older gentleman.

Moberly deftly evaded their clutches and scooped one up in each arm. "You see, Lindsey, you must outwit them."

"Mr. Lindsey!" Miss Elizabeth dashed up the hall with the two little girls behind her. "Are you all right?" Although her concern seemed genuine, she did rush past him into the nursery and grab her prize, a pink confection. "Ha." She held it high and grinned at her nieces. "I win." She popped the sweet into her mouth.

An odd but pleasant feeling filled Philip's chest. He'd never met such a delightful young lady.

Amid whines and complaints, everyone agreed Miss Elizabeth was the victor. All but Jamie. He was nowhere to be seen. A vote was taken, and they decided to reverse the ploy and not seek him out. Just the sort of thing Philip might do to his own brother.

These games reminded him of his escapades in happier times at home, and a painful dart struck his heart. He plucked it out, forbidding its poison to infect him with bitterness. God had given him a happy childhood and a beloved sister and brother. He'd be grateful for his blessings, be grateful for his brief time with this dear family and look to the Almighty for the future.

Outside her own family, Elizabeth had never known a gentleman who participated in games with children with such abandon as Mr. Lindsey. Why, he was anything but taciturn, as she'd first thought.

But in quieter moments, she also noticed his countenance became sober and sadness emanated from his eyes. Surely after these four days, with hour after hour in each other's company, she could inquire about the cause of his melancholy without a breach of propriety.

Late in the afternoon, she found him in the library reading Papa's *Naval Gazette*. Not wishing to overdo a joke, she refrained from asking why he was not reading the dictionary. Further, that sort of teasing would set the wrong tone for the more sober conversation she planned to introduce.

"Does the *Gazette* address the French issue?" *Oh, bother.* Another poor beginning.

Mr. Lindsey looked up, and his face brightened. "Miss Elizabeth." He set the newspaper aside and stood, giving her a slight bow. "I fear my mind was wandering rather than gathering information." The welcoming smile he gave her sent a pleasant shiver up her spine.

"Well then, we have something in common." She waved him back to his chair and sat across from him. "I can never find anything to keep me awake in those periodicals."

His deep chuckle wrapped around her shoulders like a cozy blanket, while the mild scent of his woody shaving balm mingled with the odors of old books and tobacco.

"Have you recovered from this morning's adventures?"

He shook his head. "Not at all. I hope never to recover from such an enjoyable experience. Your nieces and nephews are remarkable children. Utterly delightful."

"Have you been around children much?" Elizabeth's family was overrun with offspring, and she could not imagine any other way to live.

"No, to my regret." A hint of sadness did cross his eyes, reminding Elizabeth of why she had sought him out. "But," he continued, "I am close to my brother and sister, both of whom are younger than I. In these six years since our parents' deaths, I've been almost a parent to them."

"Ah. Very admirable, but a large burden for a young man to bear."

His eyes searched hers. What was he looking for? She felt a sudden inadequacy to address any matter of importance with him.

Philip could hardly resist the sympathy emanating from Miss Elizabeth's blue eyes. But as much as he wished to empty his aching soul to her, he couldn't think a young miss of eighteen years should be thus burdened.

"I sense, sir, that something other than your sister's unfortunate situation has caused you sorrow."

Ah, how she did surprise him at every turn. His emotions threatened to erupt, so he looked away and stared out the tall windows at the beautiful scenery. The storm had at last blown over, leaving the land lush and verdant, and sunlight painted sparkling emerald swaths across the dark green landscape. At home such a sight never failed to gladden his heart, but now it only brought him added sorrow, reminding him how far he was from the home he loved—and from the people in his care. They should always be his first thought and his first concern, he reminded himself, no matter how easy it was to be distracted by Miss Elizabeth's charming company.

"My valet brought sad news from home."

She gasped and moved to the edge of her chair. "Oh, dear sir, not your sister?"

"No." Her compassion sent a pang through his heart. "That would have been a blow too hard to bear." He gripped the overstuffed arms of the tapestry chair and swallowed, forbidding excessive emotion to spill out. "A dear cousin— a distant relation, but reared near us—has died."

"And these past days, you have borne it without anyone

to share your sorrow." Now her eyes clouded with tears, and they slipped down her fair cheeks like raindrops…or glistening diamonds.

Again, Philip forced his gaze away from her. "It wasn't unexpected. He never enjoyed a strong constitution."

"But that does not lessen your grief."

"No."

"Are you needed at home?"

"No." He wouldn't explain the family rift between his grandfather and great-uncle that would have prevented his attendance at Stratford's funeral, even if he'd been in Gloucestershire. No doubt every family had similar difficulties.

Miss Elizabeth dabbed her cheeks with a monogrammed handkerchief. "Will you please convey my condolences to your sister and brother?"

Philip could only stare at her, for emotion closed his throat. This exquisite creature, as beautiful in character as in appearance, was the soul of kindness. How he'd love for her to befriend Lucy. How he'd love—

"And of course—" Miss Elizabeth's soft voice cut through his short daze. "—I shall pray for all of you to be comforted in your grief."

"I thank you, Miss Elizabeth."

Their conversation turned to lighter matters for a few moments, and then she excused herself. He couldn't take offense, for lengthy private discussions between them could be deemed improper should the wrong person observe it. It would not be wise, in any respect, to encourage any belief she might hold that he intended to court her. That simply wasn't possible, no matter what she might think…or he might wish.

Chapter Twelve

"In Lindsey's honor—" Jamie stood in the middle of the drawing room holding a glass bowl containing paper "—I have invented a new word game."

Elizabeth glanced at Mr. Lindsey, who appeared as surprised as everyone else. Mama and Papa traded a look of amusement. Jamie always managed to surprise them with his antics.

"I have written a single word on each piece of paper. Everyone will draw five and make up a story using those words. Not a long story, mind you." Jamie's last instruction brought laughter from everyone, for he was the most talkative member of the family, even more so than Elizabeth. "No guessing involved. No contest. Just a simple story."

Mr. Lindsey, clearly comfortable amongst them, laughed too. "You must enlighten us, Jamie. Why is your game in my honor?"

Jamie rolled his eyes. "Well, old boy, you told me charades and riddles were not for you. And you're the one who spends his time reading *Johnson's Dictionary*."

Everyone, including Mr. Lindsey, groaned at this pronouncement.

"I do thank you, sir—" Mr. Lindsey bowed his head toward Jamie "—for creating a game I can manage with my limited intellect."

Such modesty and good humor! Once again, Mr. Lindsey demonstrated how at ease he felt with Elizabeth's family. She could not imagine Lord Chiselton as the object of such a playful quip. No one would dare attempt it. Even as a child, the viscount had not received jests well, unless he made them himself…about someone else.

Further, she could not imagine Lord Chiselton wrestling about on the floor with the twins, as Mr. Lindsey had done so wholeheartedly this morning. Perhaps the gravity of a title and the weight of responsibilities had molded Lord Chiselton's character.

Yet Elizabeth could not help but recall that Mr. Lindsey also had responsibilities. Perhaps he did not sit in parliament, but he owned land and cared for his sister and brother. And even in the midst of grief over his relative's death, he managed to be pleasant company, which was a responsibility of sorts to his host and hostess, and further proof of his good manners.

"Your draw, Beth." Jamie held out the glass bowl.

As she drew her five words, her competitive nature emerged. Jamie might have said this was not a contest, but she would make certain she crafted the most engaging story possible.

"Oh, this is easy," Mama said, taking the first turn. "I have court, heiress, ship, fan and happy." She told a short tale describing how Papa had met her in faraway America, where the heroic captain of His Majesty's Ship *Dauntless* had fallen in love with and courted an orphaned heiress, gave her a Chinese fan and made her the happiest of brides.

While everyone else applauded her lovely story, Papa

appeared to wrestle with his chosen words. At last he responded with a dramatic addition to Mama's tale, explaining how the heiress's revolutionary brother tried to blast the *Dauntless* out of the water during the war.

Mr. Lindsey listened with his mouth agape to the story Elizabeth's family knew by rote, but he rebounded well by relating how a "lost" spaniel found refuge with a "kind" cottager in the midst of a "storm" and remained there all the "days" of his "life."

"How very sweet." Elizabeth's eyes burned. She wondered whether he referred to himself as the spaniel…and whether he wished to stay forever in this "cottage." And now she was stumped. The sober tone of the last two stories dissuaded her from a humorous cautionary tale about young ladies seeking husbands at Almack's.

Even after Pru and Jamie told amusing stories that brought laughter from their listeners, Elizabeth decided to modify her original idea into a tale of gratitude for their guest.

"My words are husband, galloping, gold, chair and escape." She eyed her parents, hoping they would not scold her. After all, this topic had not been brought up since Jamie burst into the morning room days ago. "There once was a sweet young lady, one far too trusting, I fear. She sought neither *gold* nor title, just a beloved *husband* so dear. A gentleman's proposal she did receive, and even her parents were deceived. Without the *galloping* arrival of a brave friend, she would not have *escaped* a poor marriage in the end." She bit her lower lip and looked down at her clasped hands. "Forgive me. I meant no jest." She raised her eyes and saw Mr. Lindsey's bemused expression. "Just gratitude on behalf of my dear cousin."

"Well, little sister." Jamie slapped his knee and chortled. "Although you made a pretty rhyme, you left out a word—chair, so you lose."

Papa, whose expression had been surprisingly placid during Elizabeth's story, lifted one eyebrow. "But this was not to be a contest. Therefore no one loses." He grunted in his paternal way. "And I fear that in Beth's story there are no winners, either."

She was always pleased to have her father's approval, but the appreciation emanating from Mr. Lindsey's eyes was her true reward.

Finally, the time for the Bennington garden party arrived. As always, Elizabeth and Pru would spend the week at Bennington Manor so they could participate fully in both day and evening events. True to his word, Jamie planned to stay home with their guest, which Elizabeth found particularly generous. She had observed over these past four days that Mr. Lindsey's influence improved her brother's behavior and attitudes. For Jamie to choose the gentleman's company over their aunt's renowned party demonstrated a pleasing new maturity, a willingness to seek someone else's benefit rather than his own. Now she would feel better about leaving their houseguest behind. Well, not entirely better, but she could think of no remedy for the situation.

"I wish circumstances were different." She pulled on her gloves as she bade her family goodbye in the front entry hall. To Jamie and Mr. Lindsey, she said, "I should so like to have you both at the party, or have all of us stay home together."

"I thank you, Miss Elizabeth." Mr. Lindsey took her hand and placed a kiss on it, the first time he had shown that courtesy toward her. In fact, his gentle touch on her fingers lingered, as did his gaze into her eyes. "But I should be most distressed to keep you from this grand event."

A sudden wish to stay home almost prompted her to cry off. She glanced at Pru, who wore her ever-present knowing smile. Pru would not mind missing the party, for the gentleman who owned her affections would not be in attendance. But Papa had said someone from the household must attend, or Aunt Bennington would claim they'd sided with Mr. Lindsey against Sophia, thus causing a rift in the family. Never mind that the scoundrel Mr. Whitson had caused all the grief in the first place. But then, had he not done so, she would not have met this extraordinary gentleman before her. The one who still held her hand and gazed at her so kindly.

Jamie nudged Mr. Lindsey. "They should go."

"Oh." Mr. Lindsey's eyes widened as if he'd just awakened. "Of course." He released Elizabeth's hand and stepped back.

She and Pru said their goodbyes to Mama and Papa, giving hugs and kisses as if they were sailing to China, not traveling just six miles up the road. Then everyone followed them out the door where the landau awaited. Ginny, her lady's maid, stood beside the carriage with an expectant smile. The girl was fairly new to service and had never traveled to Bennington Manor.

"Have a grand old time." Jamie wiggled his fingers in a comical wave that usually indicated he planned some madcap adventure.

But it was the mischievous gleam in her brother's eyes that stirred suspicion in Elizabeth's mind as Mr. Lindsey handed her into the conveyance. What harmless nonsense did Jamie have in mind? And who would be his victim?

Chapter Thirteen

Philip stared after the departing landau until a thump on his arm turned his attention to see Jamie's rueful grin, as if the lad understood Philip's sense of loss at the ladies' departure. Fortunately, Captain and Mrs. Moberly had already reentered the house.

"Come on, old boy." Jamie beckoned him. "Let's take a ride to Portsmouth. It's always exciting to see His Majesty's fleet." The fervent look in Jamie's eyes suggested something other than ships held his interest. Gambling? Or something even more unwise?

Philip cleared his throat. "No, thanks. I think I'll just spend some time with *Dr. Johnson*." He enjoyed the way his single reading of the venerable scholar's dictionary had become a family jest. Yet another sign of how generous these people were in their hospitality.

Jamie hooted with laughter. "Better be careful, old boy. Your brainbox will explode if you keep cramming all those words into it." His expression sobered. "Don't worry. I don't plan to drag you into some nefarious undertaking. I really do like the ships." A wistful look came over his countenance.

"Ah." Philip had seen the same look in his brother's eyes,

but he'd seen no wisdom in sponsoring Charles's dreams. "Want to go to sea, do you?"

Jamie nodded. "But Father says one son serving in His Majesty's navy is sufficient. My eldest brother, Colin, is a lieutenant of eight and twenty and should soon command his own ship. I'm too old to start out as a midshipman now."

Philip gave him another fraternal slap on the arm. "Then let us go watch the ships." Anything to take his mind off of Miss Elizabeth, who would soon be in Lord Chiselton's company and no doubt many others of his sort.

Once they were properly dressed and their horses saddled, Philip and Jamie quickly covered the two miles to Portsdown Hill, where they paused to take in the magnificent view of the distant harbor. Philip had seen countless merchant ships and a few naval vessels docked in Gloucestershire, but the awe-inspiring sight of the Royal Navy could fill any Englishman with pride. Frigates, men-of-war and sloops, with sails furled to their masts, bobbed about in the great natural harbor, awaiting orders to protect British interests in some far corner of the globe. No wonder Jamie and Charles dreamed of sailing away to be a part of such a grand and noble enterprise as His Majesty's Navy.

They descended Portsdown Hill into the balmy air of Portsmouth and took a leisurely tour of the waterfront, where the smells of fish vied with odors of tar, soap and livestock, as sailors prepared their vessels for another voyage.

There in the city, Philip's concerns about Jamie were set to rest. Not once did the lad cast a covetous glance toward the taverns *or* their wenches. However, he did launch into a lengthy treatise on the various ships and how each was useful in its own unique way in battle. Never having considered the matter, Philip filed the information away for future conversations with Captain Moberly.

After a stop at a mercantile shop so Jamie could make a purchase, they took a long route back to Devon Hall, racing neck and neck the last half mile to add a bit of sport to the day. That invigorating exercise cleared his mind as nothing else could have done.

In the guest room, Philip freshened up and changed into the suit Wilkes had laid out. Then he descended the front stairs to join the family in the drawing room. But unlike other evenings, tonight he experienced no happy anticipation, for Miss Elizabeth wouldn't be there. Despite today's outing, the empty spot she left in the company deprived him of a good deal of the pleasure he took in the Moberlys' hospitality.

"Ah, there you are." Captain Moberly greeted him by the door and ushered him into the family circle. "Sit down, sir. We are to be entertained by the children once again." His merry smile bespoke grandfatherly pride. Nor could Philip miss the genuine kindness—dare he say affection?—filling the captain's eyes as he welcomed him.

"I thank you, sir." As he took the chair reserved for him and none other, Philip permitted joy to infuse his spirit. For this hour alone he would grant his imagination leave to dream of being a permanent part of this loving, giving family. Even the children's play, whatever the subject, would be engraved on his memory to enjoy after he returned home.

Frances, whom Philip guessed he should soon begin to address as Miss Moberly, as she was the only child of the captain's second son, stood with her Bible in hand. No shyness colored her fair face as when Philip had first arrived. The twins, dressed in the same ragged robes they'd worn for their last presentation, giggled in the background.

"Our text is Matthew 18:21–35. 'Then came Peter to him,

and said, Lord, how oft shall my brother sin against me, and I forgive him? Till seven times?'"

An odd nettling scratched at the back of Philip's mind, but he had no time to evaluate it.

As Frances continued to read Jesus' answer to his disciple, Helena stepped forward, appearing regal in a silk cape and feathered turban. A servant, portrayed by Guy, owed a great deal of money to his master, or in this case, his mistress. She held the power to throw the servant into prison and sell his wife and children.

Guy's usual dramatic nature took over as he groveled at his sister's feet begging wordlessly for mercy. Helena, with hand on chin, considered the matter, then extended that hand in a gesture of forgiveness. Guy made a face but kissed it.

Jumping up to celebrate, Guy caught sight of Lewis, the servant who owed *him* money. Guy grabbed his brother by his ragged robe and shook him. Helena came forward and clasped his shoulder, scowling. She pointed to a side table. With much pathos, Guy pleaded again for mercy. But this time Helena would not relent. Lewis imprisoned Guy under the table and "tortured" him with a small, leafy oak branch, bringing forth more giggling.

"'So likewise shall my heavenly Father do also unto you,'" Frances read, "'if ye from your hearts forgive not everyone his brother their trespasses.'"

The adults applauded the performance, goodnights were said and Miss Alastair guided her little flock from the room.

Philip eyed Captain Moberly, who was now engaged in quiet conversation with his wife. Had they instructed their grandchildren to present this particular scripture? Was their hospitality nothing more than a ruse to dissuade him from pursuing justice and recompense for Lucy?

The butler stepped into the room and announced supper, and everyone stood and moved toward the door.

"Well, I must say—" the captain chuckled "—one never knows what the children will come up with. I think Guy chooses the texts based on how dramatic they are."

"Undoubtedly." Mrs. Moberly joined him in laughter.

Try though he might, Philip could see no subterfuge, no guile in his host or hostess. Even Jamie, the soul of transparency, merely laughed, then launched into an account of their trip to Portsmouth.

With some effort, Philip shoved aside his suspicions. He must not permit Whitson's treachery to destroy his trust in his fellow man.

As for the biblical lesson in tonight's story, well, it simply did not apply.

Chapter Fourteen

"Ah, there you are, Miss Elizabeth." Lord Chiselton strode toward her across the large drawing room. "I'm so pleased to find you alone."

Elizabeth reluctantly closed the slender, leather-bound volume of Philip Sidney verses. The brief biography of the famous Elizabethan courtier that prefaced his writings brought a tear to her eye at the thought of his early death. Further, his noble character reminded her of Mr. Lindsey, who always wanted to set things to right.

"Good afternoon, Lord Chiselton." She pushed away her melancholy and waved him to an adjacent chair. During the three days she'd been here at Bennington Manor, she's had little interaction with the viscount. When she'd first learned he was visiting the area, she'd hoped this time would serve to bring them closer. Yet she felt surprisingly disinclined to enjoy his company, though she couldn't fathom why. He was everything she sought in a husband…wasn't he?

The viscount, who usually seated himself with a flourish, slumped into the overstuffed blue chair. His eyes filled with sadness. "It's no use, you know."

She stared at him. "No use?"

He shook his head. "No use at all. I must confess I cannot resist any longer."

Somewhat relieved, Elizabeth knew she should ask what he could not resist, but the words would not form.

A frown darted across his forehead. "I know you're eager to know what I cannot resist, so I shall tell you." He gave an artificial sniff and settled into his chair. "I have the overwhelming urge to confide in you, my dear."

"Oh." She managed a slight smile and a tiny nod.

"All my life, I have carried the weight of my title…all alone. Unlike you, I had no warm family to enfold me. No mama or papa to nurture me." He steepled his hands and rested his forehead on the apex formed by his forefingers. The pose was impressive in its pathos. "No filial affection to bolster me in difficult times."

Elizabeth's heart constricted with pity. What would she do without her beloved family? No wealth or title could take the place of those she loved. "You have all my sympathy, Lord Chiselton."

"Thank you, dear lady." His smile seemed genuine.

Now curiosity reared its head. "Is that all you wished to say?"

"There. I knew you would understand. Would care about me." He leaned forward and grasped her hands. "I do have more to say, but I should like to wait until this evening during the masquerade. Promise you will meet me in the south corner of the back terrace at midnight?"

Did he wish to propose to her? The idea should thrill her, but instead she felt almost uneasy. Why, he had not even asked Papa's permission to court her, for Papa would have told her. She gently twisted her hands from his grasp. "I cannot think it proper, Lord Chiselton."

"No, of course not." He waved his hand in a careless

gesture. "Not if we were entirely alone. But everyone will be there trying to guess who's who." He wiggled his eyebrows and gave her a playful grin. "You needn't bother trying to guess my identity, for I shall tell you. Then you'll have no trouble finding me. Tonight—" he lifted one hand, finger pointed toward the ceiling as if he were making a grand proclamation "—I shall be Mark Antony."

Elizabeth blinked. "Ah."

"I would have been Julius Caesar, for he was the great conqueror. But one always thinks of him as an old man or—" he shuddered "—assassinated. Antony holds a more youthful image." He leaned one shoulder toward her in a conspiratorial pose. "What mask will you wear?"

"Humph." Unease crept into her chest, but she managed a cheerful tone. "*That* is a secret." She told herself that she was merely teasing, responding to his flirtations in kind, but deep down, some instinct had her resolved to stay as far away as possible from Mark Antony and the south corner of the back terrace.

"What do you say, old man?" Jamie draped himself over a red damask chair in the library and munched on an apple. "I desperately need a diversion, and you could use one, too." The late-afternoon sunshine filtered in through the library window, casting a glow on his carefully arranged Caesar-cut curls.

Seated across from him, Philip closed his volume of sonnets. Philip Sidney's *Astrophel and Stella* had done more to remind him of Miss Elizabeth than to distract him, so he set the book on the mahogany side table and studied his friend. His *good* friend. The nineteen-year-old, still a restless youth, had selflessly dedicated these past three days to entertaining him. Yet Philip's melancholy remained, and he couldn't shake it off.

He had no doubt the young lady would return home affianced to that dreadful Chiselton, an advantageous match for her, to be sure. The thought filled his heart with an ache compounded by grief over his kinsman's death and his own future. If the matter of Whitson's contract could simply be dealt with, Philip could go home and enjoy the consolation of his family. But Bennington seemed in no hurry to settle the affair. No doubt he was too diverted by his garden party.

A reckless urge swept through Philip. He'd spent the last six years shouldering massive responsibilities. Why not abandon himself to enjoyment for an evening? Within reason, of course. He grinned at Jamie. "Very well. What do you propose?"

Jamie glanced around as if checking for listeners. "The masquerade is tonight. It's just the thing to stir up some excitement."

"Um, have you forgotten I wouldn't exactly be welcomed at Bennington Manor?" Despite his words, Philip could think only of seeing Miss Elizabeth again, even if just from across the room.

Jamie smirked. "Have *you* forgotten the definition of masquerade?" He tossed his apple core on the table, and juice splashed across the wood. "Masks, my good man. Masks and capes and costumes. No one will know who you are." He stood. "Let's go to the attic and raid the costume chest."

Philip pictured the rags the children wore for presenting their Bible stories, but if there were finer garments to be had, this escapade could prove interesting.

He glanced at the apple juice leeching from the core onto the smooth mahogany. In very little time, it could eat into the wood and discolor it. Drawing out his handkerchief, he scooped up the fruit and dried the table.

Jamie tilted his head and frowned. "Oh. Right. Good show." He took the core from Philip and tossed it into the dustbin by the fireplace. "Must you always be so perfect?"

His mocking tone dug into Philip. Was that how he seemed to his friend? No, he certainly wasn't perfect. And the proof was the risk he planned to take tonight just to see the woman he couldn't allow himself to love.

With the help of their lady's maid, Elizabeth and Pru prepared for the evening's excitement in their shared bedchamber. Elizabeth had brought one of Mama's old dresses for the masquerade. Made long before slender, high-waisted dresses came into fashion, the gown had wide lavender panniers over a white underskirt and a scooped but modest neckline edged with delicate lace. A powdered wig left by some Moberly ancestor provided the perfect addition to her disguise, although it did carry a slightly musty odor, despite Ginny's attempts to shake out some of its ancient powder and dust.

Pru chose a blue shepherdess costume with many underskirts. The crook she carried could prove useful, but no such weapon seemed appropriate for Elizabeth's disguise. Though she could not imagine why such a thought had occurred to her.

"I enjoyed the story Aunt Moberly told us as we were choosing our costumes." Pru tugged her gown's low neckline as high as it would go before tucking a gauzy fichu into its edges. "Who would think our parents ever faced such difficulties when they were courting?"

Elizabeth sat before the dressing table mirror while Ginny adjusted her wig and mask. "Yes, one would never know from their happy circumstances now. When I am courted, I should like less drama and more security." She adjusted the mask so she could breathe through two tiny nostril holes, then stood so Pru could sit.

"Oh, I don't know." Pru studied her reflection and continued to fuss with her fichu until Ginny took charge and secured it with pins. "A little drama might be entertaining." She tucked her hair under a mobcap that covered every blond strand. "As long as no one's life is threatened."

"Or as long as no one interrupts the wedding." Elizabeth pictured dear Mr. Lindsey's face, so filled with fear and courage at the failed wedding. Would his business with Uncle Bennington be completed before she returned home? That thought stirred a pang of regret. So far, this entire party had failed to draw her interest away from the gentleman, and now she faced the evening with no small amount of trepidation.

"Do stay close to me, Pru." She eyed the shepherd's crook, formed from a solid hickory branch.

"I shall not desert you. Humph." Pru's usually smiling lips pursed with disapproval. "The very idea of Lord…" She eyed their maid. "You may go, Ginny."

"Aye, Miss Prudence." Well-schooled by Mama's Nancy, Ginny dipped a curtsy and left without a change in her placid face.

The instant the door clicked closed, Pru grasped Elizabeth's hands and squeezed. "Imagine Lord Chiselton accosting you that day at the ruins and reminding you of your childhood infatuation with him, as if those girlish feelings obligated you to him now. And worse, telling you he had dreamed of you since those long-ago days. I do not believe him, nor do I trust him. If he was so enamored of you, why did he not come calling? He was just trying to win your good graces."

Elizabeth winced. "But for what purpose? He seemed so sincere, and you cannot discount the weight of responsibility he carries. And always has."

"To be fair, no." Pru raised an eyebrow. "Well, then, if you are so sympathetic to him, you should be prepared to accept his proposal." She wrinkled her nose. "After all, you did pray for a husband with a title." Pru's words cut Elizabeth.

"I did. But…" At a scratching on the door, Elizabeth stopped. "Yes?"

Cousin Di flung the portal open and entered, followed by her sister Sophia. Dressed in the flowing Greek robes of Aphrodite, Di carried a white feathered mask. Her thick blond hair was piled high and entwined with gold and floral strands. "Come along, my little sprites. There will be much merriment tonight."

"Do you like our costumes?" Sophia had dressed as Boudica, queen of the Iceni, who had fought so fiercely against the Roman invasion of Britain. Covered in furs and woolen leggings, she spun into the room, brandishing a wooden sword. With her full, sturdy face and broad shoulders, she did indeed look like a female warrior. "My Mr. Whitson is dressed as the Roman governor, Paullinus. Do you not think that is just the thing?"

At her last remark, Elizabeth tried very hard not to glance at Pru, but she failed and saw mirrored in her cousin's face an identical shock. How could Aunt Bennington countenance such a travesty against propriety? The Roman governor had quite cruelly defeated Boudica and her people. Is that what they hoped for Sophia and Mr. Whitson? These past three days, Elizabeth had watched the still-engaged couple cavorting about the manor as if nothing had happened to halt their wedding. As if Whitson were not a scoundrel and nothing less than a thief who had stolen Miss Lindsey's dowry.

Even Di had made a better choice of a favored male companion. Her entire countenance became animated any time the most proper Mr. Redding entered the room. If Lady Aphrodite was not careful, she would end up married to an untitled gentleman, against all her lifelong dreams. But then, what did childhood dreams or infatuations account for when a lady met an extraordinary man?

Filled with a sudden longing to be home, where Mr. Lindsey no doubt sat in Papa's library reading *Johnson,* Elizabeth marched forth from the bedchamber and into the fray. But as much as she would like to emulate Sophia's warrior identity for her inevitable encounter with Lord Chiselton, somehow she felt far more like poor Marie Antoinette on the way to the guillotine.

Chapter Fifteen

"This isn't going to work." Philip dismounted his borrowed steed in the darkened woods some fifty yards from the imposing, three-story Bennington Manor. He adjusted the heavy brown wig and broad-brimmed hat that resembled something Charles II might have worn a century and a half ago. Then he struggled to secure the ties of the ankle-length cape he'd nearly lost during the six-mile gallop, and before that, almost tripped over as he descended the stairs at Devon Hall.

Wilkes had fussed as he had dressed Philip, saying these old leather breeches were too stiff and snug and would limit his movement, as did the sword and wooden pistol at his sides. But nothing could be done, for they must make haste to the masquerade, with no time to find something more suitable.

Some highwayman he made. Philip grunted at his own foolishness in agreeing to Jamie's scheme. He'd be fortunate if he didn't get shot for wearing this ridiculous disguise.

"Of course it'll work." Jamie tied his horse's reins to a low-hanging willow branch. "Come along." His beckoning wave was barely visible in the fading twilight. The brass

uttons on his father's old uniform did catch a spark of light
rom time to time, but his short hair did no justice to the
costume unless covered by the black bicorn hat. A naval of-
icer who served during the American rebellion should have
a long queue, Jamie had complained, but no proper hairpiece
could be found in the attic.

Looking ahead to their destination, Philip took in the il-
uminated scene. At the back of the manor house, Chinese
anterns were strung across the terrace and around the vast
back lawn, all the way to a stone boathouse beside a black
ake. Countless costumed attendees mingled or wandered
about the property. It all made for a grand event unlike any-
hing Philip's family had engaged in. Was this something
every peer was expected to do?

He followed Jamie, who walked across the field toward
he house as confidently as if it were daylight. From time
o time, he stepped around a boulder or stump and tossed a
cautionary word to Philip.

Twenty yards from the lighted area, they came upon a
masked wood nymph and a hooded faun. At Jamie's "tsk-
sk," the couple beat a hasty retreat back toward the house.
Philip felt his heart sink to his stomach. Did Lord Benning-
on know what went on at his party? Did he care? What did
hat say about the claims this wasn't to be like Midsummer
Eve, where all manner of wickedness took place? More important, what did it say about Miss Elizabeth's safety?

"Quit hunching over." Jamie thumped Philip's back,
almost knocking the wind from his lungs. "Relax. We're
not sneaking in. We're walking in as if we own the place.
After all, I am an invited guest. Who's to say I cannot bring
a friend?"

"Oh. Right." Against his better nature and his former concerns, Philip gave himself permission to enjoy this adventure.

After all, he meant only to walk about and observe the fri volities, not participate. Unless offered, he wouldn't so much as taste a dessert or accept a light drink. And he certainly wouldn't dance. Faster than anything else, that would mark him as one who didn't belong here. The dance master Mama had engaged years ago had given up in despair when Philip's feet refused to cooperate.

"I see two Caesars and an Apollo." Pru stood on tiptoes and peered across the crowded ballroom. "But I don't see a Mark Antony."

Elizabeth laughed into her stiff mask and felt the warm breath gust back against her face. "How can you tell the difference?"

Pru tilted her head. "Caesar always wears a laurel wreath and a toga. Antony wears the uniform of a Roman soldier."

"Of course." Elizabeth sighed and once again felt her own breath return on her. "Oh, Pru, we've spent far too much time avoiding Lord…that person. We're not enjoying ourselves at all." She spied a newcomer dressed rather soberly in a long black coat and dark breeches. Beneath the mask that covered only his eyes and nose, she recognized his familiar smile, and his neatly trimmed brown hair was unmistakable. "Come with me." She looped an arm around her cousin's waist and shoved her toward the gentleman.

"Where? What? Oh!" Pru tried to stop, but Elizabeth propelled her forward.

"Good evening, Mr. Smythe-Wyndham." Elizabeth noted with satisfaction the young vicar's surprise and, perhaps, caution, as evidenced by his hesitation to return the greeting. "We did not expect to see you this evening."

"Ah, Miss Elizabeth." He gave her a slight bow. "I would

recognize your voice anywhere. And may I assume this lovely shepherdess is Miss Prudence?" He bowed to Pru, who seemed suddenly dumbstruck.

"You have found us out, sir." Elizabeth nudged Pru. "I was just telling my cousin we're not enjoying this evening much at all. But now that you are here, perhaps we can find a quiet spot and chat." Where she would leave the two of them as soon as possible. Then, if the vicar did not see what a jewel Pru was, he did not deserve her.

"But, Beth." Pru broke free from her grasp. "Perhaps Mr. Smythe-Wyndham wishes to…to—"

"Not at all." He smiled at her, his attention at last where it should be. "Do you know of a proper place?"

"This way." With one hand, Elizabeth grasped his forearm, perhaps a bit too familiarly for a vicar, and with her other hand clutched Pru's. Urging them through the crowded room, out the door and down the stairs, she guided them to the drawing room. There older adults played whist or talked or read. She settled them into two empty and adjacent chairs and crossed her arms in satisfaction. "There."

Mr. Smythe-Wyndham, so poised and relaxed in church, removed his plain black mask and stared at her, his high cheekbones flushed with color. Pru removed her mask, as well, and revealed a complexion infused with radiant pink.

"Beth!"

"You will excuse me? I must, um, must—" Rather than invent a lie, she spun on her heel and hurried from the room. At the door, she turned back, noting with more than a little satisfaction that her cousin and the vicar were laughing.

At last, something good to come of this evening. Mr. Smythe-Wyndham could not be a finer shepherd for his flock, but he required a shepherdess to assist him. Prudence

Moberly was a paragon of Christian womanhood, the perfect choice.

Following the sounds of a string quartet, Elizabeth strolled toward the back terrace, hoping to find a quiet but visible corner to while away the rest of the evening. She found a pleasing spot on a small stone bench near the musicians, where Chinese lanterns provided the proper amount of illumination.

Some guests had gone to great expense for their costumes. Satins and silks, wigs and hats, furs and even armor. She laughed to herself at the thought of a medieval knight trying to manage a reel or the Roger de Coverly. And there was a golden-masked Louis XIV, the Sun King resplendent in his bright yellow satins, golden shoes with four-inch heels and a high silvery wig that made him appear over six feet tall. Few men reached such height or possessed such a kingly bearing. Who could it be? Other than Papa and her Uncle Moberly, whom did she know with such an imposing stature?

Mr. Lindsey? Why, Elizabeth could just picture Jamie's machinations here. Had he not promised some mischief with his silly wave and impish eyes as she was leaving home? But where would they have found the costume? This was no mere homespun disguise.

She started to rise and make herself visible, but caution kept her seated, even as curiosity kept her eyes upon him. With an elegant turn, he surveyed his "kingdom," and when he fully faced her, he stopped. A slight nod, like Mr. Lindsey's? A hesitant step in her direction. Then a firm march.

Elizabeth's heart leapt and her pulse raced. She stood and curtsied.

His bow nearly toppled his wig, but with an artful hand he caught and righted it. Wordlessly, he reached out, and she placed her gloved hand in his, receiving upon it a kiss.

through the metallic gold mask. He gestured toward the wide terrace, and she permitted him to lead her through the crowd and across the tiled surface.

"Your Majesty." She tried to disguise her voice with a French accent, but chose not to speak that language in case Mr. Lindsey had not learned it. "How nice of you to visit our humble soiree."

He answered with a gracious nod and continued their journey. As they wended toward the south corner, a slight misgiving came over Elizabeth. She stopped.

"Your Majesty, where are you taking me?"

He placed a gloved hand over his heart and the other against his forehead, palm out, as if hurt by the question.

"We will not leave the lanterns or the sight of other people?"

He shook his head.

"Très bien." No, not quite "very good," but what could happen on the lighted terrace with other people around? She took his offered arm once again.

The back corner was darker than she'd expected, for several of the Chinese lanterns were unlit. But still, other people stood some small distance away. They stopped at the terrace's concrete banister, another safeguard, for if this proved to be no gentleman, he could not drag her into the nearby darkness. She laughed aloud at such imagining, brought on no doubt by all the costumes and hidden identities.

He tilted his head in question.

"I was just amused by my own foolishness." She gazed up at him, almost losing her hair in the process. "My goodness, how did our ancestors manage with these dreadful wigs?"

He chuckled in response, and a shiver ran down her spine. Rather than the deep baritone of Mr. Lindsey, it was Lord Chiselton's tenor.

"Oh." She stamped her foot, more frustrated with herself than angry with him. "You are quite the trickster, my lord. Mark Antony, indeed."

Now he laughed in earnest. Removing his golden mask, he snickered. "And when you did not find me in that role, did you despair?"

"Not in the least." Removing her mask, she turned to leave.

"Wait." He touched her arm. "Do not abandon me." His woeful tone stopped her. "Did I not say I have a question to ask you?"

Facing him, she offered the kindest of smiles. "Yes, Lord Chiselton, you did. But what you did not do was speak to my father first."

He blinked and gaped, a study in surprise. "Why, Miss Elizabeth, why ever would I wish to speak to your father?"

Now *she* blinked and gaped but only for an instant before realization struck her. "Clearly, I made an error." She once again turned to leave, but he wrapped one arm around her waist. She gasped. "You must let me go, my lord." Why had she ever thought this self-centered popinjay could make her happy?

He tugged her close and bent forward. "But will you not kiss me first? Those lovely pink lips—"

"And that was the question you wished to ask? You wanted to kiss me?" And no doubt, much more. This man, this peer of the Realm, had nothing but dishonorable intentions toward her. She, a respectable lady and the daughter of a British naval hero.

Tears stung her eyes as she struggled against his tight grip. He was nothing but a rake and she a silly girl who should have known better. What a harsh truth to discover that a man could possess a noble rank and yet be utterly devoid of a noble nature.

"Release me."

His chuckle was anything but pleasant. "But, my dear, I am the Sun King. By divine right, I own the world and everything…and everyone in it."

Chapter Sixteen

"Unhand her, sir." Philip gripped the hilt of his sword, more to steady himself than to threaten the overdressed golden peacock holding Miss Elizabeth to his chest in such an inappropriate manner. The way she leaned away from him and the alarm written across her beautiful face generated anger such as he hadn't felt since learning of Whitson's betrayal. But now, as then, he must control his rage or do irreparable damage.

The brigand turned and revealed his identity, but Philip experienced neither surprise nor alarm. From what he'd seen of Chiselton, his misuse of a lady was perfectly in character.

The scoundrel raked him up and down with a venomous look. "Ah, so the common highwayman hopes to rob the Sun King of his prey."

"This is hardly a game, Chiselton." Philip glanced over his shoulder for support, but Jamie was nowhere to be seen. Removing his mask, he turned back. "Unhand her. Now."

"Mr. Lindsey." Miss Elizabeth's plaintive tone both gladdened and strengthened him. "You came, after all."

She shrugged away from Chiselton and moved around him toward Philip.

"I say." Chiselton's vicious sneer as he watched her unmasked his true nature. He possessed not the slightest degree of respect for her. "Do not presume to give me orders. Do you have any idea of how completely I can ruin you?"

Philip moved between the man and Miss Elizabeth. "Ruin me, then, Chiselton. But you will do no harm to this good lady." He offered her his arm. "Shall we find your Aunt Bennington, Miss Elizabeth? She'll want to know what mischief her nephew has been up to."

"Oh, yes." She gripped his forearm as if it were a lifeline.

"Lindsey!" The threat in Chiselton's tone could not be missed.

Philip wanted to walk away. Should walk away. But somehow found himself facing the viscount again.

"My aunt will not believe you. And what does it signify if she does?" He waved his hand in a careless gesture. "Miss Elizabeth has always desired my attentions, have you not, my dear? I was merely granting her wishes."

Miss Elizabeth gasped and swayed, which gave Philip something to do rather than strike the viscount. He steadied the lady, breathed out a hot, angry breath and led her toward nearby French doors. A footman opened them, and they entered the crowded parlor.

Miss Elizabeth leaned against him, and he feared she'd faint. But even in the dim candlelit room, he could see that her flushed face reflected anything but faintheartedness.

"Are you well, Miss Elizabeth?"

"I am now." She straightened and exhaled crossly. "Very well and angry as a Fury."

Her blazing blue eyes and the prim set of her lips

confirmed her recovery. "That's the spirit." What admirable courage this lady possessed! "Shall I escort you to Lady Bennington?"

She gazed up at him, and her charming dimple appeared at the corner of her smile, lifting Philip's heart. "I thank you, Mr. Lindsey, but what Lord Chiselton said is true. Aunt Bennington would never believe him capable of anything but the most proper behavior." Her smile disappeared as she released a wistful sigh, all fire gone.

"But you are a lady and her niece. Would she not—?"

"Her niece by marriage. He is her own blood, her late sister's son." She gave a little shrug. "And, of course, he is a peer. His word would likely be taken over anyone else's."

"Lord Bennington, then? As your father's brother—?"

Again, she demurred. "Uncle Bennington has enough to manage with my cousin Sophia's debacle." She cast an apologetic glance at him. "And no matter how well-connected my father may be, I fear Lord Chiselton would win any suit."

"I have observed that inequity." Philip clenched his jaw. "Well, then, please permit me to escort you to some safe company in this immense house."

She shook her head, and her wig swayed. "Perhaps I should retire for the evening."

He read the weariness in her eyes. "Very well. But I'll escort you to someone who can accompany you."

"I say." Jamie bounded up to them, an amber drink in hand. "Where've you been, old boy? Why, Beth, there you are. Somehow I knew you two would find each other."

"Jamie!" Again, Miss Elizabeth's cheeks flushed with color, and Philip felt warmth returning to his own face.

"So, what've you two been up to?" Jamie took a sip of his drink, wrinkled his nose and set the glass on a nearby table. Although liquid sloshed onto the table, this time Philip wouldn't clean up after him. "Beastly stuff, that."

"Just so." Philip again offered his arm to Miss Elizabeth. "May I take you to a friend?" She set a hand on his sleeve.

"What?" Jamie eyed them both.

To her credit, Miss Elizabeth didn't decline to answer, but gave her brother a brief account of Chiselton's actions.

"I say." Jamie posted fists at his waist and frowned. "Shall I call him out then?"

Philip sucked in his cheeks to avoid laughing in shock at the lad's admirable but foolish offer.

"And ruin all your prospects?" Miss Elizabeth shook her head, and all joy left her face. "No, brother dear. I shall avoid him at all costs." Her forehead wrinkled. "And I shall return home early tomorrow long before he has slept off his…merriment."

With Jamie's assistance, they found Miss Prudence, who was just bidding Mr. Smythe-Wyndham *adieu*. After pleasantries all around, including an invitation from the vicar for Philip to visit the parsonage, the clergyman and the ladies said their goodnights and retired in their respective directions.

Philip watched Miss Elizabeth ascend the front staircase with a mixture of sorrow and relief. Although her posture conveyed a degree of melancholy, she hadn't been harmed physically.

Like Jamie, Philip very much desired to call out Chiselton. But for him to do so would further impugn the lady's character. And his feelings for the lady would not permit him to cause her even the lightest distress. He could deny it no longer—he loved her. And while it had not been in his plans to seek a wife at this point in his life, surely this match had the Lord's blessing. Otherwise, why would he have felt compelled to do something so rash and uncharacteristic as to barge into this party uninvited? Why, for no other reason than to save her from that beast. Yes, the Lord's hand was at work in their relationship, and that gave Philip considerable consolation over having to leave her here.

Elizabeth trudged up the first flight behind Pru, fully aware that Mr. Lindsey was watching. But she could not improve her posture or her mood, nor turn and join Pru in waving to him from the top step.

On the second floor, they made their way to their bedchamber where Ginny welcomed them, cooing pleasantries. With costumes removed, nightrails on and hair brushed and braided, they bid their lady's maid good night, sending her off for a bit of fun with the other servants. At the door, Elizabeth called her back.

"Yes, miss?"

"Do avoid the guests." Elizabeth gave her a meaningful stare. "The male guests, I mean."

Ginny's eyes widened. "Yes, miss." She bit her lip and frowned. "Never have to worry about that at Captain Moberly's house, now do I? Thank the good Lord." She spun around and hurried toward the back stairs.

Truly weary at last, Elizabeth let her eyes fill. "Yes, thank the good Lord," she whispered. For surely God had sent Mr. Lindsey just in time to stop Lord Chiselton from whatever mischief he had in mind.

Elizabeth related her sad tale to her cousin, who was a dear for not saying, "I told you so." But Pru did rise and bolt the door before surrendering to sleep.

Tired though she was, Elizabeth did not find rest. While tonight had taught her much, it also confounded her. From the first, she had tried to find Mr. Lindsey inferior to Lord

Chiselton in both manner and character, but had been unable to do so. And tonight had proven beyond a doubt who was the better man. Even before their last encounter, she had felt uneasy with Lord Chiselton, the man she had once hoped to wed.

And yet now it was the noble Mr. Lindsey whom she would gladly marry, should he but ask.

Chapter Seventeen

On the second day after his intrusion into Bennington's masquerade, Philip accepted the captain's invitation to inspect the vast Moberly grounds. Early on, they rode in silence, watching as sunrise lifted the misty shroud from the land to reveal its hidden beauties. A myriad of familiar smells filled his senses: mown grass, wildflowers and fresh morning air, all of which imparted to him an invigorating energy.

This country manor was much like his own property, with rich farmlands, lush woodlands and a quaint village at the outskirts. Flocks of sheep grazed in the verdant fields, while playful otters plagued the snowy swans floating serenely on the ponds. Wild hares scurried about the apple orchard searching for fruit fallen before its time. A blue-coated nuthatch seized an acorn from beneath a giant oak tree and dashed away with its prize. Bees and common blue butterflies sipped the nectar of wildflowers. Even the gray stone ruins of an ancient castle reminded him of his beloved home.

At a pond in the glade, a pair of fallow deer trotted to safety. A wide-racked stag paused to stand guard until his doe disappeared into the thick brush. Philip felt a kinship with the creature, for he longed to stand guard until assured of Miss Elizabeth's safety.

These past few days, first being denied her company and then rescuing her from Chiselton, confirmed to him how much he regarded—no, *loved*—her. If he were certain of her feelings for him, he'd speak to the captain now. But should she not return his affections, they'd all be uncomfortable until Whitson was dealt with. For now, he must keep his sentiments to himself. But he must also devise a plan to present to Captain Moberly of how he would care for a wife.

They paused at the summit of a small hill from whence they could view the upper floors of distant Devon Hall. The fog, which lay across the lower landscape like a snowy carpet, receded beneath the rising sun.

"Seen enough?" Reaching down to pat the neck of his bay mare, Captain Moberly eyed Philip.

"Not really, sir. Your grounds are magnificent. I could stay out here all day." Still, his heartbeat increased at the prospect of returning to the hall and seeing his lady, or so he had come to think of her.

The captain, however, seemed in no hurry to return home, and Philip began to feel ill at ease. So far, the Chiselton incident hadn't come up in general conversation, and he was confounded as to how to introduce the subject to his host.

Yesterday morning, when the young ladies had returned home, the household had rejoiced in being complete again. The children had demanded a full accounting of the events, which, of course, could not be granted. But one would have never known anything was amiss from the way Miss Elizabeth and Miss Prudence had recounted the various games and diversions they had enjoyed. With the children satisfied they'd learned everything important, they had traipsed off with their governess to their lessons. In the evening, when the family had gathered in the drawing room, no one would've guessed anything had disturbed their normal routine.

As they descended the hill, the captain guided his horse closer to Philip's. "You must tell me about Chiselton."

The question startled him. "Sir?"

"Come now, man, do you think Jamie could keep quiet about it?" Moberly scowled. "I had no idea you two rode over to the masquerade nor that there was an unpleasant incident. My son was thoroughly enraged but said you kept him from doing something hotheaded. I want to hear your account of it."

The air went out of Philip's lungs, and he had to pull in a deep breath before responding.

"Nothing much to tell on my part, sir." He sent up a quick prayer he would say the right thing. "Jamie and I put together some costumes and—"

"Jamie talked you into going."

"Yes, sir." Philip gave him a sheepish grin. "Upon arrival, we parted company, and I happened to recognize Miss Elizabeth, even though she was masked, for I'd seen her costume before she left. She was talking with a rather ornately garbed man." He refrained from referring to Chiselton as a gentleman. "This fellow led his reluctant prey to a dark corner and tried to force a kiss upon her." Or something worse. "When she protested, he wouldn't release her. I insisted he must. He was not pleased."

They rode in silence for a short distance. At last Moberly spoke, his voice thick. "Permit a father to express his deepest gratitude. No material treasure would be sufficient to repay you." The hint of despair in his tone struck Philip with sorrow. Even a heroic naval captain who'd protected British interests around the world couldn't protect his daughter from a devious peer with evil intent.

"Sir, you have befriended me in my distress and made me a guest in your home these many days. If there is payment to be made, it is I who should make it to you."

Moberly nodded his appreciation. "I will speak to my brother about this incident, but I cannot expect too much. Chiselton is a fool, but he has wealth and influence. Of course I will not permit my children to go to Bennington Manor while he remains there."

Philip could see the anger smoldering in the captain's eyes. How hard it must be to hear of the assault on his daughter and not be able to challenge the perpetrator. Were he not a Christian, Philip would ride over to Bennington Manor this very day and settle the matter.

But where would that leave Lucy? He must use good sense, no matter how hard it was to postpone his revenge on both Chiselton and Whitson. And, indeed, when the time was right, he would find some way to avenge Miss Elizabeth's affront without harming her reputation, just as he would deal with his sister's betrayer.

The morning after Elizabeth and Pru returned home from Bennington Manor, they joined Mr. Lindsey and Jamie on the east lawn for a game of *paille maille*. With Mr. Lindsey new to the little-known game, Elizabeth and Jamie demonstrated how to play with the wooden ball and mallet. Each one hit a ball down the mown grass alley in an attempt to send it beneath a small iron arch. And each one proved how out of practice they were, to the good humor and merriment of all.

To Elizabeth's delight, Mr. Lindsey managed to do at least as well as the others. Once again, he fit into the family activities as if he belonged. And of course, he cut a fine figure in his black morning coat and tan breeches. With his wavy black hair tossed about in the wind, he appeared much as he had when he had burst into the church and interrupted Sophia's wedding.

After several missed attempts, Jamie announced he would take his best shot by imagining a certain viscount's visage on the ball. He placed his ball by the first arch, drew back the mallet and smacked the orb soundly. It spun across the grass, shooting directly through the distant hoop. He executed a comical bow, complete with a flourish of his hand. "There, Lord Chiselton. What do you think of that?"

Everyone, even Pru, laughed and applauded.

"Good show," Mr. Lindsey said. "I may just borrow your inspiration."

They enjoyed the game for an hour or so until the sun grew too warm and drove them inside for a midday repast.

After a brief lie-down, Elizabeth found Mr. Lindsey in his favorite spot by the windows in the library. His broad, welcoming smile reached clear to his eyes, and she permitted herself to bask in the kindness reflected there.

He stood and bowed. "Are you rested, Miss Elizabeth?"

"Yes, thank you." She settled into the chair across from him, the better to see his handsome face. Any day he could be called away from here, and she wished to record his features so as never to forget them.

"I am glad you found me, for I've a question best asked in private." He glanced toward the open door and nodded his approval at the footman, far enough away not to hear their conversation, close enough to ensure propriety.

A pleasant suspicion tickled Elizabeth's brain. She could

trust this gentleman's question would not at all resemble the viscount's impropriety. "Very well. Do ask."

He gripped the arms of his chair, as he often did. "I'd like to ask Captain Moberly for permission to…well, I cannot refer to it as calling upon you, for here I am." He chuckled and shrugged one shoulder in the most charming way.

She laughed. Or rather, breathed out a happy sigh. "Yes."

He wrinkled his brow. "Yes?"

Now she laughed in earnest. "Yes, please do speak to Papa. And do be encouraged, for I cannot think he has permitted us to spend so much time together without having the highest regard for you." Oh, how she longed to reach out and grip his hand, but that would not be proper. "Do remember he has been approached by my two sisters' suitors, and not a one has perished."

"Ah." Another chuckle. "Then I'll do it without delay."

As if summoned, Papa entered the room, and Mr. Lindsey stood. He exchanged a quick look of understanding with her, and she jumped to her feet.

"Papa, how well you look today." But in fact, he actually looked somewhat careworn.

"Thank you, my dear." He pressed a light kiss on her temple. "Now, you must excuse us. Mr. Lindsey has received his summons to Bennington Manor, and I intend to accompany him."

Chapter Eighteen

A bow string couldn't have been pulled tighter than Philip's nerves as he and Captain Moberly approached Bennington Manor. They rode up the tree-lined drive toward the brown stone edifice, whose broad, three-storied façade was even more impressive than the rear elevation Philip had see on his previous visit. When they reached the front, two grooms rushed from the side of the building to take their horses.

After dismounting, Philip straightened his coat and inhaled a deep breath. The pleasant fragrance emanating from the nearby bed of roses stood at odds with Whitson's foul-smelling deeds he must now contend with.

"Steady, lad." Moberly clapped him on the shoulder. "My brother is a reasonable man."

"Thank you, sir." Philip tried to pray as he approached the front door, but the heavens seemed encased behind a silent wall.

A butler greeted them, an ancient stick of a man dressed in black and topped with a silver crown of close-cropped hair.

"Good afternoon, Mr. Lindsey, Captain Moberly." The man bowed to each in turn.

Philip wondered whether the old fellow was losing his grip on reality. Most certainly, the captain should have been addressed first. Philip cast an apologetic glance at Moberly, who shrugged and shook his head. Once again, the man's graciousness bound Philip's heart to him. How he prayed today's events wouldn't destroy any chance he might have to marry Miss Elizabeth.

Blevins, the butler, took their hats, then led them without ceremony up the front staircase to Bennington's first-floor library. He stepped through the open door and intoned, "Mr. Lindsey. Captain Moberly."

Pity for the old servant welled up in Philip's chest. This type of error in precedence might see the fellow set out to pasture, should some august personage complain.

Moberly nudged him into the room, and Blevins retreated, closing the door behind him. The room smelled of tobacco and, if Philip was not mistaken, bergamot, most likely from someone's over-applied shaving balm.

Across the large chamber, Bennington sat in a red, throne-like chair behind a white oak desk, his gray hair curled impeccably at the sides of his round face. Two slender, middle-aged men dressed in black were posted like sentinels on either side of the unlit hearth. Whitson stood beside the desk, his eyes wide. Philip hadn't seen him since the canceled wedding and, strangely, felt nothing at all. No rage. No fear. Certainly no charity.

"Come in, come in." Bennington waved them to the chairs in front of his desk. "Sit, sit. You, too, Whitson."

Like obedient minions, the three took their places across from him, with Moberly between Philip and his adversary.

"You're looking well, Tommy." The earl gave his brother a placid smile, then nodded to Philip. "Thank you for coming, Lydney."

Philip's chest constricted. "Lindsey, my lord."

Bennington eyed him and smirked. "Oh, yes. Of course." He shuffled the papers on his desk. "I suppose I was recalling an old political foe. Lord Lydney. Haven't seen him in years. Old age and infirmity have kept him from taking his seat in parliament these six years. Just got word through my solicitors here that the old goat has passed on at last. God rest his miserable soul."

An icy shroud descended upon Philip's head and shoulders as its watery counterpart sluiced through his veins, numbing him clear to the ends of his toes and fingers. How could one freeze and burn at the same time? Lydney dead? Now his future was sealed. There was no escape. He gripped the carved oak arms of his chair, as if that would keep him from drowning.

"Are you ill, sir?" Bennington's tone held a hint of amusement.

What possible pleasure could the earl take from another man's distress? What did he know? Anger and fear flared inside Philip, but caution doused both. "No, my lord."

"Are you certain?" Captain Moberly leaned toward him and gripped his arm. "You've gone pale. No, your color is coming back." He chuckled. "You must forgive my brother's seeming disregard for Lydney's eternal soul. He is not as coldhearted as he sounds."

"Of course not." Philip forced a casual grin. Only a brother or intimate friend would dare to direct such banter at Bennington. But Philip wouldn't be diverted from the task at hand. Shoving aside thoughts of the future, he stared unblinking at the earl, determined to avenge sweet Lucy. With a strong measure of resolve, he brought to mind her bitter heartbreak and ignored the memory of her letter stating her relief over learning of Whitson's true character. And of course, the scoundrel must not be permitted to keep the dowry.

"Shall we proceed?" Bennington beckoned the two black-suited men with an imperious wave of his hand. "These are my solicitors from London, Graves and Soames. Gentlemen, give us your report."

"My lord." Graves bent forward in an elaborate bow. Behind him, Soames copied the gesture. "We have thoroughly examined the document and the signatures—"

"My lord." Whitson's voice resonated with strain, but Philip refused to look at him for fear of at last losing his temper. "I've already admitted I signed the contract."

"So you did, my boy." Bennington's bland expression didn't mask the kindness in his tone. "Carry on, Graves."

The dour solicitor glared at Whitson over his reading spectacles. "Ahem. As I was saying, we have examined the document, and it is a flawlessly executed legal contract duly signed by those named therein."

"And there are no provisions for a *volte-face?*" Bennington's arched eyebrows displayed only mild curiosity.

"No, my lord. Nothing about a change of heart." Graves stepped back, and his colleague stepped forward. He glanced nervously between Bennington and Philip.

"My lord, according to the Hardwicke Marriage Act of 1753, a contract such as this cannot be used to force a marriage."

Force a marriage? Now Philip's latent anger rose to the surface, and he moved to the edge of his seat, ready to stand and declare they could keep their warnings, for he would never give Lucy to this scoundrel.

Captain Moberly once again gripped his arm. With difficulty, Philip settled back into the chair.

Soames gave him a smile that appeared more like a

grimace. "However, the Marriage Act did allow for Mr. Lindsey to take Mr. Whitson to court and sue him for breach of contract and thereby lay claim to the ten thousand pounds."

Whitson squeaked out some unintelligible word, and at last Philip looked at him. Pale as a winter moon, the man looked stricken. "I haven't got it."

Graves moved up beside his partner and cleared his throat. "I must say, Mr. Lindsey, I cannot comprehend your turning over the dowry to Mr. Whitson before the marriage took place. Whatever were you thinking?"

Soames's eyes widened, and he nudged his partner.

"Forgive me, eh, *sir,* I mean no disrespect."

"But it is a good question, do you not think?" Bennington gazed at Philip as if asking him whether he played billiards.

The earl's mild tone notwithstanding, Philip felt very much like a schoolboy called before the headmaster. The vast chamber suddenly closed in on him, but he managed to resist the urge to wipe perspiration from his forehead. "He said he needed the money for an investment to ensure his future. At my sister's request but against my better judgment, I trusted him, not knowing he planned to invest in a London Season." He stopped before his anger generated careless words that might insult the innocent Lady Sophia.

"Ah. I see." Graves nodded, as though it made perfect sense, whereas Philip could at last perceive what a schoolboy's error his generosity had been. He still had much to learn regarding his responsibilities and hoped Captain Moberly could advise him.

"Have you a solution?" Bennington eyed his solicitors.

The two men traded a look. Soames spoke.

"There are several options, my lord. Should you permit

Mr. Whitson to marry Lady Sophia, he can use her dowry to repay Mr. Lindsey. Should you decide against it, Mr. Lindsey has the recourse of the suit we mentioned, or—" he cleared his throat "—he can demand satisfaction on a field of honor."

Whitson jumped to his feet. "My lord, I am not a man of violence." His wild-eyed stare shot around the room, taking in all inhabitants but Philip.

Philip should have felt some degree of satisfaction to see his adversary—*Lucy's* adversary—in such fear. But no such sense of triumph filled the emptiness within.

"Well." Bennington's tone remained languid, as did his posture. He studied Whitson, who looked as if he were taking a turn before the headmaster's desk. "You'll not have my daughter or her dowry until you repay Lydney...Lindsey." The earl glanced at Philip.

Prickles of intuition crept up the back of Philip's scalp. Somehow Bennington knew about him and hoped to goad him into some reaction. But he wouldn't give the man what he wanted. At least not until this matter was settled.

"But, my lord." Whitson gaped. "I have no funds, no prospects."

"Pity." Bennington waved one hand dismissively. "Very well, Lindsey, I turn him over to you."

All eyes snapped to Philip. Now satisfaction flooded his entire being, body and soul, and he felt his lips curl upward in a sardonic smile.

"What say you, Whitson? Do you prefer debtor's prison, or shall I demand satisfaction on a field of honor?"

Chapter Nineteen

"Why are they taking so long?" Elizabeth paced back and forth across the Wilton carpet before the drawing room hearth. At each outside sound, she dashed to the front window, thinking Mr. Lindsey and Papa had returned, only to see the breeze blowing a branch against the glass or a groom exercising one of Papa's horses.

"And of course your pacing will bring them home sooner." Pru threaded her silver needle and began to embroider a blue monogram in the corner of a linen handkerchief.

Elizabeth dropped onto the settee beside her. "How can you be so patient? Until Uncle and Aunt Moberly return next month, you cannot receive Mr. Smythe-Wyndham other than as our vicar. I should go mad waiting that long." She tapped her fingernails on the settee's ornately carved wooden arm. "At least I shall have Papa's answer soon."

"And surely there is no reason he should deny Mr. Lindsey permission to court you." Pru's careful stitches began to form the letter *P*.

Admiring the work, Elizabeth leaned back to watch her cousin. As the youngest of three daughters of a man of modest means, Prudence exemplified her name. She sewed her own clothing or wore Diana's and Elizabeth's castoffs and made her own handkerchiefs from old bed linens. Due to Papa's success in His Majesty's Navy and some wise investments, Elizabeth could purchase silk and lace handkerchiefs by the dozen, and her clothing was made by hired seamstresses. How Uncle Robert Moberly would provide dowries for his three daughters was a serious question. But each of these lovely girls bore their situation with grace.

"Tell me, Beth." Pru's eyes lit with merriment. "What title should His Majesty bestow upon Mr. Lindsey to make him worthy to marry you?"

Elizabeth elbowed her cousin's arm. "Humph. Haven't *I* learned my lesson? Promise me you will never tell my children about that foolish dream."

"I would never consider it." Pru shook her head as if to emphasize her pledge. "Have we not heard often enough of peers who were no gentlemen, even in regard to wellborn ladies?"

Elizabeth leaned her head on Pru's shoulder. "Indeed. How wise your advice has always been that we should pray first for a godly husband." She laughed softly. "And so I did but never failed to add 'titled' to that petition." She lifted her head and glanced toward the front windows. No one approached. "Still, one must admit a title provides protections for a family. If Uncle Bennington sets himself against Mr. Lindsey, he is able to ruin him just as surely as Lord Chiselton threatened to do."

"Thus we must trust our futures to the Lord. If God be for us, who can be against us?" Pru tied and clipped her embroidery floss, then selected a yellow strand to thread into the needle. "There is no earthly thing worth having if it is outside of His will. And no harm can come to us if we follow His plan for our lives."

The truth of her cousin's words fell upon Elizabeth like a touch from the Lord Himself, filling her with joy. She had not always taken Pru's counsel to heart, but this was one gentle sermon she hoped to imbed in her heart forever.

"Very well, then. Whitson will find a way to repay the dowry or face debtor's prison." Bennington rose from his chair. "There is nothing more to say."

The other men also stood. Philip released a quiet sigh of relief that Whitson had chosen repayment, for the burden of killing another man, no matter how deserving of death he might be, wasn't something he wished to carry for the rest of his life.

"Whitson, you will retire to your room." The earl's sober expression brooked no objections, and the scoundrel scooted out the door like the rat he was. Bennington dismissed his solicitors with much more courtesy, assuring them that his servants would see to their comfort. "And now, Tommy, will you give me a few moments with Lindsey?"

Philip's stomach churned. Which of two topics would the earl choose to hammer him with—Whitson of Lydney?

"Bennington?" The captain's dark frown challenged the earl as only someone close to him might dare.

"Do not fear, my good brother." Bennington chuckled lightly. "I shall return him to you unscathed."

"Lindsey?" Moberly questioned Philip with an uplifted eyebrow.

"Have I a choice, sir?" Philip clenched his jaw. He wouldn't relent in his suit against Whitson, no matter what the earl said. If good men didn't stop the perpetrators of evil, no person, male or female, would be safe.

Bennington shrugged. "Go on, Tommy. We'll be only a moment or two."

"I shall call for our horses." The captain gave Philip a reassuring pat on the shoulder and left the room.

"Now, sir," Bennington said, "do you require any advice?"

Philip questioned him with a frown. "Advice?"

"Oh, come now, Lydney—"

"I say, uncle, may I have a word?" Chiselton sauntered into the library. When he saw Philip, his lips curled into a sneer. "Lindsey, what cheek of you to be here."

Philip resisted the urge to knock that sneer off his face, the way Jamie had struck the *paille maille* ball. Perhaps later. First he must tend to Lucy's situation.

Bennington blew out a harsh breath. "Not now, Chiselton. I am talking with Lydney here."

Chiselton laughed, a thin sound, edged with nervousness. "Lindsey, you mean, my lord."

Bennington leveled a harsh glare upon his nephew. "Do not correct me, boy. I am not yet in my dotage. This is the Earl of Lydney, as reported to me by my solicitors just this morning. As it was, of course, confirmed by the Committee of Privileges and soon to be in all the newspapers."

Once again the icy shroud swept over Philip. *No, Lord. Why does this have to be?* He did not want this title, this position. He possessed not a whit of ambition for the elevation many men desperately sought. If the law of patents permitted, he'd gladly hand the title and all the wealth and land that came with it to his brother or anyone willing enough to wield its power. Someone like Captain Moberly, a true and good gentleman. But alas, no such refusal was permitted. Like a plague, the title would be attached to him until the day he died.

"Ah, Lydney." Chiselton's voice, high and shrill, cut into his thoughts, while a too-wide grin split the viscount's face.

"If there is anything I can do for you, do by all means ask." His words were laced with an insincere tone. "Do let me take you around London. I know all the right gambling dens, horseracing parks. And of course, the ladies—" He caught himself in midsentence.

If the viscount's horrified expression weren't so comical, Philip would slam a fist into his aristocratic nose. As it was, he barely possessed the self-control to turn back to Bennington.

"My lord, if that is all—"

Bennington emitted another of his maddening chuckles. "Yes, *my lord,* that's all. Oh, but do remember, in order of precedence, your letter of patent is some fifty years older than mine. Do not be reticent in taking your place ahead of me. It does little for the entire peerage if one of our number pretends it does not matter. For indeed, it does."

Without responding, Philip strode past Chiselton, who continued to mutter fawning gibberish at him. Downstairs, claiming his hat from Blevins, he granted the old butler his dignity by permitting him to open the front door. Yet Philip would much rather have exhibited a courtesy due to the man's advanced years.

The thought struck him that Blevins must have overheard the news of his elevation and thus deliberately addressed him before the captain, while discretion had kept him from using the title. Servants heard everything and took great delight in being the first to pass on important information. Now everyone would know all about him. He could not escape. Perhaps Captain Moberly already knew, for he made no attempt to stop Philip as he rode his horse at full gallop all the way back to Devon Hall.

Chapter Twenty

"They're here." Elizabeth dashed to the front door, beating the butler handily, and threw it open. "Well?" She looked from Mr. Lindsey to Papa and back again as they entered the portal. A thread of concern wove through her at their sober demeanors.

"My dear." Papa kissed her temple, just as he had before they left, then moved past her toward the front staircase.

Elizabeth watched him ascend the stairs with some dismay but then turned to Mr. Lindsey.

The gentleman's frown became a smile. "Good afternoon, Miss Elizabeth."

"You may not pass until—" She stopped, realizing she had no right to demand an accounting, even if she did so in a playful manner. At least not yet. "I mean…"

He stopped mere inches from her and gazed into her eyes, his broad shoulders and height a pleasant distraction that made her heart beat faster and the breath disappear from her lungs. But the message in his eyes was unclear. Had he spoken to Papa regarding a courtship? Or had the business at Bennington Manor taken all of their attention?

"I fear we didn't have a chance to talk about..." He glanced beyond her. "Good afternoon, Miss Prudence."

"Mr. Lindsey." Pru gave him a quick curtsy and a questioning smile. "You must come into the drawing room and tell us everything."

He shrugged. "There's not much to tell. Bennington's solicitors confirmed the contract, and now Whitson must repay the dowry." A frown wrinkled his broad forehead. "The earl refused to assist him and has canceled the engagement."

"Poor Sophie." Elizabeth moved toward the drawing room door in hopes Mr. Lindsey would follow. "But I can muster no pity for a man who deceived two good families."

Mr. Lindsey remained in the entrance hall, an apologetic look pinching his fine features. "Forgive me. I should go upstairs."

To speak with Papa? Elizabeth would detain him no longer. "Yes, of course." Her heart tripped over itself, as it often had since this gentleman came to visit. "Do that."

But his weak smile and accompanying wince did not suggest he planned to follow Papa and ask for her hand in marriage.

In the privacy of the guest room, Philip sat in a straight-back chair with his head in his hands and a sick feeling in his stomach. When he'd left home in a hurry, he'd prayed only that he might stop the wedding, not thinking exactly how he would pursue Whitson legally. But today, even a hard ride on an excellent steed hadn't cleared his head. Now he must determine exactly how one went about seeing a man put in debtor's prison. That could be accomplished only by returning home to seek the counsel of his own solicitors, for he had no desire ever to see Bennington's men again.

But before he left Devon Hall, he must settle his nerves

and ask Captain Moberly for Miss Elizabeth's hand. Taking a deep, bracing breath, he stood and began to pace the room, the better to think through the matter.

"Captain Moberly," he said to the painting of some family ancestor hanging on the wall, "I understand that taking a wife is a great responsibility. However, despite my mere three and twenty years, I am certain I am prepared for it." He paced in one direction, covering the five yards of the chamber in four steps, and back again.

The Tudor-era ancestor still frowned his disapproval. Philip cleared his throat.

"If you are concerned about Miss Elizabeth's material needs, please know I possess sufficient wealth to ensure her care for the rest of her life." Another thought emerged. "*And in the style to which she is accustomed.*" And then some.

The ancestor's stare bored into him, cutting to the heart of the matter.

"Ah, yes. Of course you would be concerned about spiritual issues. Sir, my devotion to the Lord is steadfast. I shall honor my marriage vows and never betray her. I shall make certain our children are reared in our faith."

The stare softened but still posed a question.

Philip sighed. "But unless you bring up that wretched title, I shall remain Lindsey to this family for as long as possible."

"Ah, at last!" Wilkes stood in the door, his hands clasped together and his granite face lit with...joy? "My lord, congratulations!" He clapped his hands and then plunged them into the wardrobe, searching among the garments. "We must find something dashingly appropriate for you to wear to supper this evening. Ah, such good news, such very good news."

Philip strode across the room and shut the chamber door.

"Shh! Do be quiet, Wilkes. The family doesn't yet know, nor do I wish them to." He would not have his title influence the captain's decision or the way this good family regarded him.

"But, my lord—"

"Please! You must call me 'sir' until I am ready to announce it."

Wilkes's face crumpled into a frown, then molded once more into a granite façade. "Of course, sir. I beg your pardon."

"Never mind, my good man. When we return home, I'll announce to the household that you knew it first but kept it a secret according to my wishes."

"Yes, my lord…sir." The twinkle in Wilkes's eyes bespoke his pleasure over being trusted with a treasured secret.

His valet helped Philip into a fresh suit and fussed with his hair, muttering that it needed a trim. But for Philip, impatience to complete his goal overrode excessive grooming.

"I must do this now, Wilkes. You do understand."

The good fellow's façade melted a little. "I wish you well, sir. The lady is very fortunate."

"You are kind to say so." What else would a faithful retainer say? "But I am the one who is blessed to own her affection."

Philip descended to the first floor and eyed the footman at the library door. "Will you announce me, please?"

"Sir, he said you are to go in."

Not at all surprised, Philip walked on wooden legs into the room that heretofore had always felt so welcoming. Captain Moberly sat behind his desk looking far more imperious than his titled brother. Or perhaps it was Philip's fear that painted him thus.

"Come in, Lindsey." A good sign he didn't know about the title.

"Thank you, sir." Philip walked across large room, struggling to recall his planned words. He stopped before the desk and sat in obedience to the captain's gesture toward a chair.

Sir, I should like to ask your permission to propose… no…I know that a husband…would you consider—

"I am in love with your daughter."

Moberly stared at him unblinking for what seemed an eternity. "I am aware of that, sir." Somehow, his former welcoming demeanor had vanished.

As when they'd first met, Philip suddenly felt like an insubordinate sailor. Somehow he must plunge ahead.

"May I have your permission to marry Miss Elizabeth?" His voice sounded as high and thin as Whitson's had just over two hours ago. He tried to still his pounding pulse with thoughts of his own honor compared to that miscreant's scheming nature, but to no avail.

Again, an eternity seemed to pass before the captain responded. "You may not."

His words felt like a *paille maille* mallet striking his chest. Did all fathers feel the need to test their daughters' suitors this way? Hadn't he proven himself already in the Chiselton incident? "Sir, may I be so bold as to ask why?"

Moberly stared beyond him for several moments, then turned icy blue eyes that cut into Philip like a rapier. "Do you recall the story concerning Mrs. Moberly's brother I told the other evening?"

Fighting confusion and dismay, Philip scrambled to pull the shocking tale to the front of his mind. "Yes, sir. He was an American sea captain who tried to blow up your ship."

He'd not had a chance to learn further details. "I can well imagine you hold no charity for him."

"But before that, Templeton had done far worse." The captain's stare drifted back toward the window. "He came as a Loyalist friend to my father, the late Lord Bennington, a member of His Majesty's Privy Council. But he was a spy sent to steal war plans for the Americans."

Philip recoiled and could think of no response. Yet he recognized a kinship with Moberly's family, for had not Whitson sneaked into his home like a spy? No wonder Mrs. Moberly didn't wish to speak about her homeland, where her own brother had tried to send the man she loved to his death.

"While here, he won the affections of my only sister, and she ran away with him to the colonies, breaking the hearts of all who loved her."

Indignation filled Philip's chest, along with an added measure of empathy with this family. Now he understood why the captain had befriended him, for he too had seen a sister's future destroyed. "Unspeakable behavior, sir. After he fired upon your ship, did you pursue him?"

Another span of time passed before the captain replied. "No. I forgave him."

"What?" Philip clenched his teeth. So that was what this was about. His former suspicions now reasserted themselves. Moberly wanted him to release Whitson from all obligation. To set him free as if he had done nothing.

"I forgave him."

The repetition hammered the words into Philip's skull. Emotion choked him, but he managed to speak. "Why? How?"

"It took some time, but eventually I realized my bitterness took a greater toll on me than on my adversary. So, for my wife's sake and for my own, I released Templeton to God's judgment."

"Sir, you must forgive *me,* but I cannot see how this applies. In times of war, both sides must use all resources to defend their countries, whereas Whitson schemed to rob my sister of her future for no one's benefit but his own. He took her dowry and spent it to win a well-connected wife." Making the man twice the fool for not knowing what the future held, for Lucy's rank would now be higher than Lady Sophia's. "It was by half a more personal matter."

One corner of the captain's lips lifted. "A twenty-pound shot across the bow of a man's ship is rather personal, as well, especially when one's identity is clear."

Philip stood and ran a hand through his carefully combed hair. Wilkes would complain. "And so you forgave this man, this Templeton."

The captain remained seated, his icy stare once again piercing Philip. "Captain *James* Templeton, godfather of my son Jamie, and my lifelong friend."

"Ah." Philip found himself seated once again. "Then you are a better man than I am, Captain Moberly, for I shall not forgive Whitson until he repays the last pound he owes my sister."

"Until he has paid the uttermost farthing?"

"N-no." Philip's insides twisted. "Well, yes, then. Exactly like the example the Lord Christ gave in the fifth chapter of Matthew. He is utterly unrepentant and should be thrown in prison until he pays the uttermost farthing." But this was not at all like the biblical story from the same Gospel that the children had performed. For Philip owed no money or apology to any man. "So you won't give your daughter to me because of Whitson?"

"I will not give my daughter to a man whose soul is filled

with bitterness and bent on revenge." The captain rose, his military bearing making him seem all the taller. "When you have it within your power to let him go free and repay you over time."

Rejecting the impulse to feel small in this man's presence, Philip stood and returned his icy stare. What Moberly suggested was unthinkable. Whitson was a scoundrel and a thief. Society was best served by making it impossible for him to deceive and cheat another family.

"You are to make no appeal to my daughter regarding this matter." The captain emitted a mirthless chuckle. "The Moberly women, as exemplified by my dear sister, can become quite willful when they want something."

Philip's face felt pinched, slapped, for he would never stoop to stealing away with Miss Elizabeth, but he could hardly call the captain out for this affront. "You insult me, sir."

"Do I?" Moberly regarded him through narrowed eyes and with his chin lifted, as if expecting the gauntlet.

Philip glared at him, twice insulted. After several moments, he spun on his heel and strode across the room and out the door.

How could such a wise, hospitable man—a protective father of daughters—be so mistaken about how Philip should deal with Lucy's betrayer?

Chapter Twenty-One

"Gone?" Elizabeth's voice cracked into a sob. "But why?"

She had missed Mr. Lindsey at supper the night before, but assumed he was wearied from his trip to Bennington Manor. As eager as she had been to receive his proposal, she had reasoned that he preferred to be rested when he spoke to her.

And now Papa, freshly returned from his morning ride, announced over breakfast that Mr. Lindsey had left at dawn for Gloucestershire.

"He has matters to tend to at home." Papa lifted his newspaper like a shield between them.

Elizabeth glanced at Pru, whose sympathy radiated from her entire countenance. Mama gave her a sweet smile but shrugged. Jamie hung over his plate, toying with his eggs. Her brother was not given to drink, so his behavior could only mean he was as depressed as she was about their guest's departure.

"Well." Elizabeth stood and marched to Papa's end of the table to peek over the paper. "I do not mean to be impertinent, Papa, but surely we have a right to know why our guest left so early and without saying goodbye to…to *anyone*."

Papa's gaze was not devoid of kindness, but his lips drew into a thin line. "His business here was finished."

"No. No, sir, it was not." She glanced around the room. Everyone, even the footman, must know how she and Mr. Lindsey regarded each other. "He was to ask you for my hand."

Papa folded and set aside the paper, stood and pulled her into his arms. "And so he did, my dear. But I denied his request."

"You what?" She shook out of his embrace and stepped back.

His face now held no warmth. "You must trust me, Beth. I know what is best for you."

Oh, yes, just as Grandpapa knew what was best for Aunt Templeton. Elizabeth bit her lip to keep from blurting out her admiration for Papa's sister. She and her sisters and female cousins often engaged in lively discussions about that piece of family history, with Elizabeth being first to say she would never show her parents such disobedience. But now she understood exactly why Lady Marianne Moberly had run away from home for love of Captain Jamie Templeton.

She blinked back tears and excused herself. Then promptly hastened upstairs to her bedchamber to count her pin money.

Inside the velvet-lined coach, Wilkes couldn't keep his face straight. Ever since Philip granted him permission to give the news to the driver and groom, his valet had held his chin a bit higher and his lips in a smug grin. Now it was "milord this" and "milord that" from the three of them. When they reached home, they'd probably trip over one other to be first to tell the other servants.

The coach bumped along at a reasonable speed, guaranteeing another good day of travel, as yesterday had been. In this good weather, they should reach Lindsey Hall within three days even without pushing the horses.

Philip sighed. When his grandfather became estranged from his great-uncle during the Seven Years' War, no one could possibly have foreseen that this branch of the family would inherit the title. Now he must brace himself to shoulder the additional responsibilities the Lord had placed upon him, including the seat in Parliament. And all without the woman he loved beside him.

His chest felt empty, as if his heart had been ripped out and left at Devon Hall. Indeed it had been. And all he had to carry home was the memory of Miss Elizabeth's sweet face gazing up at him in trust that he would secure the right to propose to her. But he'd failed.

What else could he have said to Captain Moberly? It wasn't in him to lie and certainly not about a matter as serious as releasing Whitson from his debt. And why should he? So the scoundrel could be liberated to find some other family to cheat?

Still, Philip would have been pleased to be a part of Captain Moberly's family. Beyond the exquisite Miss Elizabeth, there was the kind, warm Mrs. Moberly, who spent many days in Portsmouth ministering to poor wounded sailors who'd served England and then been cast aside when no longer useful. There was gentle Miss Prudence, a good friend to her cousin. There was Jamie, the witty scamp who would grow into a good man like his father. Philip had actually entertained thoughts of introducing him to Lucy once her heart mended. And then the captain himself who, despite his stand on Whitson, would make a worthy replacement for Philip's own father, giving sage advice about countless matters large and small. He had lost them all.

Something nagged in the back of his brain. Ah, yes. The biblical play about the unforgiving servant. The evening the children had performed it, he'd suspected collusion within the family against him. But he could not credit that thought and still respect them as true, good-hearted Christians. No, it had been an innocent bit of entertainment with no more plan behind it than the play about the lame man. After all, in the play, the unforgiving servant had owed a great debt to his master. But what misdeed could be laid at Philip's feet that he should be indebted to any man? Had he not spent his entire life choosing the good and the right thing to do? Was he not now planning to assume unwanted duties God had ordained for him? To whom did he owe anything? No one.

And yet...

The truth came crashing down upon him like a thundering ocean wave, and he nearly drowned in the force of it.

"Homer!" He thumped his cane against the roof of the carriage and felt the horses slow.

"Aye, milord?" the driver called down.

"Turn around, man. We're going back to Devon Hall."

Elizabeth could not believe Sophie's words. Nor could she believe Di's sober agreement. The sisters sat side by side on the parlor settee, a picture of grief.

"But how can you countenance such a thing?" Pru asked.

"Don't you see?" Di appeared close to tears on her sister's behalf, exhibiting a rare concern for someone other than herself. "Whatever Mr. Whitson may have done, he truly loves Sophie. I have seen it myself."

"And you will be pleased to know—" Sophie dabbed at her tears with a silk handkerchief "—he has acknowledged that what he did was wrong. Why, he has even spoken with Mr. Smythe-Wyndham about the danger his actions may have posed to his immortal soul." She drew in a deep, shuddering breath.

"Please, Beth dear, implore your Mr. Lindsey to devise a payment plan whereby we can return the ten thousand to him over time rather than putting my dear Gregory in prison." She sniffed, and somehow her tear-covered face seemed almost pretty. Perhaps it was true love.

Elizabeth swallowed her own tears. "If it were possible, I would do so. But Papa has forbidden me to write to him." And had been far too attentive these past two days for her to run away. Not that she planned to—not seriously, anyway. She knew her Mr. Lindsey to be an honorable man who held her father in great respect. He would not approve of her traveling to his side against her father's wishes.

The glow faded from Sophie's face, but she gripped Di's hand. "At least one of us has good news."

"Aha." Pru sat up straighter. "Mr. Redding."

Di blushed prettily. "Yes. And Papa has agreed."

Elizabeth and Pru both left their seats to offer congratulatory embraces and many more tears.

"I know what you're thinking," Di said. "He does not possess a title, but he is a gentleman." Her cheeks remained a rosy hue. "I freely confess that his father was a merchant who gained his wealth during the American rebellion. There, I said it. Now tease me as much as you wish."

Elizabeth could find no cause for teasing. If one of her cousins could find happiness, what did the man's rank matter? In fact, some titled men like Lord Chiselton considered themselves above the laws of decency and propriety, reason enough to abandon her former goal. No, she wished only to marry her ordinary gentleman, a far superior man to any other. But unless he and her father could resolve the discord between them, such a dream could not come true.

Chapter Twenty-Two

The midmorning sun broke through the trees and turned the long driveway into a mottled carpet leading to Bennington Manor. The air smelled fresh and clean, with summer scents of hay and roses wafting into Philip's coach and clearing his head.

Yesterday, after he'd ordered his coachman to turn around, he'd reconsidered his destination, for he must deal with a matter of grave importance before seeing Captain Moberly. Never had he been so certain his actions were right.

At the door, a younger butler greeted him. Philip worried about old Blevins until he saw that worthy soul standing by, perhaps training the new man.

"I've come to see Lord Bennington, if you please."

The butler eyed him up and down without expression, and Philip briefly wished for a mirror to check his appearance. Wilkes had done his best to groom him at the inn this morning—

He dismissed such silly thoughts and straightened his posture.

"Please tell him Lord Lydney is here." He managed not

to stutter over this first use of his title, but indeed it did feel strange on his tongue.

The man blinked. "Yes, milord." After a glance at Blevins, whose stony face didn't change, he took Philip's hat and led him into the drawing room, a bright chamber well-lit by sunshine beaming in through tall windows.

The fragrance of lavender in a dozen vases filled the air, while an abundance of artwork captured his attention. Most prominent were the statues of Zeus and Hera guarding the giant hearth and a large painting of a battle above the mantelpiece. In the center rode a man on horseback, and from his clothing, Philip assumed he was George II defending his Hanoverian throne against Stuart forces. Behind the king rode another black-haired soldier who looked very much like Captain Moberly. Perhaps it was his father, the previous Lord Bennington.

"Ah, Lydney." Bennington entered the room with one hand outstretched. "Welcome back."

Philip accepted the greeting, noting the older man's weak handshake. "Good morning, Bennington." How hard it was not to say "my lord."

"Well, I must assume you've come to cart off the thief." Bennington's thick, gray eyebrows bent into a frown. "Shall I send for him?"

Philip hadn't prepared exactly how to execute this battle, so, staring up at the late king's portrait, he quickly devised a strategy.

"Yes, if you would be so good."

Bennington winced but rang for a footman. "Bring Whitson." He waved Philip to a chair. "Won't you be seated?"

"I'd rather stand, if you don't mind."

The older man breathed out a long sigh. "And if you don't

mind, I believe I shall sit." He eased his well-fed body into a wooden, thronelike chair with red cushions. Around his light blue eyes, a red rim indicated some deep emotion. But whether it was grief or anger, Philip could not tell.

Whitson entered the room in a halting gait as if approaching the gallows. "Mr. Lindsey, I am at your disposal." His pale face exuded no fear, only misery, and perhaps a touch of resigned courage.

His address confused Philip. A glance at Bennington, who shrugged, gave him no satisfaction. Had the earl seen fit to keep his title a secret? That was all the better for Philip's plan, for he wouldn't want his rank to influence this situation or intimidate his adversary.

"Good morning, Mr. Whitson." *Lord, give me the words You would have me speak.* "I've come to tell you that I've forgiven your debt." Behind him, he heard Bennington gasp.

Whitson swayed. "Sir?"

Philip swallowed, and his eyes burned. "As Christ has forgiven my sins with no demand for any works on my part, so I forgive you with no expectation of repayment."

Whitson stared at him, his mouth working but no sound coming forth. At last he found his voice. "Oh, thank God. I thank You, God." The man fell to his knees, his face in his hands. "I did not dare to pray for this, only for your mercy." He gripped Philip's hand. "I will be your servant, sir. Somehow I will repay the debt."

Every part of Philip cringed at Whitson's words and actions, but it would be arrogant to shake him off. "Stand up, man." He gripped Whitson's elbow and lifted, almost dragging him to a chair. "You need not repay me. It was never about the money but rather, your deceit." *And my own pride over falling for your scheme.* What was ten thousand pounds when he considered his recent inheritance? Not quite a trifle, but near it. "You may be certain that should you attempt another scheme of this nature, I shall prosecute you to the full extent of the law."

Whitson nodded feverishly. "Yes, I see. Of course. But I never meant to deceive either you or Miss Lindsey. She is a delightful creature, so kind and good and beautiful and accomplished. It seemed an advantageous match. My intention was to use the dowry money, which you so liberally provided, to make my own business connections in London so that I could provide for Miss Lindsey in the long term rather than rely on your generosity. An old schoolfellow of mine named Rigsby vouched for me at Almack's." He paused to gulp in air and breathed out a strangled laugh. "How was I to know I would meet a remarkable woman of like interests as myself and fall madly in love with her?" A look at Bennington. "Lady Sophia and I are two halves of a whole."

Surprised—and a bit worn out from Whitson's lengthy self-justification—Philip nevertheless understood the concept of unexpectedly falling in love with a remarkable woman. He prayed Whitson wasn't once again deceiving them all. But that wasn't his responsibility, rather, God's.

"Now, if you'll excuse me." Philip gave Bennington a slight bow.

The old man rose from the chair with the vigor of a twenty-year-old. He strode to Philip and clapped a hand on his shoulder. "Will you not stay and share our midday repast?"

"No, thank you, *milord*." He couldn't smother a tiny smirk.

Bennington chuckled, his pale eyes now bright with good

humor and perhaps even joy. "You cannot keep it a secret forever," he whispered. "The newspapers, servants, gossip, etc."

"No, sir. But let me enjoy my privacy a bit longer."

Bennington still held his shoulder and now gave it a slight shake. "You are an extraordinary man, my friend. I am more than a little pleased to have met you and look forward to furthering our acquaintance."

"May I return the compliment?"

During this exchange, Whitson's eyes shot back and forth between them, but no comprehension registered there. "Mr. Lindsey." He approached Philip. "You have given me back my life. Whether or not Lord Bennington gives me his daughter, I have much to repent of and much to be grateful for." He reached out a trembling hand.

Without hesitation, Philip shook it, feeling a freedom of spirit he had not experienced since he first learned of the man's plans to marry Lady Sophia.

As he made his way to his carriage, he treasured the sense of satisfaction filling his heart. But another more gratifying emotion swept into both heart and mind: his love for dear Miss Elizabeth. For now he must obtain Captain Moberly's permission to marry her…or die trying.

Chapter Twenty-Three

"My thread keeps tangling." Seated in a parlor chair across from Mama, Elizabeth tugged on her needle, but a knot kept it from pulling through the fabric.

"It's too long." Mama paused in her own sewing and eyed the blue floss. "Don't be so impatient to finish."

Feeling like a child just learning to sew, Elizabeth used the point of her needle to loosen the knot. "I do not understand why Papa would not let me go with Pru to visit Di and Sophie."

"Don't you?" Mama's dark eyes searched hers, a gentle yet knowing smile softening the lines of her face.

So Elizabeth's suspicions were correct. Her parents had somehow divined her initial intention to follow Mr. Lindsey. What they failed to discover, however, was that she had discarded the plan. Now she would never see him again, and her heart ached inconsolably.

But whether or not her parents trusted her, the experience of being tempted to do something she believed to be wrong and yet refusing to actually do it had made her stronger. Perhaps even more mature.

"You're right, Mama." She snipped her thread with silver

shears and began again with a smaller length. "I have been too impatient." This time, she had no tangling, and the monogram was quickly done.

Pru would return home to her parents soon and had not yet finished her handkerchiefs. Completing the task was the least Elizabeth could do for her favorite cousin, whose counsel had refined her own faith. As exemplified by Elizabeth's former desire for a titled husband and the calamity such a dream almost caused, at last she grasped the truth that no earthly object was worth having if the Lord did not will it for her. Not even the man she longed to marry.

"There. *P* for Prudence." She lifted a silent prayer of thanks for the prudence her cousin had imparted to her, but also asked the Lord to ease her heartache.

"Do not mention my title to the captain's staff." Philip's gaze took in his three servants, all of whom appeared wounded. Or disappointed. "This is important to me."

After receiving their resigned agreement, Philip climbed into his coach. As certain as he'd been before visiting Bennington Manor, his nerves now wound tight with uncertainty. Never had six miles gone by so slowly as the trip back to Devon Hall, where either bliss or doom awaited him.

But soon enough, he found himself standing once again before Captain Moberly's desk. The strange, intimidating glint in the man's eyes threatened to undo him, but for Miss Elizabeth's sake, he plunged ahead.

"Sir, I have been a Pharisee."

The glint vanished, replaced by a friendlier light. "Indeed?"

"While it is true I've always endeavored to do right by every man, no one can be perfect, for pride over one's supposed righteousness is the worst of all sins." He exhaled a quiet laugh. "As God forgives my pride, I must forgive my adversary for his offense against me."

The captain appeared about to speak, so Philip rushed ahead.

"The Lord claims the right to vengeance, and I will no longer usurp His authority. I have absolved Whitson of his debt. He will not only not go to prison, but he need not repay a…a farthing."

Moberly's mouth hung open for several seconds. "You need not have forgiven the debt, just given him time to repay it."

"No, sir." Philip would not be deterred. "This is what the Lord wants me to do."

The captain came close to smiling, and warmth filled his gaze. "Well done, my boy. Or should I say—" He stopped and shook his head. "Is there anything else you would like to say?"

Philip shuffled his feet. He couldn't bear another rejection. "Sir, I love your daughter. May I have your permission to propose to her?"

Now the captain gave him a full, welcoming smile. "You may."

Relief dropped Philip into a chair, yet he pulled together enough strength to fully lay his heart out before Moberly. "I will see to her every need, whether spiritual or material. The Almighty has blessed me with more than enough wealth to care for a wife and children, should He grant them to us."

Moberly chuckled. "So I have heard."

"You know?" Philip gripped the arms of the chair. "But do you know I have no desire for this elevation?"

"Yes. Bennington told me." The captain held his gaze. "Your very reluctance will make you a better leader. You will weigh issues with more equity if you have no personal ambitions. And think of the good works you can accomplish."

"Perhaps so." The thought encouraged Philip, but he did not wish to pursue the subject. Not now, at least. "Sir, if you have no objection, may I see Miss Elizabeth?" His heart began to hammer.

Moberly answered by ringing for a footman. "Tell Miss Elizabeth she is wanted in the library." He nodded to Philip and left the room on the heels of the servant.

Dizzy with relief and excitement, Philip paced the length of the room for what seemed an eternity.

And then, there she stood in the doorway, radiant in her pretty blue dress that turned her eyes into shining sapphires.

And then, she was in his arms, warm, soft, trusting…and all was well.

"Oh!" Elizabeth jumped backed. "Forgive me, Mr. Lindsey. I was overcome with…with…" Oh, my, how good it had felt to be in his arms for that brief, audacious moment.

His gentle gaze, filled with love and amusement, imparted a reassurance to her that she had done nothing amiss.

"Well, then." He grasped her hands. "I hope you will be as pleased as I am to know your father has consented to our marriage." Doubt flitted across his eyes. "That is, if you still want—"

Relief and joy bubbled up within her. "Of course I do. I am yours, Mr. Lindsey, to have and to hold, um, once our wedding vows are completed."

Now he laughed, and she enjoyed the way his face brightened. Too soon, he sobered again.

"Before you fully consent, you must know something. I cannot think to offer you a life you may find displeasing."

"Oh, do not be concerned. I shall be as happy in Gloucestershire as ever I have been here at home." Or would have been in London. "As long as we are together."

His pleasure beamed only briefly from his handsome face. "Do you recall when I received word my distant cousin had died?"

"Yes." Sympathy welled up inside her. "If you are required at his funeral, I will understand."

"No. I am certain that matter has been attended to. However, another relative has died."

"Oh, my dear Mr. Lindsey."

"Don't be dismayed. I never met the man, so my grief is the same as for the departure of any mortal soul."

"Ah, I understand. But why is this a concern?"

"My cousin was this man's heir, and now I am to receive all that was his."

"Yes?" Intuition inched into her.

"Including his title. You see, my great-uncle was the Earl of Lydney."

Elizabeth heard a squeak emanate from her own throat.

"Just so. But I cannot refuse the title."

"Nor would I ask you to do so." Elizabeth's brainbox executed a dizzy spin. She was not to be Mrs. Lindsey but, rather, Lady Lydney. She was to have a titled husband after all.

"Does this trouble you?"

"No, no." She gave him her sweetest smile. "I shall somehow manage to live with it."

Chapter Twenty-Four

"Dearly beloved, we are gathered together here in the sight of God and in the face of this congregation to join together this man and this woman in holy matrimony." Mr. Smythe-Wyndham intoned the opening words of the solemn rite from his prayer book.

This time, Elizabeth stood beside her beloved Lydney, handsome in his black suit, ruffled cravat and diamond tie pin. Papa stood on her other side, his gentle grip on her arm giving support. Soon he would hand her over to this dear, handsome earl.

The fragrance of roses from Aunt Bennington's hothouse filled the air. Elizabeth had never been a favorite of this particular aunt, but the august lady adored Lydney for his generosity in ensuring one of her children's happiness, so she insisted upon donating the flowers.

The vicar proceeded to read the explanation of God's purpose for marriage, each word of which Elizabeth devoured, determined to be the perfect wife for her perfect husband. From time to time, she glanced up and found him looking down at her, love radiating from his brilliant blue eyes.

"I require and charge you both," the vicar recited, "as

ye will answer at the dreadful day of judgment when the secrets of all hearts shall be disclosed, that if either of you know any impediment, why ye may not be lawfully joined together in Matrimony, you do now confess it."

The church door slammed open. "I made it in time." A breathless young man stood in the portal, his eyes wide, his naval uniform slightly askew. As one, the congregation turned. Several people gasped. Others chuckled.

His mouth agape, Lydney stared first at the newcomer, then at Elizabeth. "I promise you, my dear, there is no impediment…for me."

"Nor for me, my dear." Indignation flared briefly within her. "That is my eldest brother, Lieutenant Colin Moberly of His Majesty's Royal Navy. He always likes to enter with a flourish."

"Ah, I see." Lydney snickered. Then laughed. Elizabeth and the congregants joined in. Papa's deep chuckle rumbled beside her.

Mr. Smythe-Wyndham cleared his throat. With difficulty, Elizabeth sobered, although she could see Lydney's eyes still dancing with merriment.

"Forgive me, vicar," he said. "You may proceed."

None too soon, Papa gave her over to Lydney, who grasped her hands with gentle firmness. The vows were completed, the psalms read, the homily spoken and Holy Communion shared.

"Ladies and gentlemen, I present to you Lord and Lady Lydney."

Sighs and hums of admiration filled the small church. Everyone filed out, making a path outside the door for Elizabeth and Lydney to run the gauntlet. Rice and flower petals rained down upon their heads as they made their way to an open landau.

* * *

Seated beside his beautiful bride at the head of the table in the vast dining room at Bennington Manor, Philip longed to escape and be truly alone with her for the first time since they'd met. No cousins, no parents, no footmen or maids in attendance. His own sweet Elizabeth in his arms, to have and to hold from this day forward. And the sooner the better.

"What do you think?" She blinked those brilliant blue eyes, which sometimes were turquoise, other times sapphire, once or twice icy silver.

"Think? About what, my dear?" Uh-oh. His first lapse, failing to listen.

But she forgave him with a smile. "Who do you think will marry next?" She tilted her pretty blond head toward the countless Moberly and two Lindsey relatives at the long table. "I do believe Lady Lucy and Jamie are moonstruck."

Philip dutifully perused the crowd, his gaze lighting on his sister, now raised in precedence because he had been, and his wife's favorite brother. Indeed, Lucy and Jamie had instantly latched onto one another, as much as was proper, each seeming to have found a kindred spirit.

Lucy had borne up well when she'd encountered Whitson earlier in the week, even wishing him and Lady Sophia every happiness. Whitson's honest shame in her presence, along with his genuine plea for forgiveness from her, had convinced Philip he'd been right to absolve the man of his debt. Lady Sophia was determined to have him, even if they must live in poverty or, worse, move to America. Bennington, a generous and indulgent father, had given his blessing, but wouldn't bestow a dowry until they married, a lesson Philip would not soon forget. Nor did he wish to begin his life with this large family holding ill will against a kinsman. He'd never known all the reasons his grandfather and great-uncle had quarreled, but he determined never to engage in such a feud with a relative, but, rather, he would follow Captain Moberly's...and Christ's...examples and quickly forgive any offense.

"Well?" Elizabeth nudged him.

"What?" He placed a kiss on her fair cheek and nuzzled her ear for the briefest moment. "Oh, very well, I'll play your game. I am convinced Miss Prudence and Mr. Smythe-Wyndham will marry before Christmas."

She shook her head. "I have moved on from that topic, my dear. I asked if you like these custard cakes, for if so, I shall obtain the recipe from Aunt Bennington's French cook."

"Oh. Custard cakes. Yes. They are quite delicious." He bent to kiss her, but she ducked her head away.

"Now see here, Lord Lydney, you must pay attention. Do you think your mind can wander that way when you sit in parliament? Your fellow peers will think you daft."

He nuzzled her ear again and breathed in the heady fragrance of her rose perfume. Would this wedding breakfast never end? "What do I care what they think? I've no doubt they are all mad eccentrics."

"Lydney!" Shock swept over her exquisite features. "You must be serious about your position."

"Why ever must I?" Ah, what fun. Their first argument. One he'd gladly let her win, should she give him a reasonable answer.

"Why, because...because..."

He stopped her with a kiss, and she did not protest.

"Now," he whispered, "what were you saying, my love?"

She sighed and smiled, then leaned her head against his shoulder. "I believe I was asking if we would be remiss if we excused ourselves and began our wedding journey."

Philip could think of no argument against that plan.

*   *   *   *   *

Dear Reader,

I hope you've enjoyed this journey back to Regency England. This is my very first Regency story, and it was the natural progression from my three Revolutionary War stories about the Moberly family. The children of those heroes and heroines would be growing up just in time to fall in love during this unique and fascinating era, the setting for Jane Austen's timeless novels.

When I began writing it, my thoughts were all about romance and weddings, but the more I researched, the more I saw that this was a novel of manners. The social structures of the Regency era were quite confining, but true love could find a way to cross social lines. By the way, if you're a diehard Regency fan and find an error, please let me know! And please know that I tried to get it right!

Thank you for choosing *The Gentleman Takes a Bride*. As with all of my stories, beyond the romance, I hope to inspire my readers always to seek God's guidance, no matter what trials may come their way.

I love to hear from readers, so if you have a comment, please contact me through my website, *http://blog.Louisemgouge.com*.

Blessings,
Louise M. Gouge

QUESTIONS FOR DISCUSSION

1. What reasons does Elizabeth have for wanting to marry a titled gentleman? Given the social structures of her times, do you think these reasons are valid?

2. Elizabeth and her cousins are only eighteen years old and yet each one hopes to find a husband soon. How are things different for girls today? Considering the era and their social positions, would you like to be one of the three cousins? Which one? Why?

3. Philip rides in to "save the day" more than once: to stop Whitson's wedding and to rescue Elizabeth from Chiselton. What does this say about his character? Do you think he fits the image of a "hero"? Why or why not? What is your definition of a hero?

4. What sort of person is Lord Chiselton? Why does he think he can do as he wishes? Are there people today with that attitude of privilege? What are our modern protections against them?

5. Why doesn't Philip want to be a peer? Do you think his reasons are valid? Considering the responsibilities as well as the privileges in those times, would you want to be a peer/peeress?

6. This was an age in which a father had complete control over his daughter's life until she married. Why does Captain Moberly initially refuse to give Philip permission to

propose to Elizabeth? Do you agree with his reasons? If she were your daughter, what would you do?

7. Which character changes the most in the story, Elizabeth or Philip? In what ways did each one mature and become stronger? In what ways did they stay the same?

8. In the Regency era, there were no televisions or movies, and families had to make their own evening entertainment. My inspiration for having the children perform Bible stories came from my husband's and my child-rearing days, when our four children acted out Scripture and storybooks. What does your family do in the evening to spend time together?

INSPIRATIONAL

Inspirational romances to warm your heart & soul.

HISTORICAL

TITLES AVAILABLE NEXT MONTH

Available July 12, 2011

CALICO BRIDE
Buttons and Bobbins
Jillian Hart

FRONTIER FATHER
Dorothy Clark

SECOND CHANCE FAMILY
Winnie Griggs

HEARTS IN FLIGHT
Patty Smith Hall

REQUEST YOUR FREE BOOKS!

2 FREE INSPIRATIONAL NOVELS
PLUS 2
FREE
MYSTERY GIFTS

Love Inspired

HISTORICAL
INSPIRATIONAL HISTORICAL ROMANCE

YES! Please send me 2 FREE Love Inspired® Historical novels and my 2 FREE mystery gifts (gifts are worth about $10). After receiving them, if I don't wish to receive any more books, I can return the shipping statement marked "cancel". If I don't cancel, I will receive 4 brand-new novels every month and be billed just $4.24 per book in the U.S. or $4.74 per book in Canada. That's a saving of at least 23% off the cover price. It's quite a bargain! Shipping and handling is just 50¢ per book in the U.S. and 75¢ per book in Canada.* I understand that accepting the 2 free books and gifts places me under no obligation to buy anything. I can always return a shipment and cancel at any time. Even if I never buy another book, the two free books and gifts are mine to keep forever.

102/302 IDN FDCH

Name	(PLEASE PRINT)	
Address		Apt. #
City	State/Prov.	Zip/Postal Code

Signature (if under 18, a parent or guardian must sign)

Mail to the **Reader Service:**
IN U.S.A.: P.O. Box 1867, Buffalo, NY 14240-1867
IN CANADA: P.O. Box 609, Fort Erie, Ontario L2A 5X3

Not valid for current subscribers to Love Inspired Historical books.

Want to try two free books from another series?
Call 1-800-873-8635 or visit www.ReaderService.com.

* Terms and prices subject to change without notice. Prices do not include applicable taxes. Sales tax applicable in N.Y. Canadian residents will be charged applicable taxes. Offer not valid in Quebec. This offer is limited to one order per household. All orders subject to credit approval. Credit or debit balances in a customer's account(s) may be offset by any other outstanding balance owed by or to the customer. Please allow 4 to 6 weeks for delivery. Offer available while quantities last.

Your Privacy—The Reader Service is committed to protecting your privacy. Our Privacy Policy is available online at www.ReaderService.com or upon request from the Reader Service.

We make a portion of our mailing list available to reputable third parties that offer products we believe may interest you. If you prefer that we not exchange your name with third parties, or if you wish to clarify or modify your communication preferences, please visit us at www.ReaderService.com/consumerchoice or write to us at Reader Service Preference Service, P.O. Box 9062, Buffalo, NY 14269. Include your complete name and address.

LIHI1

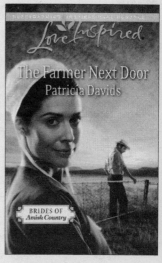